BLUEGRASS KINGDOM

by Nate Jaggers

© 2025

Dad,
I miss you...
I hope you'd be proud.
Love, Nate

Chapter One

Kenny gasped for air, each breath a sharp pull like gravel in his chest. Each inhale jagged and desperate—the chill around him was crisp, almost piercing. But fall in Kyrock could do that to a person.

Each exhale released a rising cloud that vanished into the darkness like a ghost. His chest heaved and his fingers tingled, numb from gripping something, though he couldn't remember what.

His chestnut eyes stretched wide, dilated with dread as they darted here, then there, trying to focus, but everything was a blur.

It couldn't be true, he thought. *How did this happen? And what was that noise?*

The ground beneath his flip-flops was uneven, like gravel or some kind of broken terrain. His heartbeat pounded in his ears, drowning out the echoes of nature in the night. Except for that damn sound.

He couldn't collect his thoughts; he couldn't think straight.

My God, what is that noise? The question rang through his skull, louder than whatever was making it.

His heart pounded in his chest as if urging him to move, to do something, but that sound—unrelenting—it held him in place, paralyzed.

His eyes stayed wide as memories flickered past like fireflies in the dark, there one instant, gone the next.

The sound came again. Distant at first— a slow, steady ringing, echoing somewhere just beyond his understanding.

He focused on it, trying to place it—

A sharp cry split through the night, high and raw.

Kenny flinched. The sound came again—hysteric, panicked.

A scream!

His breath caught as he turned toward it.

Then somewhere, not so far off, the scream came again!

A girl screaming. A scream that tore through the chilly Kyrock night.

His breath remained rushed, still uneven. His head pounded and his body was sluggish as if waking from a dream. Still, he couldn't piece together the why of it all.

Kenny noticed sharp bursts of light cascading down the hillside in front of him. Blinding, erratic flashes, like a broken signal desperately trying to be seen. They danced against the sky, revealing jagged silhouettes of trees and the uneven rise and fall of the land.

But that scream, it cut through everything. It came again—louder now, raw and desperate.

Kenny stumbled forward. Every step felt unsteady, like the earth itself was shifting beneath him. The flashes of light, red and blue, tangled together.

Then, he saw her.

At the top of the hill, framed in the bounding light, stood a girl.

Her back was to him, her shoulders rising and falling with panicked, uneven breaths.

In that moment Kenny's consciousness came crashing back to earth.

He opened his mouth to call out to her, but before he could she turned, and the look in her eyes made his blood run cold.

***

Earlier that day in Kyrock, Kentucky, morning came in like a whisper—quiet, slow, and easy to miss, just like the town itself.

Kyrock rested smack dab in the middle of the sticks, just on the outskirts of nowhere in particular.

It was the kind of place where porch sittin' was a pastime, and the only thing that moved faster than the autumn winds was the town gossip.

It was just another morning, the type that stretched endlessly, full of plans that felt important in the moment but faded as soon as the sun dipped below the tree lines.

High atop the infamous Bledsoe Hill, the trees that lined Ma and Pa's property stood nearly bare, and their last stubborn leaves clutched tight, afraid to let go.

The once-vibrant Kentucky bluegrass had faded to a dull brown—a stark reminder that winter was on its way, bringing with it a cold, calculated emptiness that would soon settle over everything and everyone.

The scent of chimney smoke hung in the air as it dueled with the rich aroma of fresh coffee drifting from Ma's breakfast table.

Kenny Bledsoe stood in the driveway of Ma and Pa's old ranch-style house, perched atop the hill on Bledsoe Road. His eyes swept across the property like twin lanterns carrying a single flame—full of untold stories and storms not yet named.

Much like Kyrock, the Bledsoe home wasn't much—but it was theirs.

The land it sat on, however, looked like something straight out of a Bob Ross painting—the kind with rolling hills and happy little clouds. The type that made you forget, just for a moment, how hard life could be.

Kenny's hands were stuffed into the pockets of his tattered University of Kentucky hoodie as he stared at his older brother's truck: a beat-up '05 Toyota Tundra, black once, now faded to a dull, patchy gray. The windshield was smudged, the tires caked in dried mud, and a faint dent lingered on the driver's side door—a reminder of a story he and his brother vowed to never tell.

It was supposed to be a normal day. No flashing lights, no screams, no unease crawling beneath his skin; just another crisp fall morning in Kyrock, where nothing ever changed.

But that's the thing about small towns. When something does happen, everyone remembers.

Such was the story of Kenny's life, like the air before a summer storm, it always felt unsettled and charged, waiting for a strike.

Things had happened to Kenny in his seventeen years on earth that you wouldn't wish on your worst enemy. Moments that left scars deeper than skin, events that had carved him into someone even he didn't fully recognize. The kind of things that made him question if he could ever hope to be the person a less broken person might hope to be.

Kenny swept the mess of his curls from his eyes. His hair, untamed and wind-kissed, much like the Bledsoe land itself, was wild and free.

He wore a faint scar just above his right cheek, the kind that hinted at a tale best saved for another day.

As Kenny took in the view, his eyes found their way to the giant cottonwood tree, the way they always did when looking out across the Bledsoe property.

It stood there, unwavering—one of the few constants in his life. Every morning, every season, before the world stirred awake, there it was, silent, steady, and alive.

He sighed and stuffed his hands deeper into his hoodie pocket as the cold nipped at him in quick little bites.

His fingers brushed against something—a small, folded-up note. He'd been carrying it around all morning, and most mornings since, well, before he could even remember. He mindlessly smoothed the creases of it, folding and unfolding, without realizing.

He couldn't recall the last time he'd actually read the note; he didn't need to, he knew it by heart.

Still, he toyed with the paper between his fingers, as if the sensation of it might tell him what to do on a day like today.

Much like the old cottonwood, its roots reached far beneath the surface. Perhaps he found comfort in the feeling that it wasn't going anywhere.

From inside the house, a voice called out, Ma's voice.

"Grandson, don't let this chill swallow you up. Get in here and eat before your food gets stiff," she hollered like folks from the south tend to do.

He smiled at the sound of her voice; gravelly, impatient, and laced with the kind of authority that came from a lifetime of being in charge. Ma didn't ask people to do things. She told them. And if you had any sense, you listened.

Plus, he was getting cold. Mostly his bare legs that stuck out beneath a pair of old ball shorts. Tan and lean, they were carved from basketball games and long walks on gravel roads.

Winter had Kentucky dead in its sights, but Kenny, stubborn as ever, wore his flip-flops like it was July. His toes pinked against the cold.

He climbed the steps with his long, lean frame. Although lanky at a glance, anyone who was anyone in Kyrock knew Kenny Bledsoe was country-strong in all the ways that counted.

As he trudged across the porch, each board creaked like a billy goat clearing its throat. He pulled open the heavy front door and stepped into the warmth of the house. Years, maybe decades, of photos were mounted on the walls. Happy faces frozen in time, their smiles stretched over wounds of the past.

On the mantel beneath them, war monuments sat quietly, freshly dusted, though time still clung to them in ways polish couldn't reach.

Before Kenny hit the kitchen, the smell of fried eggs and biscuits wrapped its arms around him.

Ma stood at the stove, wearing her faded blue *Jesus Loves Me* cooking apron, and like always, her wiry gray hair was pinned back in a way that somehow made her look more intense, not less.

She didn't turn from the stove as she spoke to him.

"You're up earlier than usual," she noted.

Kenny snuck a biscuit from the plate on the table before she could stop him.

"Couldn't sleep?" she questioned.

She turned and glanced at him, her sharp eyes narrowing slightly. The corner of his mouth tugged the way it always did, one side caught higher than the other, like even his lips couldn't decide between staying quiet and fighting back.

"Bad dreams?" she asked.

Kenny hesitated, "somethin' like that," he replied.

Ma didn't press, but the way she studied him made it clear she knew he wasn't telling the whole truth.

Betty Lou Bledsoe always knew things. Not because she was nosy, but because she just... knew. And right now, the way she was looking at Kenny made his skin prickle. Like she saw something in him that even he hadn't figured out yet.

Before she could say another word, the back door swung open, bringing in a sharp gust of morning air and the familiar thump of a basketball being dribbled once before getting tucked under an arm.

"Dang, it's cold," Caleb huffed, shaking out his curly damp hair as he stepped inside.

"About took my fingers off," he joked.

Caleb Bledsoe, tall and broad-shouldered, was only a year older than Kenny, but some days it felt like he'd lapped him twice. Even his hair was a little brighter than his younger brother's. It was the kind of easy golden that made people notice him first. He had a calm confidence, the way his smile came quick, the way he made everything look easy, the sort of things Kenny could never quite figure out how to fake. His face had that country-handsome look: sunkissed cheeks, square jaw, his blue eyes carrying that effortless sort of charm that made people lean in when he talked.

Caleb was the star senior shooting guard for the Kyrock Knights, a straight-A student and golden boy of the town. He didn't just play basketball—he lived it.

And in Kyrock, basketball was life.

Caleb had it all together, or so it would seem.

Even now, as he wore his practice jersey over a long-sleeve compression shirt, which hugged his muscles like he was one of those actors you can tell is twenty-five years old playing an eighteen-year-old in a movie, he had that steady, unshakable ease about him—like nothing could touch him.

His gym bag was slung over one shoulder, sweat still cooling on his skin, dripping from his curly hair. But boy, he somehow made it look good.

"You done been shootin?" Kenny asked his brother, but he already knew the answer.

Kenny's country dialect had a way of kicking the hell out of proper grammar. Often stomping it down and grinding it to dust.

Caleb grinned, flipping the ball effortlessly in his hands. "Since five thirty little brother, gotta stay sharp. You saw me hit ten straight before I came in, right?" He gestured toward Ma.

Ma, who was standing at the stove flipping eggs, didn't turn around.

"Eleven," she corrected. "But your release was sloppy on the last one," she said seriously.

"Always afraid to pull punches, this one here." Caleb joked as he hugged an arm around Ma, his tall frame towering over her. But it certainly was just that— a joke, a fib, even. No words spoken about Ma could have strayed further from the truth. Betty Lou Bledsoe was steady as a sunrise.

Ma was no timid, soft-spoken grandmother. Behind that *Jesus Loves Me* apron, she ruled her kitchen the same way she ruled everything else: with sharp elbows, a sharper tongue, and a heart big enough to carry the whole dang town.

And Ma loved basketball. She knew everything about it. She could tell you the stats of every great player from Kentucky's past and predict the outcome of March Madness before the brackets even dropped. The previous Kyrock coach had once joked about putting her on staff. She wasn't joking when she replied she'd do a better job.

Kenny, on the other hand, liked basketball just fine, but he wasn't obsessed with it. He wasn't an underachiever—he just didn't have it all mapped out the way Caleb did. And most days, being the forgotten little brother was no bother at all.

There wasn't any bad blood. In fact, more often than not, Kenny felt grateful to be able to coast in Caleb's shadow. But sometimes, when the inevitable comparisons came, he felt like he was missing something. Like everyone expected him to be Caleb, and for better or typically worse, he just... wasn't.

Caleb rested the ball on the kitchen table, on top of a scatter of envelopes—at least a dozen of them—scholarship offers, recruitment letters, all the proof that his future was lined up, waiting for him. Being 6'3" with a jump shot that reminded the people in Kyrock of some of Kentucky's all-time greats will do that for you.

"What, you didn't hit your snooze button six times this morning? You sick or something?" Caleb teased Kenny, with that crooked golden-boy grin of his—effortless, confident, like he already knew he was winning at something Kenny hadn't figured out how to start.

Kenny rolled his eyes, shoveling his last bite of biscuit into his mouth.

"You say that like I'm some kind of loser," he mumbled through a mouthful, like a second-place brother would.

"Your words, not mine," Caleb teased through a grin.

Kenny was no frail thing himself. Last summer he hit his growth spurt, and depending on if he was standing up straight or not, some might say he was now a tiny bit taller than his brother. He'd never think it, but the truth was, he had his own kind of pull—sharp features, darker hair, and a smile that came slowly, but meant more when it did.

Kenny, however, didn't have the jump shot his top-ranked brother had. But what he lacked on one end of the court he sure as heck made up for on the other: defense. Kenny took pride in putting his 185 lbs. of country strength to use. Making the other team's best player miserable for four quarters, "four quarters of hell", as Pa referred to it.

Ma swatted Caleb's arm as she passed by him on her way to the coffee pot, not hard, just enough to remind him she was still in charge. That coffee pot had been there longer than either of them could remember, and every time the boys tried to buy her one with buttons and timers, she'd wave them off and say, "Ain't no sense in replacing somethin' that ain't broke."

"Don't be startin' with your brother this mornin'. You know you're gonna need him tonight," she said sharply.

Caleb grinned. He knew she was right; Ma was always right.

He reached for the pot and poured himself a cup, pausing only for a second before glancing at Kenny again like he noticed something was off. Of all the things Caleb was—and that list was long—he was Kenny's protector first and foremost.

Legend has it that when Kenny was in kindergarten, some second-grader tried to take his lunch. Caleb, all of seven years old, marched over, shoved the kid backward, and told him in no uncertain terms that touching his little brother was a great way to meet the tooth fairy. When the kid questioned what he meant, Caleb knocked his front two teeth out.

That story, or some version of it, had been told so many times, in so many ways, Kenny wasn't sure what was actually true. But one thing was certain—Caleb always had his back.

Kenny smirked and crammed his left hand instinctively into his hoodie pocket again as his fingers curled around the note before he spoke.

"I dunno–just... nerves, I guess," Kenny said softly.

Caleb gave him a look like he wasn't buying it, and with good reason. The Bledsoe boys were always burdened with a sense that today might be the day the other shoe finally dropped. There was a melancholy in the way they lived their lives–fifty percent happy and fifty percent sad at any given moment–not by choice, but more as a shield forged to protect them from the blows life had delivered.

Or to put it simply: if the past is prologue, the prologue of the Bledsoe boys' life was nothing either of them wanted to write about.

But before Caleb could push any further, Ma clapped her hands together.

"Enough of this sittin' around; off to school you two go. I ain't no teacher no more!" she proclaimed.

Ma, a retired school teacher herself, had put in forty-three years wrangling kids at Kyrock Middle School, where word around town was that she was a ferocious hooper herself back in the day.

And while clearly the boys didn't get their height directly from her five-foot two-inch contribution to the gene pool, Ma was still undefeated in the family games of HORSE.

She shooed them toward the door, but not before pointing a finger at Caleb.

"And don't forget—their zone defense collapses on the drive. Kick it out and hit the open man, would'ya," she demanded.

Her sharp eyes then bounced to Kenny.

"And you—remind him when he starts thinkin' he can take on all five of them boys at once. What do I always say?" she asked.

Kenny smirked. "That Jesus loves us win or lose?" he teased.

The only thing Ma loved more than basketball was Jesus—and depending on the game, even that was up for debate.

She sighed, exasperated. "Pass the dang ball," she scolded.

Kenny and Caleb both mouthed along, perfectly in sync—they'd heard it a million times, maybe more.

Betty Lou wasn't a curser. In fact, the only time she ever came close was when she said, well, that.

"And you," she continued, directed at Kenny now. "You let it fly, grandson."

Kenny had only heard that one a millionie-billionie times.

As Ma passed the boys their bagged lunches she'd packed for them, a smidgen of a smile tugged at the corner of her mouth. "Now, don't you think for one second the Lord wouldn't want y'all to beat those boys from Carter Central. That awful John Deere Green! Yuck!" she said, scrunching her nose.

Caleb grinned, spinning his truck keys around his finger. "Now that's a sermon I can get behind!" he shouted.

"Hallelujah!" Kenny exclaimed.

And with that, the Bledsoe boys bolted out the door.

Chapter Two

The Whitmore home looked exactly like you'd expect the preacher's house to look. White shiplap siding, a neatly trimmed lawn and a porch big enough for Sunday afternoon gossip. A wooden cross hung beside the front door, and a sign beneath it read, *As for me and my house, we will serve the Lord.*

Caleb barely had the truck in park in the ginormous circle driveway before the front door of the palatial HGTV starter castle swung open. Sara Grace Whitmore, Sara to most—preacher's daughter, cheer captain, and owner of just about every boy's attention in Kyrock—stepped out onto the porch like she was stepping onto a stage. Sara certainly had "it," whatever that was. But she never flaunted it.

"'Bout time," she called out, her voice thick like honey with a twang of southern drawl.

Her hands were on her hips, and her brown ponytail swished from side to side as she bounded down the steps.

Now, don't let the accent fool you. Sara wasn't stupid; far from it. Too smart for her own good, maybe. She dotted both Bledsoe boys' i's and crossed all their t's. She might have sounded sweet as sugar, but she could cut like a blade.

She was dressed in her bedazzled cheer warm-ups—black and gold, Kyrock Knights stitched across the chest—**Bledsoe** in bold letters on the back.

Kenny sat in the truck watching as Caleb grinned ear to ear as he leaned against the hood of the rumbling Tundra. There was something about the way Caleb looked at Sara—like she hung the stars and gave the moon its shine; like she was the only person in the world who could keep up with him.

"You're impatient this mornin'," Caleb called out to her.

Sara rolled her eyes, stopping just short of him.

"That's because I knew you'd be late. And wouldn't you know who won the pony?" she asked behind a smile.

Caleb chuckled, reaching for her waist, but she dodged him with a smirk.

"Nuh-uh," she said. "Not until you tell me how many shots you made this mornin'."

"Oh God, there's two of them," Kenny groaned out the window from inside the truck.

Sara shot him a look. "Oh, hush now, Bledsoe," she teased.

There had been rumors once, back in elementary school, that Kenny and Sara Grace were a thing: some notes passed in class, some playground teasing about how they were "k.i.s.s.i.n.g. in a tree", or how they'd get married one day. But the truth was, they'd always just been close. The kind of close where words weren't necessary and they could tell what the other was thinking with just a look.

The kind of close where silence was never awkward, secrets were never really secrets, and no matter how much life changed around them, including the summer when Sara went from a training bra to the real thing, they never had to wonder where they stood with each other. People eventually stopped gossiping when it became clear Caleb had his sights set on Sara, and Kenny was just, well, Kenny.

Kenny and Sara were in the same grade, juniors, and growing up in Kyrock that meant they saw a whole lot of each other.

And while Kenny and Sara— or Gracie, as he referred to her, had been close since before either could remember, it wasn't until the summer before his junior year that Caleb joined in, making this a true triad.

"Your support means a lot to me," Kenny teased Sara, nodding towards the letters on the back of her jacket.

Sara smirked, flipping her ponytail over her shoulder, landing on the B in Bledsoe.

"Please. You couldn't handle this attention," she declared confidently.

Kenny smiled. "Yeah, and he can?" he asked, pointing at his brother.

Sara shot him a look and crossed her arms. "For your information, much unlike you, this man right here," she said in an exaggerated sassy voice, tucking her arm underneath Caleb's, "thrives in the spotlight."

Kenny leaned out the window and shrugged, swiping the unruly hair from his eyes.

"Well, maybe I'd enjoy a little attention from you, Gracie," he said with a playful grin tugging at the corner of his mouth.

Sara gave him a sharp look. "Oh, please! You panic when a cute waitress tries to take your order," she jabbed.

Caleb, long used to the tomfoolery of the pair, had begun checking his phone and finally looked up.

"Are y'all done flirtin', or do I need to give you two a minute?" he asked.

"Oh, Gosh!" Kenny groaned. "You know he practices standing like that in the mirror," Kenny shouted. "He's got a whole rotation of dramatic poses."

Caleb smiled and Sara laughed, tossing her petite arm around Caleb's waist as they glanced over at Kenny.

"Don't be jealous now Kenny, I'm sure there's some poor, lonely, desperate woman out there for you, somewhere. God have mercy on her soul," she said behind a mischievous smile. One that said she enjoyed messing with Kenny just a little too much.

Kenny rolled his eyes as he leaned back inside the truck. He couldn't help but grin. Some things never changed with these three, and as far as this third wheel was concerned, that was perfectly fine.

***

The cab of Caleb's truck was tight, tighter than a pair of church shoes after a summer growth spurt. Elbows knocked and knees pressed, and the engine growled beneath them as Caleb steered down the familiar crooked roads of Kyrock.

"Tell him, Gracie," Kenny said, mid-conversation, turning in his seat. "It's wheel burra—like you're moving somethin' that's been burrawed in the ground. Ain't it Gracie?" he asked.

Caleb cackled, nearly swerving the wheel from laughing.

"You idiot, it's a will-barrrel. Like a barrel that you're willin'. I think that's it, right, Sara Grace?" he asked as he turned to look at her.

Sara rubbed her temples as she sat in the middle seat irritated.

There was a pause in the conversation as she looked at Caleb, then at Kenny, then back at Caleb again.

"You absolute block heads. It's a wheelbarrow. It's an old English word," she said with confidence that only came with being the "knower of things" in this little trio.

Caleb turned again; his eyebrows raised.

"Wheelbarrow? Nahhh, that can't be it," he said softly.

Kenny chimed in with his deep thought on the matter.

"An old English word? Ain't that what we speak?" he asked, country as cowboy boots.

Sara pressed her thumb and index finger between her eyebrows. "Oh, how I mourn for our future bloodline," she huffed dramatically.

"And while we're on the subject," she continued, placing her hand on the rearview mirror of the truck, "this right here is a mirr-*or*." She elongated the second syllable pointedly. "It's not a *meer*. Believe it or not, there are two whole syllables hidin' in there, so start findin' em' would ya?" She sassed, clearly mocking the brothers now.

So it was with these three every morning; the conversations and radio stations might have changed, but the rest, the comfort of it all, remained.

Caleb sat behind the wheel, Sara in the middle, and Kenny to her right.

Riding with Caleb and Sara always felt the same for Kenny, like being part of something, something real.

Sara had her legs crossed, flipping through the radio stations as she liked to do in the old truck.

"Too much static, too much country, ugh, too much Jesus," she muttered.

Kenny watched her out of the corner of his eye as she fidgeted with the pendant on her necklace.

Sara glanced down at his bare legs and flip-flops, shaking her head. 'Lord have mercy, Kenny... do you even *own* socks?' she asked, laughing as she nudged his calf with her sneaker.

As Sara flipped through the stations, static crackled between bursts of music and commercials until a familiar voice cut through.

"And we're here with Coach Wills, the new head coach of the Kyrock Knights. They are off to a great start this season with eight wins and zero losses, with what has to be their biggest game in decades coming tonight in the Kyrock gym. As they face off with the #1 ranked team in the state of Kentucky, Carter Central. Coach, how's the team feeling heading into tonight?"

"Oh, come on. Turn that crap off," Caleb groaned.

Sara reached out and turned the volume up.

"What? You don't wanna hear them gush over you?" she teased.

Kenny leaned his head against the window, half-listening as Coach Wills' deep, steady voice filled the truck.

"Well, I'll tell you this," Wills said with confidence, *"these boys have worked their tails off. This town's got a lot to be proud of. And of course, it helps when you've got a leader like Caleb Bledsoe."*

Caleb shook his head, but Kenny caught the way his brother's lips curled into that effortless golden-boy smirk.

"He's the real deal," Wills continued. *"You give a kid like that the ball, and he's gonna make things happen. But honestly, I'm more proud of the young man he is off the court."*

Kenny stared out the window as his jaw tightened slightly. No mention of him. No surprise there.

Sara must have sensed it as she shot him a glance. "Bet they talk about you next," she said lightly.

And this time, for a change, they did.

"Now you're no fool, Coach. You know everyone on your schedule this year is gonna plan on attacking you by cutting off the head of the snake and trying to shut down Caleb." The radio interviewer, a long-timer with a voice as distinct as the jingle of the old station itself, carried on.

"Now folks shouldn't sleep on the rest of our boys, especially Kenny Bledsoe," Coach Wills added. *"That kid's on his way to becoming something special. He's got instincts you just can't teach. When he puts it all together, look out."*

Kenny blinked, caught off guard. He wasn't sure he'd ever heard a coach—not even Wills—talk about him like that.

Sara nudged him with her bony elbow, grinning. "See, I told you," she said with a smile.

As much as Caleb was Kenny's protector, Sara was his balance. She had a way of keeping him in check without ever making it seem like she was trying. Whether it was a quick-witted joke, a knowing glance, or the knack she had for wrangling him back to earth when he got lost in his own head. Sara had always been the one to steady him.

"Alright, so let's talk game plan," Sara said as she reached for the dial and turned the volume down.

Caleb groaned. "Sara Grace—"

"No, don't you middle name me," she sassed, pointing a finger at him. "Carter Central is cocky, and they've got good reason to be. You need to break their zone early, or they'll trap you all night," she continued.

Caleb smirked, one hand on the wheel. "You think I don't know that?" he asked condescendingly.

Sara shot him a look. "I think you like to play hero ball is what I think," she said, full of grit and glitter.

"Girl knows ball," Kenny jabbed from the passenger seat.

Caleb glanced over at him. "Well, maybe if I had a little help, I would pass–," he said.

Sara and Kenny both turned and shot him a look.

"Well, some," Caleb muttered.

Kenny rolled his eyes. Sara shook them both off.

"Focus now boys. Caleb, if you drive and force them to collapse, then you kick it out to D, he'll be open in the corner. And if they rotate quick, he'll swing it to Kenny, then...bang!" she said matter-of-factly.

"Well, there's the fatal flaw in your plan, babe," Caleb teased, directed at Kenny's lack of three-point shooting.

"I'm serious," Sara said, jabbing Caleb's arm.

Caleb sighed, but nodded. "Alright, coach, anything else?" he asked sarcastically.

"Yeah, pass the dang ball," she said with a grin.

Kenny couldn't help but smile. For all her bossiness, Sara knew her stuff. She probably got it from her dad, Earl Whitmore, the preacher, or as Kenny referred to him, Preach. Earl was on the last and only Kyrock team to ever win the State Basketball Championship in 1993.

So maybe it was an apple–tree situation, but whatever it was, Sara certainly knew her stuff when it came to basketball.

And no matter the subject, Sara had a gift for making Kenny feel like she was looking out for him rather than telling him what to do. It was just who she was. She pushed, she prodded, but at the end of the day, right or wrong, she had his back— both their backs.

When Sara Grace Whitmore was in on you, she was ten toes in.

Kenny leaned forward, resting his arms on the dash.

"You see, brother? Somebody appreciates my skills," he said out of the corner of his crooked grin.

Caleb smirked. "Yeah, well, she's also a Louisville fan so, you can't really trust her judgment, can you?"

Sara Grace, a University of Louisville Cardinals fan, which in most parts of Kyrock, especially this particular truck, was a huge RED flag, school colors, pun intended.

"He's got a point there," Kenny agreed.

At that moment, Caleb's smirk vanished as his eyes went wide.

"Shi—!" he let out under his breath.

From out of nowhere, a deer shot across the road. For a split second, it stood frozen, its wide eyes catching all three of theirs.

Caleb tensed as he smashed down hard on the brakes and gripped the wheel with all his might.

Sara let out a sharp gasp, bracing herself with one hand on Caleb's leg and the other on Kenny's arm. Kenny, who had been leaning forward, smacked into the dash with a grunt.

The truck came to a jerking stop in the middle of the road as silence lingered between the three.

Then, as quickly as it had appeared, the deer bolted, vanishing into the trees, leaving nothing behind but the smell of hot brakes and the sound of their racing hearts.

Kenny exhaled first.

"Well, damn!" he eloquently mustered.

Sara put a hand over her heart. "I think my heebies are jeebied," she breathed.

Kenny let out a short laugh. Sara could always make him laugh, whether she was trying to or not.

Caleb, usually the coolest in the room, always the one who was never rattled, exhaled sharply and ran a hand through his still perfectly styled hair. His mood shifted, like he'd seen a ghost. He didn't speak, just lifted his foot from the brake and pressed the gas.

Kenny sank back into his seat; his fingers drifted into the pocket of his hoodie. He found the folded-up note, the paper soft and worn from years of handling. As the truck rolled through downtown Kyrock, the place looked like someone's faded memory of a small town—familiar yet distant, like a story passed down rather than a place truly lived in.

That's the thing about small towns: the towns are, well, small, but it's the people and the stories that make them larger than life.

21

Chapter Three

They pulled into the school lot just as Kyrock High came alive that morning.

There were kids hanging off tailgates, leaning on car hoods, voices tangled in laughter, and music woofing from some speaker like it was trying to outrun the day.

It was another typical day in Kyrock, and Kenny moved through it all with a familiar burden heavy on his chest. Like the air was stalling, biding its time.

As the trio exited the vehicle, Caleb didn't speak; he snatched his backpack from the back of the truck and bolted towards the school's entrance.

"Oh, sure. You have a good day too, sweetheart!" Sara yelled sarcastically in Caleb's direction, but he didn't turn around.

"What crawled up his butt?" Sara asked Kenny, turning to him.

"Ahh, now that's one of life's great mysteries," Kenny joked.

But he knew what had shifted in his brother. He didn't want to talk about it though, not even with Sara.

"Hey, look who's waitin' for ya," Sara said, nudging Kenny's shoulder. Sara's eyes bounced over to Kate and her sun-caught blonde hair and that effortless, put-together glow she always seemed to have. Sara wasnt jealous, just annoyingly impressed.

Kenny glanced over catching sight of Kate standing on the front school steps with her girlfriends. Her blonde hair draped over her shoulders, soft and sunlit. It wasn't messy—just unbothered, natural, and perfect in every way.

Kate Covington, a junior, was co-captain of the Kyrock girls' basketball team. She had a magnetic pull about her and Kenny couldn't help but gravitate to her. Kate managed being popular without, how would one put this delicately, being a bitch.

She didn't demand attention; she simply made everyone feel like they belonged in her orbit.

She was the kind of person who knew how to balance ambition with kindness, giving everyone their moment to shine. It was a quality that Kenny admired from afar, unsure of how someone like him—quite often overlooked—could ever fit into her world.

But the way her eyes locked onto Kenny's made his stomach flip. Kate had a way of unraveling boys: making their stomachs teeter, then totter. Not because she was cheap or easy, but quite the opposite: elusive, unattainable. A look from Kate made Kenny feel like he was the only person in the world; it was the way he watched Caleb and Sara look at each other.

Kate was impossible to ignore and even though she wasn't even trying, it was like the universe had decided to give her a head start on being the girl everyone noticed.

Her eyes were bright, mischievous even; they carried a certain slyness about them, the way they seemed to catch the light with her every glance. They were a clear, steady blue that quietly had Kenny reconsidering whether Kentucky-Wildcat blue was still his favorite shade.

And as sweet as Kate was off the court, on it she played like she had grudges laced in her sneakers. Underneath that sun kissed hair hid two chips, one for each shoulder.

Sara, detecting the pair looking at each other, smirked.

"You know, if you two were any more obvious, we'd have to start callin' you guys captain," she joked.

Kenny rolled his eyes, trying to play it cool. "It's not like that, Gracie," he said. But as he stared across the parking lot at Kate, he didn't fully believe himself.

Kenny's delusion aside, he most certainly had developed feelings for Kate, and here's the real kicker: Kate had always had a thing for Kenny, implausible as it seemed to him.

Kenny never realized just how lovable he was, which was one of his many adorable traits.

Be that as it may, Kate and Kenny's will they, won't they, was one of the things that everyone at Kyrock High knew but never said out loud.

As Kenny and Sara made their way across the parking lot, Kate approached them, a smile tugging at her glossy lips. Her steps deliberate in her faded blue Levi's, curvier than the s's in Mississippi.

"Mornin', Bledsoe," she called out, her voice flirtatious without trying to be.

Kenny let out a breath he hadn't realized he was holding, offering her an awkward smile.

"Hey, Kate," he muttered in a voice cracking like a prepubescent teen.

She didn't waste any time closing the distance between them, slipping in just close enough to make Kenny hold his breath again.

"Big game tonight?" she asked, glancing between him and Sara. "You're gonna make all those other guys jealous with a smile like that," she said confidently.

"Uh oh, you better watch out, Kenny. Kate's making a move," Sara teased.

Kate tilted her head, her smile grew wider.

"I'm just sayin', you're a hard guy to get a hold of these days. What's a girl gotta do to spend a little time with ya?" she asked as she reached out and grabbed one of the straps from Kenny's backpack. Her fingers lingered on the strap for just a moment, and she couldn't help but notice how the muscles in his shoulders moved beneath it—how his face, gentle and familiar, had a way of softening every time he looked at her.

Kenny cleared his throat and shifted uncomfortably. "I don't know about all that, Kate," he replied softly.

Sara, watching the exchange, couldn't help herself. "Careful now Bledsoe, you don't wanna say too many cool things all at once," she quipped with a smile.

Kenny shot her a glance. "I can handle myself, Gracie," he said, knowing full well he most certainly could not.

Kenny felt Kate's eyes locked on him, but he kept his gaze focused on the ground and his energy on readjusting the straps of his backpack over his broad shoulders.

"Well, I'm just saying don't make a girl beg; it's not very lady-like," Kate joked.

After a long beat, Sara stepped in and broke the silence.

"Alright, alright, that's enough, you two," she said as she winked at Kate. "Every mornin' it's the same thing with y'all. Step up Kenny, and put your big boy pants on," Sara teased.

Kenny shot her a look, but he couldn't help but laugh. He knew she was telling the truth.

Kate laughed too—they both knew this little dance they'd been doing had just about run out of steps.

"Oh, he looks like he can handle himself," Kate said leaning closer to Kenny, making his heart skip like a record.

Kenny finally lifted his eyes to meet Kate's, trying to play it all off.

"You're always so...sure of yourself huh, Kate?" he asked.

Kate grinned.

"What can I say? I know what I want," she said behind a playful smile. "Question is," Kate paused for a second and tugged on Kenny's straps one more time, "what do you want, Bledsoe?" Her grin could melt the morning frost off a cold windshield.

Sara raised an eyebrow as she watched on.

Kate wasn't usually like this. Actually, that's putting it mildly. She was never like this. But she knew Kenny was harmless, and more than that, she knew she could trust him. Even if a big part of her actually meant the things she said.

Before Kenny could respond, the sharp sound of the school bell rang out signaling the start of another day at Kyrock High.

"Well, good luck tonight, Kenny. I'll be watching," Kate said, her voice carrying an edge of something playful.

As she turned to walk away she glanced over her shoulder, giving Kenny one last lingering look before her graceful stride carried her into the school, her figure disappearing through the large black double doors.

Kenny stood there for a moment, watching her walk away, reeling in the electricity of the moment.

Sara, as golden-hearted as she was, couldn't help but let one last teasing arrow fly.

"Awe, somebody better call the doctor," she said with ease.

"Huh, what?" Kenny asked, snapping from his trance.

"Looks like you got a bad case of the puppy wuwv!" she joked, pleased with herself, grinning ear to ear.

Kenny, not so pleased, turned to face her. "You're so...stupid!" he said as if every other word in the world had eluded him except that one. "I can't believe you're gonna be a Bledsoe one day...breaks my heart really," he teased.

Sara, never the one to lose a fight, even one as playful as this, turned her head and fluttered her eyelashes before saying, "Well, someone needs to sweeten this family up!"

Without missing a beat, Kenny replied, "Yeah," he shot back with a grin, "you're more like early-onset diabetes."

Sara stared at him, stone-faced. "It makes me sad, you know," she said.

"What's that?" Kenny asked.

"That there's no cure for stupid," she said, her delivery flat as a pancake.

Kenny bobbed his head, unfazed. "Yep," he said, "I think I'm terminal."

Sara couldn't help but smile as Kenny's grin met hers, easy and instinctive. There was a comfort in the rhythm of these two—like a song they both knew by heart.

"See ya in class," Sara said, still smiling as they made their way inside the school.

"Later Gracie," Kenny replied.

Kenny paused for a moment; his eyes lingering on the empty hallways. He stood still, taking in the hum of distant voices and the soft flicker of the fluorescent lights overhead.

It was as if he needed this brief moment of solitude—just long enough to gather his thoughts before the whirlwind of the day began. He reached into the front pocket of his hoodie. His fingers brushed against the familiar crumpled paper; the heft of it felt different today, like it carried a secret waiting to be told.

Tonight was the night where everything could fall into place. The Kyrock Knights were ranked for the first time in thirty years, led by a pair of brothers from a family desperate for this moment. It felt as if the entire town was holding its breath, craving something more. The burden of that kind of expectation was onerous, but it was also electric.

Kenny wanted it, but he wanted it more for his brother than he did for himself. No one on earth, not Sara, not even Ma, knew the kind of shit the Bledsoe brothers had to eat in their life. So yeah, Kenny could taste how sweet it all would be: Caleb taking the game-winning shot, the crowd roaring, the flashing lights, the screaming fans, and Kate. Yeah, the thought of her pretty little face slipped into that mind of his, too.

Chapter Four

The metal creaked under Coach Wills' solid frame as he leaned back in his desk chair, arms crossed and eyes sharp.

Jackson Wills was a man's man: the kind who looked like he'd been carved out of a block of granite, broad shoulders and no-nonsense. His hands, thick and calloused, told stories of years spent on the court and in the weight room. A lifetime of competition lived in the lines of his face: the kind of wear that only came from chasing victory and coming up short just enough times to make you hungrier.

And in a town like Kyrock, where old ways ran deep and faces rarely changed, the fact that Coach Wills was a black man stood out just as much as his reputation.

It wasn't something he ever had to say out loud, but it was there. There in the way people watched him just a little too long at the grocery store, or how some parents took their time warming up to him. He carried it like he carried everything else—with an unshakable steadiness, like a man who had long since learned that respect wasn't given, it was earned.

His steady eyes swept across his desk taking in the small 5x7 picture frame with the photograph of his family in it. So dang perfect you might have thought it was the picture that came with the frame. Wills' "picture perfect" family made the journey to Kyrock with him, of course.

Along with Wills came his wife, Janine, and daughters, Naomi and Bianca. But it was his son, Deron, who had the locals in Kyrock buzzing: a junior point guard with a sharp handle and a smoother shot. Deron had led his previous team, Louisville Christian, in scoring last season, proving he wasn't just along for the ride with his father—he was looking to build something of his own in Kyrock.

Coach Wills wasn't a ra-ra guy. In fact, like Kenny, he didn't speak much when he didn't have to. He wasn't the loudest in the room, and he didn't believe in drawn-out speeches or empty motivation. What he did believe in was toughness, discipline, and doing things the right way, even when no one was watching.

People thought he was crazy to leave his assistant coaching job at Louisville Christian, the perennial basketball powerhouse in Kentucky with a deep talent recruiting system and even deeper pockets from boosters. Most importantly, the team that knocked off the Cinderella boys from Kyrock in the semi-finals of the state tournament last year.

But what they didn't know—what they couldn't see—was what Wills carried with him from his seat on the bench that night: sometimes, even in defeat, greatness shines through.

Caleb was obvious, the golden boy, the leader, the kid with the kind of talent that made people talk in barbershops and at gas pumps. But Kenny, Kenny was the one people overlooked. The one who didn't shine quite as bright, at least not yet.

Wills saw it, though. The way Kenny moved, the way his mind worked a step ahead, the way he played like he had something to prove. He wasn't polished like Caleb, wasn't the kind of kid who turned heads the second he stepped on the court, but Wills knew that sometimes those were the kids who ended up being the most special. Because when you've spent your whole life in the shadow of someone great, you either shrink—or you find a way to make your own light.

Wills exhaled through his nose and reached for the desk phone. His thick fingers punched in the code for the school intercom. The speaker crackled to life allowing his steady voice to cut through the halls.

"Kenny Bledsoe, report to Coach Wills' office."

A few seconds later, the intercom clicked, leaving only the low hum of the lights overhead and the rhythmic tock from the clock on the wall.

Wills leaned back in his chair, rubbing his jaw as he stared at the door, knowing exactly how this conversation would go.

A few moments later Kenny stepped into Wills' office and pulled the door shut behind him. Wills didn't waste time. He leaned forward and cut right to the point.

"Take a seat. Look, I know you don't love basketball," he said.

Kenny froze for a second, caught completely off guard. He had expected a talk about the game plan, maybe some push about being more aggressive on offense—but not this.

Wills gave him a measured look. "And that's okay," he continued.

Kenny shifted in his seat. "Uh... okay?" he muttered.

Wills smirked slightly. "You remind me of myself," he said.

Kenny's ears perked. He didn't know much about Wills' playing days, just that he had been a name once, back before a knee injury cut his career short.

"I played because I was good at it, because people expected me to. But love?" Wills shook his head. "Nah. I never loved it the way some guys do. The way your brother does."

Kenny swallowed, not sure where this was going.

But what struck him most wasn't what Wills was saying—it was how he was saying it. Kenny was used to people being nice to him just to get closer to Caleb. Scouts, coaches, even teammates, all treating him like an extension of his brother. Like getting on Kenny's good side might earn them favor with the golden goose himself.

But with Wills, it was different. If anything, it felt like the other way around. This coach didn't see him as Caleb's shadow, and he didn't act like he was lucky just to share a last name with his brother. Wills was interested in him, and at this moment, only him.

"But here's the thing, Bledsoe," Wills continued, leveling him with a look, "you don't have to love somethin' to be great at it. You just have to decide whether or not you give a damn. That's the dirty little secret about life that no one wants to share. 99.9% of people will never be Michael Jordan, but they can exceed their wildest expectations just by giving a crap. By wanting to be a good father, husband, janitor, or whatever. By just deciding to care, that's it son."

Kenny stared down at his flip flops, his fingers brushing against the frayed edges of the note still stuffed in his hoodie pocket.

Wills sighed, leaning back. "You've got a gift, son. You see things on that court before they happen. You play smart and you play hard. God, you play hard. Maybe harder than anyone I've ever coached. Like people owe you somethin'. But still, you're holdin' back. And I'm tellin' you right now, if you just don't hold back life will reward you, son. I can see it. I can see it clear as day."

Kenny sensed the conversation had shifted from basketball to something bigger. He swallowed hard, but he didn't say anything.

Wills let out a slow breath. "I know you feel stuck and I know it's not easy, but you gotta figure it out and make a choice. Or one day you're gonna wake up and realize life ain't waiting on you. It doesn't wait on anyone. Because sooner or later, life's gonna choose for you."

For a second, neither of them spoke.

Wills leaned forward and smiled. "Now, that being said, if you wanna start by making Central wish they never stepped foot in Kyrock tonight, I wouldn't be mad about it," he joked.

Kenny couldn't help it—he smiled, just a little.

Wills nodded, satisfied. "Okay. Go on, get outta here would ya? Don't ya know I've got a big game to plan for here?" he asked with a wry smile.

Kenny stood, pausing for a moment before turning toward the door. His fingers brushed over the note once more, and for the first time in a long while, he wondered if—just maybe—his past didn't have to be the prologue.

***

Later that day Kenny slumped slightly in his chair, arms crossed. His eyes bounced between the clock and the window. The classroom buzzed with the low murmur of students half-engaged in their assignments, the scratch of pencils, and the occasional whispered joke filling the space.

Outside, the autumn winds carried leaves past the glass, swirling in bursts before settling in uneven piles along the edge of the school parking lot. Kenny focused on that, on the way the wind made everything move, unpredictable and restless—kind of like how he felt inside.

Ms. Lillian Carter, known to most students as just "Ms. Lilly," moved between the rows of desks with a calm, effortless authority. Something about the way she carried herself—firm, but not harsh. Her presence demanded respect without needing to ask for it. She was one of the few teachers at Kyrock High who didn't just lecture from behind a desk. Instead she engaged, challenged, and made students think instead of just memorize.

Her warm smile was framed by a sweep of blonde curls and a pair of glasses she was always nudging back up her nose.

"Kenny," Ms. Carter's smooth voice called out.

His name being spoken jolted him out of his thoughts. He turned toward the front of the room, where Ms. Carter stood with a book in her hands and one eyebrow raised. He hadn't realized she was looking at him; he hadn't even realized she had asked him a question.

"Sorry ma'am," he said, straightening slightly in his chair.

"I asked what you think the author is trying to say here," she held the book open, one finger tapping against the page, "in this passage."

Kenny blinked, his mind scrambling to catch up. He hadn't been paying attention, but he knew better than to admit that outright. His eyes darted to the book on his desk—*Of Mice and Men*. He let out a slow breath and took a guess.

"Uhm... maybe he's saying that...uhh... people carry more troubles than they let on?" he asked, hoping.

A flicker of something passed through Ms. Carter's eyes—approval, perhaps. She nodded. "That's an interesting take, and it's a good one," she said.

"Well, you don't have to sound so shocked about it Ms. Lilly," Kenny said calmly, trying to ease the ripple of tension.

A few students chuckled under their breath, but Ms. Carter ignored them. She leaned against the edge of her desk, flipping the book closed.

"That's the thing about burdens," she said. "Some people carry them out in the open. Others keep them buried so deep you wouldn't know they were there until it was too late."

Kenny swallowed hard as he fidgeted with the note in the front pocket of his sweatshirt.

Until a hushed exchange from across the room caught his attention.

Kate and Sara.

They sat diagonally from each other, just close enough to trade quick smiles and share eye rolls every time Ms. Carter droned on about the topic of the day. Today, though, there was a different energy—lighter, like the air before a summer rain, waiting to burst.

Sara leaned back in her chair, twirling a pen between her fingers, a teasing grin dancing on her lips. "So, Kate, since you're basically the queen of English class, what do you think Steinbeck was trying to say?" she asked, her tone playful.

Kate, half-doodling in the margins of her notebook, glanced up, smirking. "I think it's about loneliness," she began, shifting her eyes toward Kenny across the room. "Like how some people," she paused dramatically, "think they're mysterious and brooding when really, they're just bad at saying how they feel." Kate's basketball quarter-zip fit snug against her frame, the black and gold fabric tracing the easy confidence she carried on and off the court.

Sara's laughter bubbled up, and she shot a look at Kenny. She tapped her pen against the desk, the bright gold polish on her nails catching the classroom light with every flick—flashy, bold, and impossible to ignore, just like her. "Sounds familiar," she chimed in, raising an eyebrow at him.

Kenny blinked, pointing to himself. "Whoa, whoa, how'd I get dragged into this?"

Sara leaned forward, her ponytail swinging. "Well, if the shoe fits, Bledsoe."

"Or the flop," Kate added with a grin, bumping Sara's arm lightly. Sara caught the way Kate's eyes brightened whenever Kenny talked—hazel and warm, framed by lashes that could probably win their own homecoming crown.

Ms. Carter, sensing that Kenny could use a lifeline, cut in; her voice steady but pointed.

"You know, tension can be just as telling as dialogue," she mused. "Writers use it all the time. That suspicion that something's lurking beneath the surface, even if no one is saying it outright."

Kate and Sara looked at her, and for the briefest moment, Kenny swore he saw a flicker of amusement in Ms. Carter's eyes. Like she knew exactly what was going on and was content to let them sit with it.

Truth be told, Kenny wished Ms. Carter would've shared whatever insight she might have had, because, in that moment, he felt like the only one left out of the loop.

"Alright," Ms. Carter said, breaking the moment with a clap of her hands. "Let's get back on track. Page seventy-two, everyone. Let's identify if Steinbeck has anything else to teach us about people who carry things they don't say out loud."

As the class shifted back into focus, Kenny glanced over once more at Kate and Sara. Those two always had a way of making him feel one step behind, and he didn't mind. In fact, he knew those ladies would keep his life interesting in ways he hadn't even begun to imagine.

Chapter Five

The Bledsoe house was still and quiet, a sharp contrast to the roaring gym the brothers would soon be stepping into. The scent of thyme lingered soft as a Sunday morning hymn, a gentle reminder of Ma's homemade soap. It mingled with the stout smell of coffee she invariably had brewing, no matter the time of day.

Caleb sat on the edge of Ma's worn-out recliner with a basketball tucked under one arm. His knee bounced, and his hand trembled ever so slightly. Kenny stood near the window, his hands shoved in his pockets, staring out at the darkening sky.

Ma sat on the couch, her hands folded in her lap, watching them both with her sharp, knowing eyes.

"You boys ready?" she asked.

Caleb grinned, slapping the ball in both hands. "Always," he said.

Kenny glanced back, offering a half-shrug. "Guess we'll find out," he replied.

Ma nodded with her lips pressed together like she was holding something back. She reached out and patted the space beside her. "Come here now, both of you," she beckoned.

Caleb obeyed first by plopping beside her. Kenny followed, slower, settling in on her other side.

She looked at them, really looked at them. And in that no-nonsense way of hers, she said, "Listen to me now. You boys play hard and you play smart."

Caleb and Kenny both chuckled.

But her expression softened as she reached for their hands and squeezed them tight. "I don't care what that scoreboard says tonight. You hear me? Y'all are my boys: my Bledsoe boys. And that means something," she said.

Kenny swallowed hard and Caleb nodded.

Ma had a routine of listening to the games on the radio. She said being there made her too nervous, so she chose to pace in the living room instead, wringing her hands like she could will the ball into the basket from miles away.

But the boys knew it wasn't just nerves keeping her home. Pa needed her. His memory wasn't what it used to be, and leaving him alone for too long wasn't an option anymore. When people at church would ask about it, about Henry, she would wave a hand like it didn't bother her. Like she could just brush away the dust of sorrow.

"Y'all know I'll be listenin'. Carryin' on from my chair like we're in a revival," she said with a grin.

Kenny nodded. "Yeah well, just don't get the sheriff called...again," he joked.

"Oh hush now, I told y'all that was nothin' but a big misunderstandin'," she replied.

Caleb leaned down, pressing a quick kiss to the top of her head. "We'll make it a good one for you, Ma. I promise," he said.

She patted Caleb's cheek and squeezed Kenny's hand. Her thumb had been worn to a nub by time or tale gone wrong but, perhaps, that's a story for another day.

"I know you will, my boys. Pa would be so proud of you both...he is proud of you both," she corrected herself.

Ma gave Kenny's hand another firm squeeze. It felt as if in that tiny, weathered grip lived the strength of a hundred little old ladies. As she looked between her grandsons, her expression tightened in a familiar way—the one that signaled she was about to say something that ran deeper than just basketball.

"You boys know what Pa always says?" her voice soft as a cotton field breeze.

Kenny nodded, but it was Caleb she was looking at.

"Don't let the past decide your future," she said, with what was left of her thumb absently rubbed over the back of Kenny's hand. "You're more than what has happened to you. Don't y'all ever forget it."

Her words hung in the air.

Kenny glanced down, his jaw tightened. He knew what it meant—what it always meant when Ma and Pa said things like that. The things they never actually talked about. The things that had shaped him and Caleb in ways even time couldn't unravel.

Caleb stood and moved beside him, reaching out a firm hand and clasped it on the back of Kenny's neck. Kenny exhaled, slowly.

Ma stood and cleared her throat.

"Now," she said, forcing some joy into her tone, "y'all go win that game. You let it fly, grandson!"

Her eyes caught Kenny's. Then she turned her attention to Caleb. "And for the love of everything holy, pass the dang ball," she finished.

Caleb was the first to step out of the house as the screen door creaked shut behind him. But as Kenny headed towards the door, Ma's pale, tired hands, the same ones that had stitched a lifetime of quilts and smoothed back his hair when he was little, pulled him in close.

Her grip was firm, approaching urgent, as if she could press the load of her worries straight into his bones. Her voice, usually steady as a church bell, wavered just slightly as she whispered.

"You look out for your brother, you hear me? Somethin' don't feel right." She didn't explain, but she didn't have to. Kenny felt it too. There was a chink in his brother's armor, creeping in like the turning of the tide. It had happened before, like the quiet shift of seasons, when the world changes without warning.

"Yes ma'am," he said as he nodded. But for the first time in a long time, he saw something in Ma's eyes that scared him.

Kenny joined Caleb on the front porch; the cool night air wrapped around them both, and for a moment, neither of them said anything. The heaviness of Ma's words still lingered.

Caleb took a deep breath and rolled his shoulders like he was shaking something off. Kenny buried his hand deep into the pocket of his hoodie as the two brothers stood together on the long front porch that wrapped around the house like a hug.

Caleb finally broke the silence between the two. "You remember that time we tried to sleep out in the barn?" he asked.

Kenny huffed out a laugh. "Yeah, we didn't even last an hour," he replied.

Caleb grinned, shaking his head. "We swore we were gonna tough it out; thought we were real men, sleeping under the stars and all that," he said looking out toward the old barn.

Kenny laughed. "Then we heard that roar in the woods and ran screamin' like little girls," he said.

Caleb chuckled, the sound warm, slightly unfamiliar to Kenny.

"Ma said we woke half the county. Made Pa come out there with his shotgun," Kenny said while smiling.

"To look for a monster!" Caleb said, laughing.

Kenny couldn't help but think how good it felt to hear that sound again before his brother continued. "We said whatever it was had to be huge. Because it roared like a lion!" Both brothers laughed together. "I still remember the look on Pa's face when he found that little kitten," Kenny said.

"Yeah, that might be the only time he ever looked disappointed in us," Caleb chuckled.

Kenny laughed, but the memory settled somewhere deep in his chest, buried underneath others that were no laughing matter.

Fear had always been something neither of the Bledsoe boys could outrun. It wasn't that simple. Not after what they had been through.

"You know, I still catch myself looking for it sometimes," Caleb said, his voice low.

Both of them glanced toward the driveway where their mother would park her car when they'd come for a visit, back before all of it.

"Like maybe she'd come rolling back up that hill like nothing had changed."

But it had, everything had changed and neither of them ever talked about it.

Kenny, noticing his brother's hands starting to shake, something that only afflicted Caleb when stress was eating at him, finally spoke. "Hey," he said, his voice quieter now. "We got this."

Kenny didn't trust himself to say too much. He had learned the hard way that sometimes the best thing you can do for someone is shut up and listen. And unlike everyone else, he'd always been there when Caleb's golden boy veil had slipped.

Not even Sara knew, not really. She saw Caleb in the spotlight: the leader, the protector, the kid with the easy grin with the world at his feet. The whole town did. That's not to say that it was an act. It wasn't. But Kenny had seen Caleb's cracks, like steam from a kettle left too long. The other side of Caleb that was usually hidden.

The nights he couldn't sleep, when he'd sit on the edge of his bed staring out at nothing. The way he'd pluck and pinch at his eyebrows until there was barely anything left. The way his hands would shake sometimes when he thought no one was looking.

Kenny saw it all, but he never asked. And Caleb never said.

But Kenny knew, because he felt it, too. He just didn't hide it as good as his brother.

Neither brother spoke for a moment. The silence sat like unspoken prayers before a revival of the soul, until Kenny leaned forward, his eyes wide. "Oh shoot, dude—your nose," he said, his voice laced with concern.

Caleb raised a finger to his face, touched above his lip gently, then pulled back to see a trickle of blood streaked across his skin bright as summer berries.

"Dang," Caleb said, his voice low, almost ashamed.

Kenny pulled a tissue from his pocket and handed it to his brother. His eyes dropped to the dirt, like he was laying something down gently—giving his brother the space he needed as he turned and made his way toward the truck. But as he did, Caleb's voice rose behind him, not loud, just enough to hold him in place: mid-step, mid-thought, mid-heartbeat.

"Hey Ken," Caleb said in a tone Kenny rarely heard from his big brother.

Kenny's eyes leveled with Caleb's, giving him his undivided attention.

"I want you to promise me somethin'," Caleb said as he wiped the blood from his nose.

"Yeah?" Kenny replied.

"No matter what...I want you to promise me, you'll always do what Ma says and let it fly."

Kenny gave a half smile. "Okay, sure," he said, joking. But he could see in his brother's eyes that this was no joke.

"No, I'm serious, Ken. You gotta promise me you will," Caleb demanded.

"Okay, okay, I got it," Kenny replied, a little exasperated but not wanting to let his brother down.

"Because..." Caleb's voice trailed off, waiting for his younger brother to finish the line.

"Job not finished," Kenny said, a line he'd repeated a thousand times before, his voice steady, like it was the only promise he knew how to keep.

"I love you, man," Caleb said softly and sincerely.

He held his brother's gaze for a second longer like he was making sure Kenny heard him; making sure he really felt him.

"Always," Kenny replied as he looked at his brother and gave him an easy nod. Caleb nodded in agreement.

That was the thing about them—about brothers. Sometimes the words didn't need to be big or complicated. Sometimes "always" and a simple nod was enough.

Chapter Six

<<<<<

A familiar voice cut through the night air, warm and sure, just like it had dozens of times before. "Step into it, baby. Elbow up!" Ma yelled.

Kenny stood in the batter's box, dirt caked on his cleats, with the smell of popcorn and fresh-cut grass lingering in the air. The metal bleachers rattled under the strain of restless parents, and beyond the outfield fence the last traces of sunset melted into the Kentucky hills.

The glow of the setting sun spread across the Kyrock Little League diamond, and Ma's confidence filled the ballpark.

"Hey, batter! Come on now! We need a big hit!" she shouted.

Kenny, seven years old, stood at home plate, his helmet too big and his grip on the bat too tight. He could hear the other team's chatter from the dugout; he could feel the heaviness of too many eyes on him. His stomach was in knots.

From behind the chain-link fence, Caleb's voice scored through the noise. "Just like we practiced Ken, keep your elbow up!" Caleb shouted.

Kenny turned slightly, catching sight of his older brother leaning against the fence. Caleb wasn't just watching—he was willing Kenny to succeed like his belief alone could carry his baby brother.

Kenny tightened his grip on the bat and narrowed his eyes on the pitcher. His oversized jersey hung loose on his small frame, brimming with dreams bigger than he. The word *Braves* stitched across the front—Caleb's and his favorite team.

The pitcher wound up and fired it in. The ball came screaming toward him, or more like wobbled, with purpose. The best an eight-year-old's arm could do.

Kenny closed his eyes and swung.

CRACK!

The ball shot past the second baseman, bouncing into the outfield.

For a second, Kenny froze, stunned that he'd actually hit it. Caleb's voice came again, stronger this time. "Run, Kenny! Run!" he screamed.

Kenny took off, his cleats kicking up dirt as he rounded first, the sound of cheers ringing in his ears. By the time he slid into second, safe by a mile, his grin was so wide his face ached.

Kenny's eyes immediately went to the dugout and there was Caleb, fist raised high in the air, beaming like he'd been the one to get the hit.

From the bleachers, Ma clapped her hands together hard, letting out a whistle that could put any coach to shame.

"That's my boy!" she hollered, shaking Pa's arm like he hadn't been watching the whole thing unfold himself.

Pa, always the quieter of the two, chuckled, rocking back in his seat. "Look at that," he said, voice thick with pride. "We got ourselves a ballplayer."

Kenny had never felt lighter, never felt more like he belonged. He turned to look for Caleb, expecting another yell of encouragement, but his brother was already heading to the dugout, grabbing his glove for the next inning.

In Caleb's mind, Kenny was always supposed to succeed. It was never a question of if. It was just a matter of when.

***

The game was over. The adrenaline was fading. Out in the parking lot, the suffocating summer air felt wet. As small towns tend to be, the night was stitched with soft voices, slipping just beneath the threshold of another's ears. Not meant to be heard, but impossible not to be.

"There they go…" The whispers continued. "Those poor boys…"

Kenny heard it, same as always. He didn't have to turn his head to know it was the usual: the same murmured words that followed him and Caleb like shadows. He could sense it. Even at such a young age he always felt it. The stares, the sympathy, the curiosity, and the unspoken fascination of what it did to them. It was second nature now, stitched into him like an old patch on denim—always there.

Caleb, like always, walked a step ahead. He never flinched, never acknowledged it—at least not when he thought anyone was watching.

Kenny stuffed his tiny hands into his oversized pants. His fingers grazed the note crumpled inside as he tried to keep up with his brother.

He kept his head down as the murmurs settled into his chest like stones. It wasn't fair. They didn't know. They didn't really know. They just liked to talk, to pass around the story like it was some ghost tale told around a campfire instead of something that had actually happened to him and Caleb.

His fingers curled into fists inside his pockets. For a second, he let himself sink into it—the grief, the unfairness, the why us?

Caleb sensed it before Kenny even said a word and clapped his hand on Kenny's shoulder.

"Nuh-uh," Caleb said, shaking his head. "Not here. Not us."

Kenny kept his gaze on the pavement and his jaw tight.

"You wanna feel sorry for yourself, fine, do it later," Caleb continued. "But right now, we walk outta here with our heads up. That's what Ma and Pa taught us. That's what he would've wanted."

Kenny swallowed hard. He didn't have to ask who HE was.

Caleb nudged him. "C'mon, Bledsoe. You're tougher than this," he said.

And because Caleb believed it, Kenny did too.

Caleb turned to face him fully now, his voice quiet but edged with something unshakable. "We can't help what people say. They're always gonna talk. But we ain't the tragedy they think. You hear me?" he asked.

Kenny swallowed, staring at a crack in the blacktop.

Caleb knocked a fist against Kenny's chest, right over his heart. "Like Pa always says, we're not what we lost. We're what we got left."

Heavy words for an eight and seven-year-old to carry, but that was the hand the Bledsoe boys had been dealt.

For a second, neither of them spoke. The sounds of the parking lot swirled around them—engines rumbled and laughter spilled from car windows.

Until in the distance, Pa yelled out. "Y'all boys coming or what? Those Dairy Queen blizzards ain't gonna eat themselves now, are they?"

Caleb and Kenny turned to each other grinning ear to ear as they sprinted for the truck.

"That's my boys! My Bledsoe boys," Ma hollered, her eyes alight with pride as the boys ran toward her.

Sunburnt and grinning, no matter how hot or dusty the day had been, there was no dimming Ma's pride for her grandsons, her boys.

She hugged them both tight before they piled into the back of the shiny black Tundra. And for a moment the Bledsoe boys got to be just that: boys.

***

>>>>>

The sound of the game filled the otherwise quiet living room. Ma's eyes darted from the radio to the faded, picture-covered walls—each frame holding a memory and a piece of their story.

That same fire that burned inside her all those years ago at the ballpark still burned in her soul as she heard the radio announcer call out Kenny's name. Her hands clutched the arms of her chair like she could will the radio to speak louder, even though the announcer was nearly shouting.

"And another 3-pointer by Kenny Bledsoe, he has been on fire tonight. The Central coach has seen enough and will take a timeout to try to slow this Knights' run. Your score with 1:18 left to go here in the 4th quarter is Central 66, your Kyrock Knights 65. Kenny Bledsoe now has 31 points to go along with his 8 rebounds and 6 steals. Yes, folks you heard me correct, six steals on the night for the talented junior forward. He has been a man possessed out there, picking up the slack for his older brother who has been in somewhat of a slump–at least by his lofty standards. Shooting 1 of 12 from the floor with only 5 points, but he does have a career-best 11 assists. We'll take a quick break and be right back with the closing action."

In her next breath, Ma was pacing again; her footsteps were quick and uneven as she tried to burn off the anxious energy that was eating at her. Her heart raced and her mind jumped from one place to another like a hummingbird darting between flowers, never landing long enough to settle.

"Lord, Jesus," she mumbled under her breath, her eyes closed tight. "I know you got bigger fish to fry than a silly ole basketball game, but if you could just spare a little extra mercy for them boys in black tonight, well... I'd be much appreciative."

She paused for a second, her hands still clasped tight before she continued.

"And Lord, I know you healed the blind man, so if you could make those referees open their eyes, I'd count that as a double blessing. Amen," she finished sincerely.

"And here we go folks. Central pushes the ball up the floor. They swing it over to Jones who dumps it inside to Taylor. Kenny picks him up in the paint. Taylor dribbles, backing Kenny down. He turns, kicks it out to Cooper for 3, he shoots it...and it rattles in! Oh my! Tough break for the Knights there as Bledsoe played great defense on the All-State big man and Cooper just made a tough, tough shot. It's 69-65 and Central has a sliver of breathing

room. Coach Wills is gonna take a timeout here for the Knights. And with 38 seconds to go we will be right back after this quick break."

By this point, Ma had all but stopped breathing as she listened, her fingers clutching the frame of the window she'd cracked open to let in a breath of much-needed air.

As she stood under the glow of the blue Kentucky moon, anxious, waiting for the next play, she got an unexpected surprise. Pa emerged from his bedroom, his slow, deliberate footsteps shuffled against the hardwood floor.

Ma turned, startled, but immediately softened.

"Go on back to bed now Henry, you need your rest," her voice was gentle but firm, the way it always was with Pa these days.

To her astonishment, as if the world had tilted just slightly, Henry's eyes were clear—sharper than they'd been in months. He wasn't trapped in some fog of a memory or gazing through her like a ghost; he was present, he was really there.

"Our boys versus Central, Betty Lou," Pa said. His voice was steadier than it had any right to be. "Ain't no way I'm missin' this."

Ma swallowed the lump in her throat, blinking as fast as she took him in—his eyes clear, his posture strong, his mind, for once, not lost in the past. For tonight at least, it appeared Alzheimer's had met its match.

"Well, get over here and listen," passion surged through her voice—the very same it carried some sixty years ago when Henry was courting Betty Lou—as if not a single day had dared to pass since.

"Ok folks, let's see what Coach Wills has drawn up here. Wills made his bones as a defensive guru at Louisville Christian, but he's gonna need some baskets here if our Knights are gonna pull this one off. Caleb Bledsoe will inbound the ball here. He throws it into Wills, Deron dribbles to the left side. He passes over Carter. Carter uses a screen from Kenny. Carter dribbles back to the middle. Passes over to Caleb."

Back at the Bledsoe house, Ma and Pa squeezed each other's hands so tight it was hard to tell where one ended and the other began, both holding on like the outcome of the game depended on it.

"Caleb fakes, he drives, throws up a pass to Kenny. Oh! He dunked it in. Kenny Bledsoe dunked it in off the beautiful lob pass from his older brother and this place is rockin'! What a pass, what a play call by coach Wills, and what a night from the younger Bledsoe brother. As he cuts the central lead to 2, 69-67, with 16 seconds left to play here in Kyrock. And Central has used their final timeout."

Ma and Pa nearly jumped up and down. Well, mostly Ma, although Pa did manage to lift his tired arm for a triumphant fist pump. But it was his heart that pumped fast, pounding and full of pride.

For tonight, and perhaps for the final time, this game had given them something beautiful, something bigger than basketball.

Perhaps this night would be an answered prayer.

***

In the Knights' huddle, Coach Wills was calm. He spoke loudly, but only to cut through the deafening noise of the small-town gym. His words, like always, somehow seemed like something you'd hear in a sports movie: scripted, yet authentic. They carried with them truth and a fire of belief.

"Are you scared?" he asked his team. His voice calm, unwavering.

Unsure of how to answer, the team looked to Caleb, who didn't reply.

"Are you afraid?" Wills asked this time, and still no reply.

"Well, I know one thing, gentlemen... If your dreams don't scare the hell outta ya, then they just ain't big enough." Wills finished.

Wills looked around the huddle, letting the meaning of his words wash over his players.

The team, restless before, now sat still. Their hearts pulsed like sonar. The roar of the crowd beyond the huddle grew distant.

As the players rose from the bench, Caleb grabbed Kenny's arm.

There was a brief pause between the two before Caleb captured his younger brother's full attention.

And with fire in his eyes, he said to him, "Let it fly, baby brother, let it fly."

Then, with a single clap, it was Kenny who stepped forward with his eyes locked on his teammates.

"Knights on three," he commanded them.

"One, two, three, Knights!" the team shouted together.

As their voices and hands rose and fell in unison, the noise of the gym crashed back over them like a wave.

***

Ma and Pa stood in their living room with their arms linked tight, hunched over the radio like it was the only thread tethering them to the outside world.

"16 seconds left to play here in Kyrock, and Central will inbound the ball. They will most certainly be looking to get it into Jones, the All-State guard who shot 92% from the free-throw line last season."

"Here we go folks. Central inbounding, looking, nothing there. Oh my, Central throws a long pass out to the mid-court line. It's tipped by Caleb, it's loose. It's scooped up by Central's Jones, and oh no! He's got a wide-open path to the basket. He drives...and it's stolen away! Kenny Bledsoe from out of nowhere stole it away!"

"Kenny pushes the ball past mid court and swings it to Caleb. He's double-teamed. 7 seconds left, Caleb throws it back to Kenny. He dribbles, he's trying to free himself, oh no! Kenny dribbled it off his foot. 3 seconds, the ball is loose, it's picked up by Caleb. 2 seconds, he has three defenders all over him. 1 second, Caleb turns, he fires!"...

Chapter Seven

The air was crisp, the way it always got when summer finally gave up its fight. A young Kenny stood at the edge of the grave; his small fingers gripped a folded note so tight the paper wrinkled beneath his touch. He didn't know what to do with it—didn't know if he should read it again, tear it up, or just leave it behind like some kind of offering.

He sniffed hard as he swiped his tiny nose with the sleeve of his too-big jacket. He was just a boy. A five-year-old wasn't supposed to know just how deep six feet really is.

Footsteps crunched behind him, and then Caleb was there, like always.

Caleb was taller than Kenny but still just a boy himself, barely old enough to understand what they'd lost.

While Kenny was just old enough to comprehend the gravity of it all, Caleb was the one who carried the burden. The one who kept their world from completely unraveling, just an innocent boy who took on the kind of responsibility no child should ever have to.

Neither of them spoke at first, until Caleb exhaled a breath drawn deep from within as he stared at the headstone.

"Come up with anything good to say?" he asked his kid brother.

Kenny shrugged his small shoulders.

After a moment, Caleb stooped slightly next to him. "You know if you're waitin' for him to answer, he won't. But that don't mean he aint listenin'," Caleb said.

Kenny swallowed hard, an angry breath left him as he spoke to his brother. "How do you know?" he asked.

Caleb gave a small, lopsided smile. "Because I talk to him too," he replied.

Kenny looked at the monument; his grip on the note loosened just a pinch. The wind kicked around them, carrying sounds of the world moving on. But for a moment, standing there together, Kenny didn't feel so alone.

Back at the truck, Ma and Pa stood and watched the boys, their voices were low but carried in the quiet of the evening air.

"They're just babies, Henry," Ma whispered, her arms folded tight against the chill. "They shouldn't have these crosses to bear."

Pa exhaled, his voice rough but steady, "They're Bledsoe boys, Betty. They're our Bledsoe boys now. We won't let it crush 'em."

Ma shook her head, her eyes never leaving her grandsons. "I just don't want 'em to lose themselves in all of it," she said, her words tight with worry.

Pa was quiet for a moment, then he placed a gentle arm around her.

"They won't," he replied softly. "'Cause they got us, and most importantly, they got each other. We'll make sure they know that's all they need."

Ma approached the boys as she wiped tears from her eyes with the sleeve of her sweater.

"Come on now boys. It's startin' to get chilly out. Let's get on home and get y'all some supper," she said softly.

Kenny reached out his tiny fingers and traced the letters carved into the cold stone:

Michael Hawkins
Loving Father to Michael, Caleb, and Kenny.

***

>>>>>

Silence engulfed the gym as the ball left Caleb's hands. Every eye in the place followed its arc. Every hope, every fear balanced on its descent—hypnotized, as if it were a brown leather shooting star. No roaring crowd, no squeaking sneakers, and no pom-poms waving from Sara and the cheerleaders. For a single breath, the world stopped.

Back at Ma and Pa's, the moment seemed to hold endlessly. Ma clutched Pa's hand, her knuckles white, while the radio crackled. The announcer's voice hung in midair, caught between anticipation and fate.

"Bang! He put it in! I don't believe it! Caleb Bledsoe with the shot of his life! He put it in from almost mid court and the Kyrock Knights have knocked off the #1 ranked team in the state 70 to 69!

"It's bedlam here in Kyrock as the students are rushing the court. Heck, it looks to these old eyes, that everyone is rushing the court. What a shot! What a game! What a night!"

Down on the court it was indeed bedlam. Bodies rushed the floor with a wave of roaring voices and high fives. Cheerleaders screamed, students leapt over railings, and even the school principal was somewhere lost in the mix. But Kenny and Caleb only saw each other.

They pushed through the chaos, fighting against the tide until they reached each other at center court. For a brief moment, it was just the two of them. Caleb grabbed Kenny's jersey and pulled him in close, forehead to forehead. Both of them breathed hard, their chests rising and falling in stereo.

Kenny fought for his breath, "You did it," he finally mustered.

Caleb shook his head, a breathless grin broke across his face. "WE did," he said.

"I love you brother!" Kenny yelled as he began to be ripped away by the screaming mob of people.

"Always!" Caleb shouted in return.

The people of Kyrock had waited ages for a moment like this. And it was the Bledsoe brothers that had delivered it at their feet.

As quickly as it came, the moment was gone. The noise swallowed them whole as the celebration raged on. But for one fleeting moment, it had been just the two of them—just like always.

Chapter Eight

Later that night, the gym was unrecognizable—the earlier chaos replaced by an eerie stillness. The party had moved on to other corners of the small town, leaving behind only a few stragglers and the occasional echo of a bouncing basketball.

After answering what felt like a million questions from reporters from all across the state, Kenny finally slipped away, his mind still spinning.

That's when he spotted her. Sara.

"Gracie," he said, running a hand through his tangled, damp hair. "You seen Caleb?" he asked.

Sara, still glowing from the night's energy, nodded toward the locker room. Her cheeks donned with the number 21, Caleb's number, written in marker.

"Last I saw, he was in there," she said, as she picked a loose string off of Kenny's jersey and tucked a strand of his hair gone awry behind his ear.

"Okay, cool. I'm headed in there now. I'll let him know you're waitin' on him. You guys are gonna take your car, right?" Kenny shouted as he started to jog away.

"Yeah...and tell him I'm the one who gets to make the other wait while we're gettin' ready in this relationship," she yelled, her voice laced with sarcasm.

"Will do, Gracie!" he shouted.

"Hey, Kenny!" Sara's voice rang out across the gym, piercing through the quiet.

He turned, slowing his jog as he glanced back at her. "Yeah?"

She smirked, tucking her hands into her jacket pockets. "Good game tonight, Bledsoe."

Kenny smiled. He held her gaze for a second longer before nodding. Then he turned and bolted into the locker room.

"Hey, Caleb!" Kenny called out, his voice loud now as he burst past the old metal door, his sneakers squeaking on the tile floor. He scanned the room, his eyes searching for any sign of his brother. The thrill of victory still rushed through his blood.

There was no sign of Caleb. No signs of anyone, which he thought was a tad strange.

"Caleb?" he called out again, louder this time. Still no response.

He stepped out of the locker room, scanning the hallway that led there. It was still empty and he quickly decided that it was nothing. Caleb was just being Caleb, probably off doing something. Maybe he snuck out to grab some air or just to relax and get out his own head for a while. Caleb had a habit of doing that, especially after big moments. Maybe he just needed a break from all the attention, the noise, all of it. He grabbed his phone from his locker and decided to shoot Sara a text.

Hey I didn't find Caleb in here. Let him know we've got some celebrating to catch up on! See y'all later.

After Kenny had showered and quickly changed, he grabbed his bag and picked up the note he had carefully placed in his locker earlier. He ran his fingers over it like in some way he had exercised some demons; if only for one night. He slid it into his wallet, took a deep breath, threw on his flip-flops and exited the locker room.

As Kenny made his way towards the exit his flip-flops slapped against the court, echoing throughout the empty gym. He shoved the heavy doors open, desperate for the cool night air on his warm skin.

But before he could take a step, someone was there. Right in his path stood a shadowy figure.

Chapter Nine

"Sweet baby Jesus!" Kenny shouted.

His heart hammered in his chest as he recoiled and stumbled backwards.

His breath caught somewhere between fear and disbelief. But he quickly regained his bearings as realization dawned.

It was Kate.

There she was, standing in the shadows. Even in the dimness of the parking lot, she was beautiful. The way her eyes reflected in the haze from the distant street lights and the soft curve of her smile. Kenny was taken aback, momentarily frozen.

"You scared the heck out of me," he muttered, shaking his head in a bit of embarrassment.

"Well, nice to see you too, Bledsoe," Kate joked.

"I mean yeah, it is… it's just…you…you scared me…you…you're so pretty," Kenny said unwittingly.

"Thank you. I think," she replied, though she couldn't hide the smile tugging at her lips.

"You look pretty good yourself, Bledsoe. I especially like the flip-flops, it really rounds out the whole look you got going here," she teased with a smile that could calm a thunderstorm.

"No seriously you're really…pretty," Kenny let slip. As his mouth fired off words, well, a word, before his head could catch up.

Kate smiled as a faint flush came to her full cheeks. "Yeah, you mentioned that."

Kate was typically quick on her feet, never one to get tangled in a verbal back-and-forth. But Kenny kept going.

"I'm sorry I'm not really sure why I'm saying all these...," he paused as he desperately fought in his mind trying to find the perfect word. "Words," he finished.

Kenny didn't realize it, mostly because he couldn't shut up, but behind Kate's perfect smile, she was—maybe for the first time in her life—struggling to find the right words too.

Maybe it was the endearing way he kept stumbling all over himself just to talk to her. Or maybe it was his eyes—those bright brown eyes, like a jar of honey held up to the light. Like old love letters, full of things he'd never quite say out loud.

Either way, Kate gazed at him the way you'd watch a baby horse take its first wobbly steps on the bluegrass of Kentucky—equal parts amused, charmed, and totally helpless to do anything but smile.

And much to her delight, Kenny kept talking.

"It's just the game, and now you're here, and... it's you, and... you're gorgeous. Shit!" Kenny covered his mouth wishing to take back that last line.

Kate let out an audible laugh. "Well, we've graduated from pretty to gorgeous. I'll take that. I can't tell if you're the cutest thing I've ever seen or the most broken," she said, still grinning from Kenny's jibber-jabbering. She reached her hand out taking Kenny by his. "C'mon. Let's go for a walk and see what other adorable Tourette's outbursts you have in you."

Kenny chuckled, but the second her fingers brushed against his a quiet rush surged through him, undeniable and electric.

Kenny walked side by side with Kate across the school parking lot as their footsteps crunched the gravel underneath them. As they approached her car, Kenny glanced over at the spot where Caleb's truck was usually parked. His stomach dropped when he saw it—empty.

"Wait a minute..." Kenny muttered, looking around as if the truck might magically reappear. He ran a hand through his unkempt hair, as his frustration mounted. "Caleb must've took it?" he asked as his southern dialect pummeled the English language into submission. "He was 'spose to leave it for me."

Kate glanced over at him, a sly smile curled on her lips as if a spark had ignited in her pretty little mind.

"Well, guess you're stranded now...goodnight," she said, as she turned and walked away from him.

Kenny sighed and paused briefly before he called out to her, sheepish. "So uh, any chance you'd give me a ride?" he asked.

Kate paused and raised an eyebrow. She slowly turned back around to face him and crossed her arms like a gate closing on her curly-haired friend.

"Hmm, well, I'd love to help, but I've got plans." She paused for dramatic effect before adding with a wink, "I got a hot date waitin'."

"A hot date? With who?" Kenny asked as he scrunched his face and played along just enough to leave Kate wondering.

She shrugged, her grin never leaving her face. "Oh, you know, just someone adorable, super charming, and really good at basketball... a real catch if I do say so myself. I really should be going now," she teased, jiggling her car keys as she made her way beside the driver's side door.

Kenny couldn't help but laugh, the chemistry between them stuck to the air like heat on a July Kyrock night. He leaned against her car, fully committed to the bit now.

"Oh, I'm sure your mystery man won't mind. I think it shows what good character you've got there Kate, offerin' a ride to a stranger like me. Ya know, Good Samaritan and all that."

"Yeah, you're right. I guess it would be a bad look to leave the Great Kenny Bledsoe stranded on the night he played the game of his life and took down those scoundrels from Central," Kate teased.

The two exchanged a smile across the roof of her car.

"You think I'm great, huh?" Kenny asked, his voice carrying a flicker of confidence that even he didn't know he had.

Kate, caught somewhere in between flustered and flattered, shouted, "Oh, just get in the car would ya?"

"Yes, ma'am," Kenny obeyed.

Chapter Ten

As they traveled the winding roads of Kyrock, the mood inside Kate's car was light. It felt like two long-lost friends restarting a conversation where they'd left off. It wasn't awkward, which in itself, felt...surprising.

But Kate, never one to beat around the bush, came right out with it.

"So, why don't you see me?" she asked, straight from the chest with fire and grace.

Kenny, not entirely sure what she meant stared at her for a moment, as his mind raced for an answer.

"What do you mean?" he replied, in the way only a lost 17-year-old boy would.

Kate gripped the steering wheel tight as she turned and gave him a knowing look, her voice danced between playful and serious.

"You know exactly what I mean. We've been dancing around...whatever this is... for a while now, and it's like," she paused for just a second before dropping it again, "you don't even see me. At least not..." Her words hung in the air, as she wrestled with whether to finish the thought or leave it.

She glanced over at Kenny, waiting, hoping for him to fill in the silence.

Kenny opened his mouth to respond, but the words caught in his throat. He wasn't sure how to answer. Part of him wanted to deny it, the other part knew she had a point.

"It's Sara, isn't it?" Kate exclaimed, her voice artificially light with a hint of uncertainty. She didn't look at him; her eyes stayed fixed on the road as if bracing herself for his answer.

"What would Gracie have to do with anything?" Kenny replied, chuckling as the words came out of his mouth.

"Uh, that YOU LOVE HER, dummy," Kate shot back, her tone like thunder in the distance, both fierce and soft. She gave him a sideways glance, waiting for him to deny it—or not.

"Gracie?!" Kenny exclaimed, his voice incredulous. "She's... I don't even know where to...Oh, I know! How about she's my brother's girlfriend and the love of his life?"

He shook his head as if the whole thing didn't make any sense.

"Oh my God," Kate replied, her voice dripping with disbelief. "Dude, you call her Gracie."

"That's her name," Kenny slipped in like he knew the right answer to a question on a pop quiz.

"Yeah! The name you gave her that no one else calls her, except...YOU!" Kate's voice marveled in his innocence. "You really don't even see it, do you?"

Kenny's confusion deepened, but he couldn't help the frustration that crept into his voice now. "See what?" he asked, still not fully grasping what Kate was getting at. "She's like my..." Kenny started, trying to find the right words again.

"Sister," Kate interrupted, finishing his sentence with a smirk. "Yeah, like the hottest sister in the history of sisters," Kate teased, her grin widened as she glanced at him. "I mean, it's okay man, I don't blame you, no one would," her tone playful, "I mean, we are in Kentucky right? And Sara's freakin' perfect."

"Just stop, would ya?" Kenny said, cutting her off, his voice rising slightly. "I'm not in love with Gra—I mean, Sara!...whatever!"

He paused for a second before he turned the tables.

"And you," his tone shifted to playful. "Let's talk about you, miss I like to be chased but heaven forbid someone actually catch me! I mean the great Kate Covington might actually have to feel something...ahh, the horror!" Kenny dramatically teased.

With those words Kate swerved the car to the side of the road and slammed it into park. Her eyes flashed with a mix of surprise and amusement as she turned and faced her curly haired foe in their playful joust.

Kenny opened his mouth to say something, but before he could get the words out, Kate unlatched her seatbelt, leaned over the console, and kissed him.

It wasn't a long kiss, but it wasn't short either.

She pulled back slightly, her gaze soft but intense.

"Do you see me now?" she asked gently, her voice curious, as if waiting for him to finally understand.

A brief moment of silence filled the car before Kenny replied.

"I've always seen you, Kate, always," his voice was laced with vulnerability.

As the two leaned in for another kiss, Kate pulled back sharply, her breath shaky.

"I can't do this, not with you," she said, her voice tinged with uncertainty, as if the moment had one-upped her. She did her best to avoid his eyes as her hands gripped the steering wheel tight. "Listen, I'm not some kind of slut okay!" she exclaimed, her voice rising, a mixture of frustration and embarrassment. "I don't do... whatever that was," she added quickly. She turned her face away from him, trying to steady her breath. "I just—this isn't how I want things to go."

"Oh, okay- I mean I know you're not...I didn't expect...," Kenny stumbled through his words as he slumped into the passenger seat. "I gotta say though Kate, you sure know how to make a guy feel special," he said condescendingly.

"No...it's not that... that's not what I—" Kate paused, flustered by her thoughts before continuing. "I want to kiss you, trust me. I've wanted to kiss you since...forever. But not like this. Not...." She took a breath, attempting to steady herself. "I want to show you something," she said, more calmly than she felt.

"Okay," Kenny shrugged softly.

With that, she fastened her seatbelt, turned the ignition, and pulled the white Honda Accord back onto the road.

As the car disappeared into the Kyrock night, Kenny rummaged through a bag on the passenger-side floor, his hand sifting through the contents until he pulled out a notebook.

"Hey, what's this?" Kenny asked, holding it up.

"Don't touch that! That's my diary!" Kate yelled, her voice sharp with mock indignation.

Kenny dropped the book like it was a hot pan, his eyes wide with surprise.

Kate burst out laughing. "I'm just kidding," she teased, the laughter still dancing in her words.

"Well, I didn't wanna...," he trailed off, eyeing the notebook as if it carried some sort of disease.

"I mean, I'm not eight," Kate said, rolling her eyes. "It's not like I sit with my favorite gel pen and start... *Dear Diary, today I confess my deep, unending desire to be with Kenny Bledsoe,*" she teased in her best little girl voice.

"That's not what I....I didn't think...," Kenny muttered flustered, as he gently placed the notebook back in her bag.

It was quiet for a minute after that. The hum of the road beneath them faded and Kenny's thoughts shifted back to a place where everything was whole, where love grew wild like the garden surrounded by the white picket fence that framed the quaint little house with its matching blue shutters.

The Hawkins' place wasn't just a home; it was a heartbeat. The smell of freshly mowed grass and blooming flowers drifted through the air, mixing with the laughter of young boys and the steady scratch of a pen against paper.

Bathed in a golden kiss of an afternoon sun, Kenny, Caleb, and their older brother Michael, raced barefoot through the grass. Their father's voice echoed across the yard as he tossed a Frisbee their way. Their mother sat nearby on the front porch, lost in the pages of her journal.

A smile played on her lips, softer than a lullaby sung from a brand new mother.

Kenny was just old enough to remember. Maybe this was his first memory—the first perfect moment he ever held onto.

Their father sent the Frisbee sailing through the air, its bright yellow edge spun in contrast against the deep blue Kentucky sky. Kenny tracked it as his heart pounded with excitement. Without hesitation he leapt higher than he ever had before. He soared over Michael and Caleb, his fingertips brushed the plastic edge before he clutched it and pulled it in tight against his chest.

He hit the ground with a thud and rolled through the soft grass before popping back up, grinning ear to ear.

"Did you see that, Momma?" he shouted, breathless, hoisting the Frisbee high in the air like a trophy.

His father clapped his hands together.

"That's my boy! You got some serious hops in you, Ken!"

Michael shook his head, "Lucky catch," he said with a smirk.

Caleb, still sprawled on the grass, laughed. "Nah, that was sick," he said.

Their mother glanced over her journal as she watched them with quiet admiration, the kind of gaze that said she was memorizing the moment, storing it away where time couldn't touch it.

"Way to go, Kenny boy!" she beamed with pride.

Kenny didn't know it then, but this was heaven.

Chapter Eleven

The memory faded like the last flickers of a dream, replaced by the quiet hum of the car engine. Kenny stared out the window as the sleepy roads of Kyrock slipped past him.

Back in the Accord, the world felt different—heavier. The warmth of that perfect afternoon with his family was gone, replaced by the weight of something unspoken between him and Kate.

She hadn't said much since she'd pulled back onto the road; her fingers gripped the steering wheel like she was holding onto a secret.

Kenny shifted in his seat as he stole a glance at her.

"So," he said, breaking the silence. "Wanna tell me where we're goin'?"

Just as he'd asked the question, Kate flipped the left turn signal of the Accord. Its rhythmic clicking echoed through the quiet car. Kenny watched as she turned onto a dark gravel road, the tires crunched over the loose stone.

At the end of the road, barely visible in the dim glow of the headlights, stood a thin green sign that read:

CHALYBEATE CEMETERY ROAD.

Kenny's stomach tightened. He tore his gaze from the sign and looked at Kate. She didn't say anything, just kept her eyes ahead, her expression unreadable.

"Kate," he said slowly, his voice quieter now. "Why are we here?"

He didn't need to ask where—that much he already knew.

Kenny knew this forgotten road all too well.

This was where his father was buried.

Kenny's voice came stronger now, cutting through the hum of the engine as he searched for the why.

"If this is some kind of joke, it isn't very funny, Kate," he said as his hands curled into fists in his lap and his pulse quickened.

He didn't want to be here. Not tonight. Not ever. The thought crossed his mind to reach for his wallet. To hold the note—his note—but he left it tucked away. He wasn't ready to face the questions that would inevitably come the moment it left his pocket.

Kate finally broke her silence, her grip on the wheel loosened a bit. "Look, I know your dad is buried out here, but that's not why we came, okay? I promise." She glanced at him, her voice softer now. "I just... I knew if I told you, you would've said no, please don't be mad," she said softly.

Kate sighed as her eyes flickered between Kenny and the road ahead. "I just really want to show you something, something I've never shown anyone," she said, almost pleading.

If Kenny's memory was heaven, this most certainly was his hell on Earth.

The tension in the air was suffocating, as the headlights of the car stretched long shadows across the gravestones. Every inch of Kenny wanted to pull away, to jump out of the car and run as far from this place as possible. But something in Kate's voice held him there, tethering him to the moment, even as his heart pounded out of his chest.

As they stepped out of the car, neither said a word. Silence wrapped itself around them like a straight-jacket—heavy and inescapable. It filled the spaces where words should have been, magnifying every breath, every step, and every heartbeat, broken only by the popping of gravel beneath their feet and the soft slap of Kenny's flip-flops as they crossed the wide, secluded yard.

The cold continued to creep in slow and steady, settling in their bones as they walked shoulder to shoulder, the sorrow of the cemetery pressed in on them from all sides.

Kate led him toward the far back corner of the cemetery. Kenny, though familiar with the place, had never ventured to this part before. Then again, it's not like people take laps around cemeteries just to see the sights.

As they approached a large stone, Kate shined her phone's flashlight upon it. The beam illuminated the giant monument and the words etched across it read:

Vicky Covington
Beloved Mother and Wife

The moment hit Kenny like a punch to the gut. The stone, stark and cold, stood as a silent testament to someone he had never known, Kate's mother.

Kenny knew she'd passed away not long after Kate moved into town a few years back, but it wasn't something she ever talked about. And Kenny understood. Some things weren't meant to be pried open before their time. Grief had a way of closing itself off, waiting in the dark until the heart found the strength to face it again. It always returned on its own terms, quiet but certain, in the still moments when the world finally stopped moving.

Kate finally broke the silence; her voice pushed past her lips, tender and aching. "Watching someone you love forced to fight a losing battle... it's devastating," she sighed.

Her words stirred something inside of Kenny, like they had been pried loose from her heart.

Kate's eyes stayed fixed on the stone, her expression unreadable, but Kenny could hear the rawness in her voice—the kind that only came from knowing that type of pain firsthand.

As she continued her voice was steady, but distant, like she was speaking more to the night than to him.

"There aren't any words that make it better and time doesn't really heal the pain. You just... learn to carry it...make room for it somewhere inside of you, and after a while, it just...sorta becomes a part of who you are," she whispered in a voice like she was offering up a prayer.

A few beats passed before Kenny spoke.

"I guess I've never really figured out how to do that," he said in a voice quieter than he had intended.

His gaze remained locked on the gravestone, but his mind was elsewhere—back to the little house that once felt whole. Back to laughter in the yard, and back to the moment everything changed.

Kate glanced at him as her expression softened.

"No one really ever does," she said. "We just do a good enough job pretending we have so the world doesn't see how broken we truly are. One thing I have figured out though: it's not about replacing those missing pieces. It's about finding the people that can help you hold on to them," she offered.

The moment held its breath, dramatic in its hush. The air between them expanded with the ache of words unsaid.

Without thinking, Kenny reached out his fingers and brushed them against Kate's before gently taking her hand in his. A quiet intensity settled between them, unshakable and raw. In its own way deeper than the kiss they had shared just a few minutes prior.

The two stood facing the monument, paying their quiet tribute. Each deep in their own thoughts of all they'd lost.

Finally, Kenny spoke, trying his best to lighten the mood.

"Dang, we're broken," he said, shaking his head, his laughter tangled in the truth.

Kate gave a small smile like the wind bending through poplar trees. Her eyes flickered briefly to him before returning to the stone.

"Yeah," she said softly before continuing, "we should probably stick together, me and you."

Kenny wrapped his arm around her shoulder and pulled her in tight, offering a silent comfort that spoke more than words ever could. At that moment, there wasn't a need for anything more.

It was just the two of them standing together in the stillness of the night, somewhere, in the stillness of life.

Chapter Twelve

The back roads of Kyrock twisted and turned like old stories as the bright headlights of the Accord sliced through the darkness. The tension from before was gone, replaced by an easy silence that settled comfortably between them. The melancholy of the night felt distant now, like a dream forgotten by waking.

Kate glanced over at Kenny, a nervous smile tugged at the corner of her mouth.

"Can I play a song for you?" she asked in a playful tone. Before he could reply she continued. "You have to promise you're not gonna laugh though!"

"I wouldn't dare," he said, but the crooked smile curling on his lips begged to differ.

Kate shot him a glance, her playfulness faded. "I'm serious, you have to promise me," she said again. "You can't laugh; promise me, on my dead momma. I mean you wouldn't laugh at someone who's fifty percent orphan, would you?" she asked, fifty percent seriously.

Kenny blinked, caught off guard. "Playin' the dead momma card, dang," he said, the teasing edge still in his voice, but with a touch of understanding behind it. "Well, what if I raised you with the dead dad card?" he joked.

Kate raised an eyebrow, clearly amused. Like the world had whispered a joke only meant for the two of them.

"Touché," she replied, as a small laugh escaped her.

Kenny grinned, as his voice returned to seriousness. "Alright, you've got my word, no laughin'. I promise." As he said the words, he held out his clenched fist with his pinky finger extended.

"A pinky promise," Kate scoffed. "Aren't we a little old for that?"

"Hey now, if the pinky's out, there ain't no doubt," Kenny said, dead serious.

Kate rolled her eyes, but extended her pinky anyway.

And there—somewhere in the middle of Kyrock, in that white Honda Accord—the two of them came to an unspoken understanding, sealed by crooked smiles and crooked pinky fingers.

Kate unfolded her sun visor, and in a move straight out of the early 2000s, she removed a CD from a holder. "I know, I know," she said, shrugging her shoulders. "Who even has CDs anymore?" she joked, as a playful smile spread across her face. But Kate had them.

Much like compact discs, Kate was a relic from times gone by—something classic. But unlike them, she was something that never truly went out of style. She was sweet like tea from a mason jar, with a heart half wildflower, half barbed wire. And that smile—mercy—could talk a boy into trouble quicker than a June bug to a porch light.

As she slid the CD into the outdated player, the click of the disc spinning echoed for a moment before the first notes of a song filled the car.

"So, this is my, 'the world sucks and everything sucks, so I just wanna sing and be happy' song," she said with the happiest of grins.

"Wow, that really rolls off the tongue there, Covington," Kenny teased sarcastically.

"I think we both could use it right about now," she continued, ignoring Kenny's remarks on the matter.

Hold On, by Wilson Phillips started to play, filling the Accord with its familiar, upbeat melody.

Kate started to sing along,

Just open your heart and your mind, (mmm)
Is it really fair to feel this way inside? (woah)

Kate glanced at Kenny with a grin. "Sing with me," she said, her voice light and playful.

Kenny grabbed at the back of his neck and chuckled as Kate continued to serenade him.

"Now I agreed to not laugh, which, by the way, I'm really strugglin' with here," he said through a smirk. "But singin'? That was certainly not part of this here deal."

Kate continued to sing right over the top of Kenny's excuses, performing for her audience of one.

Someday somebody's gonna make you wanna turn around and say goodbye...

Until then, baby are you gonna let 'em hold you down and make you cry?

Don't you know, things can change

Things'll go your way

If you hoooooold....on for one more day

Can you hooooold....on for one more day?

Things'll go your way...

Hold on for one more day!

She finished the chorus in a high pitch, slightly off key, give or take a few octaves.

As the second verse began to play, Kate held out an imaginary microphone, her eyes wide with playful pleading.

"Come on, you know you want to," she teased. "I know you know this one," she shouted.

"My mom loved this song." Kenny said, barely audible over the music.

As the song built to its catchy chorus, Kate grabbed Kenny's hand, kissing it gently, her expression imploring him now.

"Sing with me, Kenny Bledsoe!" she exclaimed, her voice full of playful enthusiasm. "Don't you feel bad for me?" she pleaded through pouty lips. "My freakin' momma died!"

Kenny shook his head slightly as a grin spread across his face. "Right this second I feel bad for my eardrums!" Kenny shouted over her singing. "But I don't sing for anyone, Kate Covington...and I ain't startin toni–"...

Before Kate knew what was happening, Kenny quickly reached out and snatched the imaginary microphone, holding it close to his mouth. He began belting out the words like he'd been holding them in his whole life.

Someday somebody's gonna make you wanna turn around and say goodbye...

Until then, baby are you gonna let 'em hold you down and make you cry?

The two began to sing full throated together now:
Don't you know, things can change
Things'll go your way
If you hooooold....on for one more day
Can you hooooold....on for one more day?
Things'll go your way...
Hold on for one more day!

Kenny, seizing his moment, leaned over the console, closing the space between the two as he went in for a surprise kiss of his own.

But just as their lips were about to meet, Kate shrieked. "Oh, shhhhh-!" She jerked the wheel of the Accord hard to the left, the tires screeched against the pavement.

The car skidded to an abrupt stop.

Kenny, incredulous at what had just transpired, turned his head back and forth finding the side mirror and then Kate.

Kate exhaled a sigh of relief. "Oh my gosh! Are you okay?" she asked.

Kenny nodded.

In the rearview mirror, the flicker of emergency blinkers pulsed through the night.

"That car," Kate continued, her voice shaken. "It's just sittin' in the middle of the road back there. I... I never saw it around the curve—they could've killed us!"

"I should go check on them," Kenny said, his voice uncertain.

"Yeah, you're probably..." Kate began to answer, but before she could finish, a loud *THUD. THUD. THUD* of knocking on the driver's window snapped them out of the moment like a gunshot in the dark.

Chapter Thirteen

"Ahhhh!" Kate shrieked, her hands flailing in the air as she leapt in her seat.

The mystery knocker leaned their face closer to Kate's window. Kenny squinted through the darkness. His breath caught.

"Gracie?" he yelled incredulously.

Kate rolled her window down, and Sara Grace leaned in, her face streaked with tears and mascara.

"Oh my gosh! Are you okay?" Kenny asked, his voice filled with worry as he leaned closer.

Sara, choking back tears, muttered, "It was that stupid deer... probably the same one from this mornin'."

"You hit a deer?" Kenny asked, his voice tight with concern. "Are you okay?" he asked again.

"Yeah, but my car..." Sara replied, her voice shaky and anxious. "It's totaled. My dad is gonna kill me."

At this point Kenny unfastened his seatbelt and leapt out of the Accord racing to Sara's side.

"Did you call the sheriff?" Kate asked, concerned.

"There's no dang service out here," Sara replied, the frustration clear in her voice. "And there hasn't been one car come through until you guys! Ugh! God, I hate Kyrock," she exhaled, carrying the weight of anger and sorrow woven together.

Kate and Kenny both quickly checked their phones, only to meet the same fate as Sara Grace—no service.

"Okay, well get in. Let's get you out of here before you get killed," Kate said to Sara.

Kenny helped Sara into the back seat gently and said, "As soon as we have signal I'll call ya a tow."

As the three started quietly down the dark roads, Kate and Kenny didn't look at each other, though they both fought the urge to. The presence of a third wheel now felt undeniable. The car was quiet until Sara leaned forward, peeking her disheveled face between them. Wedged like the unwanted filling in a Kenny-and-Kate sandwich, she broke the silence.

"So, what have you two been up to tonight?" she asked in a calm voice, as if the chaos of the last ten minutes had never taken place.

Kenny and Kate glanced at each other, unsure of how to answer. But before they could respond, Sara plopped back into the back seat and exclaimed, "And I stopped to get you guys your favorite pizzas!" as she threw her hands about in frustration.

"That stupid deer—ugh!" she groaned. "If I ever see it again, I'm gonna kill it!"

There was a brief pause before Kenny smirked.

"Well, judging by the look of your car, I guess we should congratulate you on a job well done," he joked.

"Shut up," Kate whispered, jabbing his shoulder.

"Yeah, what Kate said!" Sara agreed from the back seat as she leaned forward getting in a smack of her own.

The two girls laughed softly together, and for just a moment, the mood inside the car lightened. But only for a moment. As they began the climb up Bledsoe Hill, they started to notice something—the distant flicker of lights, red and blue.

By the time they reached the top of the hill and pulled into the driveway, they were met with the blinding lights of ambulances and Kyrock Sheriff vehicles. Kenny's stomach twisted. He jumped out of the Accord, slamming the door behind him, searching for any signs of what was happening.

That's when he saw Ma sitting in the back of one of the ambulances. She was crying, but it was more than that. She was completely inconsolable as a medic tried to tend to her.

As Kenny's eyes met Ma's she opened her mouth to cry out, but only one word found its way through the ache in her throat.

"Pa," she whispered, pointing toward the house, but then her voice gave way to sobs and the tears fell like rain from a sky too heavy to hold them.

"Oh God, Pa!" Kenny cried out.

At that moment, an officer approached Kenny, attempting to stop him from entering the house. But Kenny, all six foot three inches of him, shoved the officer aside with a force fueled by panic and desperation. He barreled past him, rushing towards the house, his mind a whirlwind of chaos.

I didn't even get to say goodbye... why tonight? Desperate thoughts echoed through Kenny's mind, louder with each passing moment.

His heart pounded in his chest as he pushed through the door. The house was eerily quiet, the kind of silence that felt wrong. The air felt off, charged with a sense of impending shift. Every step he took felt heavier, as if the house itself was pulling him into something he wasn't prepared for.

He spotted two figures standing in the hallway, just beyond the living room. His legs carried him forward before his mind could catch up, his breath ragged, as he called out.

"Pa? Pa, what–?" Kenny gave him a look of worry that asked a dozen questions.

Pa was being held by another officer as if he was propping him up. Kenny reached out to grab Pa's shoulder, clinching the worn fabric on his pajamas.

"Pa, you're okay—thank God. What's going on?" Kenny said, confused.

Pa shook his head, his face etched with sorrow. His voice broke as he reached out his trembling hand.

"He's gone, Kenny," Pa sobbed.

Kenny froze. The air in his lungs vanished, replaced by a hollow ache spreading through his chest.

Kenny turned sharply, his eyes falling on Caleb's bedroom door, left slightly ajar. The dim light spilled out, quiet and cold. Inside, he saw Caleb—his brother—lying too still on the floor, the kind of still that made the world stop.

A silence, thick enough to choke on, hung in the air. On the floor beside Caleb, two empty pill bottles lay on their side, tipped over like they'd been dropped mid-thought.

Kenny's vision tunneled; his breath hitched in his throat as the world around him began to blur. The walls of the house began to close in on him.

"Cale-"

A strangled sound tore from his throat as his body moved before his mind could catch up. He stumbled back, nearly tripping over his own feet. Before he knew it, he was running out the front door, past the flashing lights and past the voices calling his name. The cold air hit his face like a slap, but he didn't stop. He couldn't.

The ground beneath him blurred into darkness as he tore down the hill, past the driveway, past the last remnants of home, toward the woods—towards anywhere that felt far enough away.

Kenny's breath came in ragged gasps as he descended further into his spiral. His mind was a blur of panic and disbelief, and the world around him seemed to be stretching and shifting, warping in ways that made no sense. His feet pounded the earth, his legs moving with no direction, no purpose—just running.

He couldn't think. He couldn't breathe. His heart pounded so hard it felt like it might rip from his chest.

Amidst the chaos of his racing mind came a noise, a scream. Sharp, raw, and unmistakably human, it tore through the night like a jagged knife.

Kenny's breath caught in his throat, his spiraling snapped to a halt. His body locked up for a moment before instinct took over. His flip-flops slapped against the cold earth, carrying him toward the sound, back toward the inevitable.

That's when he saw her.

At the top of the hill, framed in the flashing light, stood a girl.

Her back was to him, her shoulders rising and falling with panicked, erratic breaths.

He opened his mouth to call out to her, but before he could, she turned. And the look in her eyes made his blood run cold.

Sara. She was standing, but everything about her looked shattered, as if she were made of a million broken pieces waiting to fall apart.

The realization hit him like a freight train as the night seemed to close in around him.

"Caleb?" Kenny gasped, taking a step forward before falling to his knees. His voice was lost in the hollow ache that rapidly filled his chest.

His brother, the person who had always been there… wasn't anymore.

"He's de—" Sara cried out, the word catching in her throat, unable to fully escape.

Kenny wanted, with every ounce of himself, to run to her, to be her protector, but he couldn't find the strength to move.

In that moment, the world seemed to blur into insignificance. The boy who had once shared the same bed, the same hopes, and the same dreams, was gone.

The only thing that remained was the truth: Caleb was dead.

Chapter Fourteen

<<<<<

The morning sun poured through the tall windows of the school's front office, spilling long gold streaks across the worn floor– quiet light bearing witness to the beginning of something new.

Ma sat at an old wooden desk, her hands steady despite the taxing worries she carried. It was the first day of kindergarten and preschool for Caleb and Kenny, respectively. They had grown fast, and as Ma looked down at the registration forms, her heart swelled with pride. They might have their burdens to bear, but they were her boys now. So, no matter how heavy, they would carry them together.

Beside her, the two brothers squirmed, restless as always. Their little shoes tapping against the floor in a quiet, unspoken rhythm. Both had inherited that restless energy, thrust upon them by circumstances beyond their control.

Mrs. Lillian Carter, the new teacher, stood across from them, a bright smile on her face. She looked fresh out of college, the lines of experience yet to carve themselves into her features. But there was something about her—something unshaped, something genuine, like she truly cared about each child who came through that door.

As Ma signed her name, the conversation took a turn.

"Ma'am, I see your boys' last name here, says Bledsoe," Mrs. Carter began, her voice gentle but firm. "But, as a school policy, we like to ensure the name on their birth certificates matches the one we have on file. I just want to clarify—Hawkins is the name they're using?"

Ma's pen paused midair. She knew the question was coming. She'd felt it stirring long before Mrs. Carter's lips gave it form.

"No ma'am," Ma said, sitting up taller now, as tall as her small frame would allow. Her voice steady, though her hands tightened a touch around the pen. "They are the Bledsoes."

Mrs. Carter's gaze flickered for a moment, her expression faltering as she glanced at the paperwork. "But their certif—"

Ma cut her off, her voice low but clear. "Ma'am, they are Bledsoes. Their father's gone. Their mother's gone. They are my Bledsoe boys."

There was a pause in the air, like the breath spring takes before a storm.

Mrs. Carter's eyes softened as she studied Ma for a moment, trying to read the depth of her words. Her gaze then drifted to Kenny and Caleb, who were playing quietly by the window, oblivious to the adult exchange.

"But," Mrs. Carter began carefully, "the birth certificates—"

"They're Bledsoes," Ma interrupted again, her voice gaining strength. "They always have been. And they always will be. No matter what."

Another pause filled the room, one of those critical moments where everything seemed to hang in the balance.

Mrs. Carter nodded slowly, "Alright, Ma'am. I understand. I just needed to ask, but I respect your decision." She continued, "My husband is stationed overseas in Iraq, and he's not...gone."

"I am aware of your husband's...situation," Ma replied.

Both ladies clearly knew more about each other's circumstances than they felt comfortable speaking out loud.

Ma turned to the boys, a small smile tugging at her lips.

"Bledsoe it is then," she said.

Kenny and Caleb, now aware of the attention, turned their heads, with eyes wide and innocent. They didn't fully grasp the significance of the conversation, but they understood the pride in their grandmother's voice when she said their name. They exchanged a look—a quiet exchange of understanding and comfort.

Caleb turned to the young teacher and said, "Yeah, we're Bledsoe boys!" as he beamed with pride. Kenny, as he always did, mimicked his older brother, though his voice a tad softer.

"Yeah, we're Bledsoe boys."

Ma smiled and her voice softened now as she glanced at the young teacher. "Thank you, Mrs. Carter. I assume that'll be all?"

Mrs. Carter nodded, offering a kind smile, "It's not always about what's on paper, but what's in your heart, right?"

Ma's eyes glistened, but she held herself together. "Exactly," she said, soft but proud.

With that, the discussion ended, and the registration process continued. But Ma carried a quiet pride that day, knowing her boys had the one thing that would never be taken away: their name.

And with it, hopes of a new beginning, a new story. A tale they could carry in their chests, no matter where the long and winding road of life chose to lead them.

***

>>>>>

The memory of that day, the first time they fought for their name, lingered in the back of Kenny's mind as he sat in the swing that hung on the porch of the Bledsoe house. Looking out over the rolling hills, Kenny felt the gentle breeze of the late fall morning brush against his face, carrying with it the scent of places far away, somewhere with joy perhaps.

Kenny leaned forward in the old metal swing, beneath a sky full of cumulus clouds—those big, puffy ones that looked like God Himself had stacked up scoops of ice cream just for show.

His hands clutched a folded paper, light as a feather, yet heavy as the whole world. Like it knew every sorrow he'd ever carried. His fingers traced the name at the top: **Caleb Henry Bledsoe**. It was the program for his brother's funeral.

Kenny was disheveled; sleeping on a porch for two days will do that to a person. His mind began to drift, slipping in and out of memories—times when he and Caleb would sit in the swing, talking about basketball, girls, or whatever was on their minds. Times when Pa would tell the story of how he and Ma had been struck by lightning in that very swing. "Can't happen twice," he would always joke. But now, the seat next to Kenny was empty, eerily vacant—a cold reminder of the silence that had replaced their once joyful conversations.

It was at that moment Kenny heard the rumbling of tires on the long gravel driveway. Through the dust, he could make out the familiar shape of Kate's white Honda Accord, slowly making its way toward him. As Kate parked the car and stepped out, Kenny didn't look at her—at least, not really. His gaze stayed fixed on the empty swing beside him.

As Kate climbed the steps and made her way across the porch, Kenny finally looked at her. Her face was soft, comforting even, a hint of hesitation in her eyes. She paused when she got close to him, before asking, "Okay if I sit?"

"Of course," Kenny said, patting the empty space beside him.

The two sat in silence for a while—maybe twenty minutes, maybe two—before Kate gently took Kenny's hand, placing it in hers. Kenny, who had been numb for the past few days, allowed himself to savor in the brief comfort of just a flicker of forgetting.

The two sat hand in hand before Kenny finally broke the silence.

"A program, that's what they call it?" his voice tinged with anger. "It's all just so matter of fact. Like, hey, first we do this, and then we'll do that. Bullshit. This isn't normal," Kenny continued, his voice growing more bitter. "This world is so full of it! YOLO and love with all your heart..." he scoffed, shaking his head at the notion. "But when it's over, and it's time to stick that love in the ground, you're supposed to take three days and just...move on? Why would I want to do that?"

Kenny let his head fall onto Kate's shoulder, as his voice fell softer. "Why does everyone and everything I love leave me? What's wrong with me?" he choked out, his words weighted with pain and confusion.

"Nothing," Kate said, her voice soft as dusk, but firm as the porch beneath their feet. "Nothing is wrong with you," she said as she pulled him closer. Her hand gently rubbed his back, trying her best to ease the ache inside of him.

"Oh, God," Kenny said, sitting up straighter and doing his best to dry his eyes. "Now you're here and you feel like you have to help me."

"I don't feel like I have to do anything," Kate said sharply, her voice unwavering. "I want to be here. I just know there's nothing I can say that will…" she paused briefly. "So I just wanna sit with you. As long as you want me to. I'll sit here with you until you're ready to throw me off this porch," Kate added with a small, teasing smile.

"Never," Kenny said softly, then he glanced sideways at her. "I do gotta ask. How do I know you're not some kinda stalker? You obsessed with me, Kate Covington?"

Kate scoffed, nudging him lightly. "Watch it, Bledsoe."

The two shared a small laugh, and to Kenny, it felt like a gift from God—a fleeting moment of warmth in the cold, hollow emptiness that had settled over him.

His phone began to ring, cutting through their conversation like one of Pa's pocket knives.

When Kenny answered, his voice immediately tightened with worry. He stood from the swing, his posture shifting.

"No, I haven't," he said, pacing slightly. "Okay… okay, yes sir, I will right now. I will. I'll let you know as soon as I hear anything."

He ended the call, his grip still firm around the phone.

Kate started to ask, "Is everything al—," but stopped herself, realizing how inappropriate that question felt on a day like today.

Kenny exhaled sharply. "Yeah, I just—I have to go." His voice was abrupt and distracted. "That was Preach… Grac—Sara's dad. They can't find her."

Kate hesitated for a moment before nodding. "Oh gosh… well, let me know if you need anything," she said gently, sensing this might not be the time or place for her.

"You can come if you want," Kenny said, glancing at Kate.

She offered a small, understanding smile and shook her head. "No… I think this is more of a family thing," she said softly.

Kenny nodded, not pushing the matter. And with that he was off, a cloud of dust kicked up in his wake as the truck disappeared down the long gravel drive.

Kate stood there for a moment, watching the Tundra disappear into the distance. As she turned around and took in the sprawling beauty of the property, something clicked inside her—a quiet realization pressed against her chest.

She was in an impossible situation, and even though she didn't know how she'd ended up here—she had. And truth be told, she wanted to be. But deep down, she knew—some truths you just can't outrun. No matter what she did, or how hard she tried, she'd always be second to the girl with the ponytail. Sara had his past, and maybe even his heart.

Kate had spent her whole life guarding her heart tighter than she ever defended any ball on a court—and Lord knows, she didn't let much slip past her. But here she was, knee-deep in an unwinnable mess, wrapped up in a boy she had no defense for.

No play to run, no move to make—just her heart wide open. And whether he knew it or not, Kenny was the point guard now—calling the plays, holding the pace, with her heart in his hands.

Chapter Fifteen

As Kenny whipped the Tundra down the gravel road, his mind wasn't flooded with memories of the times he'd shared with his brother in the truck. Instead, he was singularly focused.

He knew, somewhere deep within him, where Sara would be. As he neared the end of the drive, he took a sharp left and veered onto a dirt road. It was a path he'd traveled countless times before. Maybe it was seven hundred fence posts to the east, or maybe it was seven million. Truth is, it didn't matter.

The only thing that mattered was it was the only place he'd go when he didn't want anyone to find him—the perfect place, the pond.

Sure enough, as Kenny's tires slowed and he pulled onto the dusty embankment, he saw a black Lincoln Navigator—Sara's mother's vehicle. And there she was, sitting on the small broken dock, staring out at the pond.

As he made his way toward her, she didn't turn to greet him; her eyes stayed locked on the water. Kenny paused for a moment before sitting beside her. The hush between them lingered as long and wide as the Kentucky sky. Until at last his voice broke through the silence.

"Everyone's looking for you, ya know?" he said, his voice low.

"You of all people don't have to come down here and be sorry for me," Sara said, her voice soft. "I mean, I should be taking care of you," she reasoned.

She sat with her arms folded, resting easy atop her knees.

"It's not a competition," Kenny replied, his tone light, joking. If such things still existed.

"Right," Sara agreed, her voice tight. "I wish someone would tell that to the endless line of people at my house, all telling me how sorry they are, or how he was such a good kid. Or my personal favorite—"

Kenny interrupted, "Well, he's in a better place now."

Sara huffed, her frustration palpable.

"Yep, that's the one" she said, her voice thick with sarcasm.

"Like telling me God had a plan for this makes it better. I mean, I know people mean well," she continued, her frustration building, "but all those stories about how much he meant to you, or some crap about whatever, it's just for them. It's just so..." She trailed off, searching for the words.

"Pretentious," Kenny said calmly. "Artificial, phony... uhh...bullshit."

"Yeah, that sums it up," Sara agreed, on the verge of smiling, though her heart wouldn't let her face follow suit. "How'd you know I'd be here?" Sara asked.

"How could I not know?" Kenny replied.

"He hated this place." They both blurted out, practically saying the words at the same time.

Kenny smirked. "He always thought it was such a waste of time being out here. Like takin' a few hours to be a normal kid would somehow keep us from going to the NBA or somethin'," he said softly.

Sara sighed as they both sat still on the edge of the dock. Their thoughts, however, were anything but still.

"I'd always ask him to bring me down here, ya know. He'd say if I wanted water, he'd take me to the beach someday. So, I'd tease him about not being able to swim. I asked him what kind of country boy can't even float a little?" she said, smiling at the memory. "And the smartass he was, he'd always somehow turn it around on me. He'd tease me about not being able to start a fire or...ride a bike," she scoffed behind a smile.

There was a pause before Kenny asked, "Wait, you can't ride a bike?"

Sara gave him a small punch to his shoulder, as her smile faltered and Kenny chuckled softly.

"I guess he just always felt guilty, like us havin' fun meant we were forgettin' about them... ya know?" Kenny said tight roping a question, like he hoped Sara would tell him it all made perfect sense.

Silence settled over the two as Kenny wrapped his long arm around Sara's shoulders, pulling her in close. He watched quietly as tears welled in her eyes and began to fall. Her fingers fidgeted with the pendant on her necklace—a small blue basketball hanging from a silver chain, swaying gently, lost in the stillness of the day.

As they sat there together, lost for words, their feet dangling just above the water's surface, barely skimming the quiet ripples beneath the dock, memories played like old film reels in their minds.

"Where do we go now, Kenny?" she asked, her voice just above a whisper.

"I don't know, Gracie," he replied softer. "I don't know."

The two sat together on the old wooden dock for the rest of the afternoon, comfortable in each other's presence, but their hearts rudderless—nothing in the world to anchor them except memories and each other.

Chapter Sixteen

<<<<<

The sun blazed overhead, higher than high noon, as if noon had come and gone without telling anyone. The laughter of teenagers echoed throughout the gigantic backyard as splashes of water mixed with the sound of music drifting from speakers. It was one of those perfect summer days, when hours felt like seconds and everything else felt distant. Like nothing could touch the simple ease of, well, being young.

Sara Grace's summer pool party was in full swing at the McMansion known as the Whitmore house.

Kenny and Caleb sat on the edge of the giant pool, their feet dangling in the rippling cool water while the sun cast silhouettes off their rippled physiques. The rest of the basketball teams and the cheerleaders swam, threw around a beach ball, and goofed off, free from all cares.

Kate was there, wearing her usual playful grin and a bikini that had the boys practically breaking their necks to sneak a peek. Her two-piece wasn't flashy, but somehow she still managed to look like summer wrapped in a smile. Kate was doing some peeking of her own from behind her oversized round sunglasses, she was looking toward the far end of the pool. Her gaze was directed at Kenny and she let her eyes linger a touch longer than she meant for them to.

But who could blame her, his hair was wet and wild and his sun-warmed skin glistened, bronzed beneath the watchful eye of the day. And she couldn't help but notice just how well the look suited him.

Kate turned with a smirk toward her friend. "I think I'll go see what's up with Bledsoe, flash him a little smile, flirt a little…just for fun," the last line a playful fib she spun from her lips, even if she didn't know it.

She swam over to the edge of the pool where Kenny and Caleb were chatting and pulled herself up out of the water, doing her best Pamela Anderson impression as she brushed against Kenny's shoulder. Kenny turned, immediately apologizing.

"Oh, 'scuse me, bumped you there, didn't I?" he said in a concerned voice, completely oblivious to anything beyond his polite demeanor and his desire to counsel his brother.

Kate couldn't help but laugh. She shook her head at how easily he'd missed the obvious.

Caleb sat beside him, quiet, his eyes focused on Sara who was talking with a few friends at the opposite end of the pool. Her bikini was modest, but her smile outshone the sun. Every so often, Sara would laugh, and Caleb's heart would trip all over itself.

"Man, you gonna keep starin' at her all dang day, or you gonna grow some and go over there?" Kenny teased, nudging his brother with his elbow. "If you don't, I might have to go down there and scoop her up," he said with no intention of doing so.

Caleb shifted uncomfortably, as he tried to mask the nerves that were clearly eating at him. "I don't know, Ken. I just…what if she doesn't even like me like that?" he asked as his hands started to tremble.

Kenny leaned back on his hands, a half-smile tugging at the corner of his mouth. "Look I'm tellin' you, Gracie is a sweetheart, she's…" he paused for just a second. "She's the best," he said, looking at her across the pool. "Besides, you're not gonna get anywheres by sittin' here like a frog on a log, brother. Just… go over there and say…heck, say anything. I'm telling ya, she's into ya. She's just waitin' for you to make the first move," Kenny said confidently.

Caleb sighed, his face scrunched in hesitation. "Yeah, but what if I mess it up?" he asked.

"Then you mess it up," Kenny said, shrugging his shoulders. "But it'll be better than sittin' here wonderin' what could've been. And for gosh sake, just don't fall in the deep end in front of 'er. Your baby brother havin' to rescue you from drownin', well, that might just mess it up," Kenny teased with his perfect smile.

Kate, always the curious soul, who may or may not have been eavesdropping, caught the last part of the conversation. She couldn't help herself as she walked over and slipped into the space between the brothers like it was assigned to her.

"You know, if you really want to impress her, you should just tell her you couldn't help but notice what a nice smile she has. That always works," she said as she flashed Kenny a smile like a sunbeam through clouds, daring him to notice the spark behind it.

Kenny reciprocated her grin, but remained oblivious to her advances.

"That's what I've been tellin' him. He just needs to take a chance, right Kate?" Kenny asked.

Kate smiled. "Yeah, you never know what might happen if you just take a chance," she said, practically batting her eyelashes at Kenny now.

Caleb stood up abruptly as if finally finding a spark of courage. "Alright, alright. I'm gonna do it," he said as he stood and began his long walk to the other end of the pool.

Kenny chuckled as he watched his brother; he ran a hand through his wet hair. "I swear that boy is so oblivious sometimes, he wouldn't know a good thing if it jumped up and bit him right on the keister," he said through a grin.

"You don't say?" Kate said condescendingly.

With a deep breath, Caleb walked toward Sara, who was sitting on the edge of the pool. Her tan legs dangled in the water. He walked with an awkward confidence; he wasn't as uncertain as before.

Kenny watched him for a moment, then he turned to Kate with a smile, beaming with pride.

Kate, close to being caught up in Kenny's cuteness, gathered her thoughts. "I thought you and Sara Grace were a thing?" she asked. "You guys are like, inseparable," she said as if asking another question.

"Me and Gracie?" Kenny scoffed, shaking his head. "Nah, it's not like that."

At that moment, he turned to look at Sara. His eyes found hers through the sea of people in the pool, and she gave him a soft wave, her fingers dancing his way. Her eyes were a deep, steady brown, dark and beautiful like creekwater catching a sliver of moonlight on a calm Kentucky night. Kenny waved back to her, his smile matching hers sparkle for sparkle.

"Well, that's good to know, you've got your options open," Kate teased, her tone soaked in flirtation.

Kenny's eyes were still locked on the other end of the pool as he nudged Kate with his elbow.

"Hey, watch this," he said.

Kate followed his gaze, then glanced back at him. "What exactly am I looking at?" she asked.

He grinned. "It's not every day you get to witness the beginning of something that'll last forever," he said matter-of-factly.

They both watched on as Caleb sat down beside Sara and the two began chatting.

Kate couldn't help but notice the pride in Kenny's face.

"You really think so, huh?" she asked.

"Yeah," Kenny said, his voice certain. "I know it will." And he meant it.

Chapter Seventeen

The sun dipped low, sinking lazy and slow on a late fall evening too warm to be trusted. The Kentucky sky wore the color of a Georgia Peach, and the earth seemed to breathe in that strange stillness that comes when the season forgets itself.

Kenny and Sara made their way back toward their vehicles in silence as Kenny reached for the door handle of the Tundra.

He leaned in and picked up the program he had tossed in the passenger seat earlier. He paused as he turned to Sara.

"You know what? None of this feels right," Kenny said, his voice firm as he looked down at the flimsy sheet of paper. "This isn't what he would've wanted," he continued, showing the folded paper to Sara.

Before she could respond, Kenny jumped in the truck, fired the engine and shouted over his shoulder, "Follow me!" as he tore out of the dirt.

When they both arrived back atop Bledsoe Hill, they were met with a sight that stole their breath—dozens of cars and trucks lined up in the fading light. The entire basketball team was there, waiting. His teammates, his brothers, and standing among them was Coach Wills.

Kenny barely had time to put the truck in park before he was met with open arms, one hug after another, his teammates embracing him without a word. Ma stood on the porch, watching, the pride evident in the soft smile she wore.

Kenny turned to the group, his voice steady. "I'm glad you're all here. He loved each and every one of you," he exhaled deeply, as if trying to release a breath that had been catching in his chest the past few days. "But I hope you're ready to work," he said.

He stepped away from his teammates for just a moment, climbing the steps of the porch and whispered something into Ma's ear. She gave him a quiet nod of approval.

Without another word, Kenny strode toward the side shed, disappearing inside. When he emerged, he carried two shovels. With a practiced toss, he flung one toward one of his teammates, who caught it instinctively. Then he stepped inside, grabbed another and gave it away also.

The group didn't say much outside the old shed, but when Kenny had passed out all the shovels he could find, he turned to his teammates and said, "This," his voice unwavering, "is what he would've wanted."

Kenny, followed by his teammates, Sara, Ma, and Pa—who had now emerged from the house wrapped in a warm sweater—made the long, daunting walk to a far edge of the property. Their footsteps were quiet. Pa's strides were slow as he and Ma trailed behind the group, a steady purpose in each step, as if he were carrying the pride of all the years this land had seen, passed down to him by his father and his father before him.

Finally, they reached it—the towering cottonwood tree, its massive trunk weathered and strong, bearing the silent tales of generations past. The tree stood like a guardian over the land, its sprawling branches reached outward as if embracing the memories it had witnessed. Beside it ran a small, quiet creek, its waters weaved gently around the roots of the old tree. There was innocence to it, a quiet grace untouched by the decays of the world. It moved as it always had, unaware of sorrow, unbothered by time—just flowing, existing.

Without saying a word, Kenny drove his shovel deep into the earth. The soil was cold, unyielding, much like the ache in his chest. But with each thrust of the tool, the ground gave way, unlike the grief in his soul.

As time passed, the boys and coach Wills took turns digging—except for Kenny, who never stopped.

As the hours unwound like thread from the spool of time and the sun had all but set in the western Kentucky sky, Kenny finally stopped. The air was unmoving with silence—it had been all along—but it was Kenny that finally broke it.

"Tomorrow morning. Nine a.m. We say goodbye," he said, as he wiped the sweat from his face.

Those were the only words he spoke—anything more felt too much. With that, he let the shovel fall from his hands.

Without another word, he turned toward the house, and one by one, the others followed. Together, they made the quiet, solemn walk back—back toward the house, back toward a life without Caleb.

Chapter Eighteen

The spray from the shower washed over Kenny like a quiet release, steaming against his skin, but doing nothing to ease the pain pressing in on him. The water spiraled down the drain, murky with dirt—the same earth Kenny had shoveled now washing away, though the pain still clung to him.

As Kenny made his way to his room for the first time since that night, he knew he wouldn't find sleep or comfort. So instead, he did what he had done hundreds of times before. He sat on the edge of the window, staring out at the night, letting the silence wash over him.

It was in moments like this that Kenny always had one constant, one thing that somehow kept him tethered to reality and carried him through times when he thought he wouldn't make it. The note.

That's when it hit him like a bolt of lightning. He jumped from his seat by the window, frantically searching through his dresser drawers, his heart pounding. For the first time in as long as he could remember, he couldn't remember where he'd put it.

"It has to be here," he muttered anxiously, as he flipped through some used laundry at the foot of his bed. But in that moment, an unwilling memory surfaced—he remembered bursting out of the house that night, that awful night. He remembered running down the hill, into the field, and vividly recalled removing the note from his wallet and dropping it, watching it flutter away in the wind.

Kenny quickly threw on a tattered hoodie and a pair of flip-flops and unfastened the seal on his window. Without hesitation, he leapt out.

Kenny had often exited his room this way since he was young—not that he needed to sneak, but because, well, that's just how he did it.

Armed with nothing but the light of his phone and the glow of the moon, Kenny set off. As his flip-flops slapped against the cold ground, his heart began to race. He wasn't sure why he needed to find the note so badly. He could recite it word for word, backwards even, but he just needed it.

He made his way down the hill, toward the spot where he remembered being that horrible night. *This is a lost cause,* he thought to himself. *There's no way.* Yet, he scoured the earth inch by inch, his mind focused solely on the search.

Suddenly, in the stillness, he heard a noise—a faint rattle in the distance. Raising the light of his phone, he froze, startled by a figure emerging from the shadows. It was a familiar, though unexpected, sight—a deer. Small in stature but bold, standing out against the night like a silhouette carved from moonlight.

For a moment, it was as if the deer and Kenny locked eyes, both still, each aware of the other's presence. Slowly, Kenny began to move toward it, his steps soft on the earth.

A branch snapped in the distance, breaking the stillness. The deer startled, used its powerful legs to launch into the night, disappearing into the darkness.

Kenny sighed, his head dropped as he stood there. Lost in the moment, in everything. It was then that something caught his eye—a flicker in the moonlight, as if a ray of sunshine had somehow crept its way through the night.

He knew exactly what it was before he even began to move closer. It was the note..

He bent down; his fingers brushed against the earth as he picked it up. He unfolded it and again, like he had so many times before, he began to read the words written on it: *I love you 4 more! Always.*

Six simple words that had carried Kenny through countless moments. He wasn't sure why his father had left it for him on the night he took his own life. Or why he chose to place it on Kenny's pillow instead of his mother's.

In fact, many times it made him angry. Why leave those six words for a five-year-old boy to carry? Why not stay and fight for your wife, for your sons, for your family?

But in a strange way, the note had been the one thing that helped Kenny navigate the tragedy of losing his father. And for that, he felt an odd sense of gratitude, despite all of it.

Would Caleb still be here if their father had chosen to stay and fight instead of giving up? he thought to himself. *If only things had gone differently.*

But slowly, Kenny was beginning to understand something deeper. Maybe this fight wasn't a fair one.

Maybe it was a battle his father couldn't win, no matter how hard he might have tried. And maybe it was a battle his brother never stood a chance at.

Caleb had been left to fight his battles in silence— the way he kept his pain hidden behind a mask of defiance, the way he struggled alone—try as Kenny might to be there for him.

The weeks of isolation, the therapy sessions Caleb had resisted, the silent tears Caleb thought no one noticed. Kenny had watched his brother go through it all, even when Caleb thought he was hiding it so well. Kenny had always known.

He had tried to reach him, tried to break through, but sometimes it felt like Caleb was too far gone. Maybe he was too young, or too tangled in his own web of pain to understand how deep his brother's fight ran. But now, with Caleb gone, the silence left behind felt louder than ever. Kenny questioned just how much he had ever truly understood.

As he carefully placed the note back into the front pocket of his sweatshirt, the burden of it settled within him. It was his and his alone to carry.

He paused for a moment, taking in the quiet around him. There was calmness in this place, a kindness in the wind that wound its way through the cottonwoods and pines. Almost as if the land was calling Kenny to lay down the pain his brother and father could not carry before it buried him too.

So, in that brief moment, standing under the stars of a Kentucky night sky, Kenny allowed himself to let go. Not to say goodbye, but to find the strength to pick up another broken piece of his soul and keep moving forward.

***

As Kenny made his way back to the house, he climbed through his window and onto the hardwood floor. But as he stood, he was startled by a shadowy figure waiting for him in the darkness of his bedroom.

"Ahhh!" Kenny yelped, his voice hushed so as not to wake Ma and Pa.

"Shh! It's me, it's me," the shadowed figure whispered. The familiar sound of Sara's rich country accent instantly calmed his restless heart.

"Gracie?" Kenny whispered, "What the heck? You scared me."

"Sorry," she murmured, as she slipped through the moonlit room, dressed in a baggy long-sleeve t-shirt and pajama pants. As she moved closer, the moonlight spilled through the window and illuminated her face more. It was soft and weary.

"I couldn't sleep," she said softly. "I saw your window open and figured you couldn't either... I didn't want to wake Ma and Pa. I just... I'm afraid to close my eyes, Ken," she admitted softly. "Is it okay if I crash here tonight?"

"Of course," Kenny replied without hesitation, quickly moving to clear a comfortable spot on his bed for her.

"I can't take your bed," she protested.

The thought of sleeping arrangements hadn't even crossed Kenny's mind. Back when they were younger, Sara would stay over all the time—during church revivals, snowy nights with no school the next morning, and long weekends when her mom and dad would go out of town. Ma would help them drag every blanket in the house into the living room, draping them over chairs to build forts that turned into castles by morning. Kenny would fall asleep under a ceiling of quilts and flashlight stars, with Ma snoring softly from the recliner, keeping one slippered foot propped on the coffee table just to remind them she was there.

But now... things were different. The house felt smaller. And Sara wasn't the same barefoot kid who used to steal his pillow and hum herself to sleep beside him. She was here in the dark, hair loose, eyes tired, the tremble in her voice making his chest ache.

He rubbed the back of his neck. "You can take the bed," he said quietly. "I'll grab the floor. It's not a big deal, it's not so bad down there anyway," he fibbed.

"Kenny, I'll sleep on the floor. I'm not takin' your bed," she insisted.

"Gracie, either you sleep up there, or no one does," he shot back, leaving no room for argument.

As the two settled into their spots, Sara spoke softly.

"Where did you go just now?" she questioned.

"I was looking for somethin'," Kenny replied.

"Did you find it?" she asked, her voice carrying more meaning than the words alone.

"Yeah," he paused before continuing, "actually, I did." His words were weighted with something unspoken.

"Good. I'm glad," Sara murmured.

Silence settled between them again until Sara reached her hand over the side of the mattress. Kenny, noticing, reached up and took it in his.

"Ken," Sara whispered.

"Yeah?" Kenny replied.

"How are we gonna make it?" Sara asked quietly.

Kenny rubbed his thumb gently over her palm, staring up at the ceiling.

"Together," he replied in a voice softer than hers.

Chapter Nineteen

<<<<<

The room was warm as the hush of the evening poured through the open windows of the Hawkins' place, bathing the scratched wood floors with pale light.

The sky was soft and dull, like it couldn't make up its mind. Out past the porch, the clouds had that look—like it might rain, but then again, spring in Kentucky was always good at bluffing.

Inside the house, Kenny stood in front of a mirror; his small hands fumbled with the tie around his neck. His father knelt beside him, guiding him with practiced patience.

"Just like this, bud," his dad said, looping the fabric with ease.

Kenny scrunched his tiny nose. "Too tight," his tiny voice complained.

His mother walked by, the click clack of her high heels echoed throughout the home. She paused in the doorway and gave Kenny a soft smile.

"My little handsome man," she cooed, smoothing his wild hair before continuing to the tall mirror on the opposite end of the space.

From across the room, his older brother Michael snickered. "Don't worry, Ken. No amount of fancy clothes is gonna fix that face," he teased.

Kenny groaned, and their father shot Michael a warning look. "Hey, knock it off," he gruffed, but amusement crept into his voice.

Michael grinned. "I'm just sayin'," he teased with a lopsided smile.

"You look...breathtaking, honey," their father said as he locked his gaze toward their mother.

"You look…," she paused good-naturedly, "acceptable to stand next to me." She tilted her head just so, as a crooked grin, the same one her boys wore like a hand-me-down, spread slowly and surely across her face.

"Why do we have to go, Momma? Can't we just stay with Ma and Pa?" Kenny whined, still tugging at the tie around his neck.

His mother arched her brow and crossed her arms. "Well, that certainly makes momma feel loved," she shot back at her tiny opposition.

Across the room, Caleb was busy fidgeting with his own outfit, struggling with the buttons on his too-starched shirt. "I don't wanna go either," he mumbled. "This thing is chokin' me," he said in defiance.

Their father sighed, pulling at the sleeves of his sports coat. "Boys, we're goin', and that's final. Now quit complainin'," he barked.

Kenny exchanged a look with Caleb, both silently agreeing that this night was shaping up to be the worst.

"You boys are too young to understand what a big night this is for your mother," their dad said as he stepped in behind their mother. She adjusted her small earrings in the mirror.

"But one day, you will," he finished.

He pressed a quick kiss to their mother's cheek, earning a chorus of groans from the boys.

"Ewwww," they complained in unison.

Their father chuckled, shaking his head. "And one day, you boys will understand that too," he added with a smile.

"Momma, I do love you," young Caleb reasoned, "but books are just…sooo boring!"

"Yeah, we might die of boredom," Michael added dramatically.

"Yeah, Momma—die!" Kenny mimicked, throwing his hands in the air for effect.

The three brothers dropped to their knees, hands clasped together in exaggerated pleading.

"Please don't make us go!" they begged in unison.

"Enough, boys!" their dad boomed, finally putting an end to the protest. "You're goin, and you're gonna have big smiles on those cute little faces while you're there," he said, tugging at young Caleb's cheeks. "And when your mother reads her book to those publishers you're going to sit and listen like it's John Calipari readin' to you," he said in reference to the University of Kentucky head basketball coach.

His eyes landed on Kenny. "And that especially goes for you, mister man," he threatened while trying to keep a serious face. At last, the cuteness radiating from the tiny human broke through almost instantly, and he was forced to resort to more drastic measures.

With a playful growl, their father scooped Kenny up in his arms. "Or you're gonna get tickled by the Tickle Monster!" he shouted. Kenny's high-pitched laughter spilled through the house as he squirmed in his father's arms.

Their mother paused in the kitchen doorway and watched all of her boys with a soft smile. She breathed the moment in and tucked it away deep in her heart. Warm as it may have been, it was far from perfect. It was something better than perfect; it was theirs.

***

>>>>>

When the morning sun peeked through Kenny's bedroom window, it laid a soft light on the dusty room and on the heavy parts of his heart—the ones still bruised from all he'd lost. As the rising sun stretched across the old wooden floor, it carried with it quiet promises of a way forward, settling gently on Sara's sleeping form. She was curled up, her breathing steady, one hand still loosely draped over the edge of the mattress where Kenny had held it the night before.

Kenny was already up and dressed. He had carefully slipped back into his room, making sure not to wake her. He stood in front of the mirror as he adjusted the collar of his black dress shirt, neatly tucked into his black dress pants. He paused for a moment as his fingers lingered at the collar, as if he could still feel his father's hands guiding him through the motions from all those years ago. The memory flickered, brief but powerful, before he shook it off and turned and looked at Sara.

Kenny blinked against the light. Exhaustion filled his bones, but there was no rest to be found. With a quiet sigh, he rubbed a hand over his face as he looked at her. She stirred slightly but didn't wake.

He would let her sleep a little longer. She deserved that much.

As Kenny slipped back out of his room, he made his way to the kitchen in search of some much-needed coffee. He was surprised that Ma was up, sitting at the table with her own cup in hand.

"Mornin'," Kenny said casually, as if it were just another day.

"Whitmore girl in there?" Ma asked, though it was clear she knew the answer.

"Ma, it's not like that," Kenny replied, pouring himself a cup.

"Didn't say it was like anything, did I?" Ma said, taking a slow sip. "Just asked a question," she continued.

Kenny sighed. "She's having a rough time with all of it, Ma," he grumbled.

"Well, her and half the county sweetheart," Ma replied, her voice a low drawl laced with the dry dust of sarcasm. "My concern ain't that girl. My concern is you, grandson." She said as her tone softened a bit.

"I'm fine," Kenny muttered. "Saw it might snow a bit this mornin'," he added, as if the weather was the most pressing topic of the day.

Ma stared at him over the rim of her coffee cup. "Mmmhmm," she said a tad sourly. That's what you gonna talk about this mornin'? We're puttin' your brother in the ground today and now you're a channel thirteen weatherman all a-sudden?" she sassed.

She set her coffee down, then stared at Kenny like she was reading a story written across his face. "Ain't no fine to any of it," she said, steady as the old cottonwood.

Kenny swallowed hard, gripping his cup like it might hold him together.

"You wouldn't have been outside partaking in a cigarette now, would ya?" Kenny asked, trying to lighten the heaviness in the room. Ma shot him a look solid enough to punch straight through drywall. "Oh, what is this now? You think you're Matlock all of a sudden?" They both almost smiled... almost. Ma might've been hell-bent and heaven-bound, but every once in a blue moon even a saint needed a smoke.

"This family...," Ma paused as her voice wavered just a little. "I ain't about to lose you too, ya know."

"You're not gonna lose me, Ma. I promise," Kenny said, his voice quiet but firm.

Ma held his gaze, steadfast, unwavering—her eyes brimming with something pure and tender.

"Grandson," she said, "you're just a boy, and you've seen pain that would bury a million men. Lord knows how hard we tried with your brother. I just, I just never thought...." she trailed off a bit.

Kenny dropped his head. He didn't know what to say, didn't know how to tell her that sometimes he felt exactly that—buried.

Ma sighed, as she stood and reached across the table to place her weathered hand over his. "I know you're tryin' to hold it all together for me, for that girl, for all of us." She shook her head. "But you don't have to carry it all, Kenny. And I should've done a better job makin' sure your brother knew that."

Kenny swallowed hard, his jaw tightened as he stared into the black swirl of his coffee. "If I don't carry it, then who will?" he asked, his voice barely above a whisper.

"That's not for you to figure out, baby. Life's heavy enough without you pilin' on more troubles that ain't yours," she said, giving his hand a firm squeeze, as if willing him to see the truth. Ma's voice settled into the quiet of the house like a prayer. She wasn't just talking, she was pleading. Her words were soaked with a love so fierce her voice nearly ached.

"I was five years old when we lost my baby brother. His name was Earl Ray...I'll never forget what it did to my momma—burying one of her babies. That kinda grief don't leave a person, not never. But that was life way back when. It was hard and full of loss, but we was really livin'.

Nowadays...I just don't know anymore." She paused for a moment, shaking her head.

"It might not feel like it now, or maybe ever," she continued, her gaze drifting toward the hallway, toward the room where Sara was still fast asleep. "But it's okay for you to live, grandson, to go on livin'. It's okay to be young, make mistakes, and to love. No one will fault you for livin' your life."

She paused, before she finished. "What do I always tell you, grandson? Sometimes, you've got to just let it fly." As she spoke, her eyes shone with something between heartache and grit.

Kenny swallowed hard. He nodded, but her words felt like smoke, impossible to hold onto.

Ma studied him for a moment, let out a long breath, and eased back in her chair. The old wood creaked for her, like it knew she was too tired to do it herself. "Well, if you're bound and determined on carrying the world, at least eat somethin' before you do."

She made him a plate and set it on the table in front of him: biscuits and gravy, the kind Caleb would wolf down like he'd never eat again. And for the first time in three days, Kenny lifted his fork and took a bite. It wasn't much—just a small mouthful. Not nearly enough to fill the emptiness inside him, but he forced himself to swallow.

Because maybe Ma was right, he thought to himself. *Maybe moving forward didn't mean forgetting. Maybe it just meant surviving—one bite, one step, one breath at a time.*

Chapter Twenty

Sara Grace stood at the edge of the creek, a stick in her hands raised high in the air. Her body still, as she locked onto something just beneath the water's surface. The cotton candy haze of dusk crawled through the trees, like it was worn down by the day, as it reflected off the trickling water.

For a beat, everything held its breath, the air thick with anticipation.

Splash! She struck down hard, the blow breaking the silence of the evening.

"That's it Gracie girl, you're a frog giggin' fool!" Kenny hollered.

"I got it! I got it!" Sara shouted, grinning as Kenny waded forward to inspect her catch.

"She's a natural, Caleb," he shouted to his brother playing in the distance under the old cottonwood tree.

Sara lifted the frog triumphantly, water dripping from her hands as she beamed. "Told you I could do it," she said, full of confidence.

Kenny laughed, shaking his head. "Never doubted you for a second, Gracie," he said.

Caleb, with his natural easy-going stride, joined the two, uninterested. One hand tucked in the pocket of his jeans and the other arm wrapped around a football. "What are y'all doin' down here?" he asked.

"Kenny's teachin' me how to gig," Sara said. Her face was alight with excitement.

Caleb let out a low chuckle, glancing between them. "Y'all are some-thin' else," he laughed.

"Ma says it's about time to wash up for dinner. I'll let her know you're here, Sara," he said before heading back the way he came.

The creek babbled beside them, the evening air full of summer. And for that moment, everything was easy—just them, the water, and the fading light of a day they'd never get back.

"What do we do now?" Sara yelled at Kenny.

"Now we eat," Kenny said with a grin.

"Uhh, no. We most certainly do not eat," Sara protested, wrinkling her nose.

Kenny smirked. "Well, if you ain't gonna eat it Gracie, you're basically just one of those big game hunters—killin' for the thrill of it," he teased. "I mean that frog had a family. Probably had a wife and kids, Gracie," Kenny said, needling her further.

"Shut up Ken, that's not funny," she shot back. Her gaze fell to the lifeless frog on the razor-sharp stick and her expression softened. "Aw dang, what if he did have kids?" she said, only half-joking. "I ruined everything."

"Yeah, looks like you're a widow-maker now," Kenny teased.

Sara groaned, "This is horrible!"

Kenny grinned. "Well, there's only one thing to do then," he quipped.

She eyed him warily. "And what's that?" she asked.

"Eat it," he snarked, as he nudged her with his elbow. "Come on," Kenny said. "I'll start us a fire."

As the two preteens sat around their makeshift fire, Kenny held the frog over the flames, roasting it on a stick. The smell of smoke filled the air as he carefully pulled the charred toad free and passed a small piece to Sara.

Sara reluctantly took it in her fingers and eyed it skeptically.

Just as Kenny was about to help himself to a taste, she cut him off. "Wait!" she shouted.

Kenny paused, mid-bite. "Wait for what?" he asked, confused.

"We should say something," Sara continued.

"You mean like a—," Kenny didn't finish his thought from before.

"A eulogy," Sara interrupted, "Think of the children," her expression serious despite the absurdity of it all.

"Okay, then...go right on ahead, preacher's daughter, speak from the heart now," Kenny said, sarcastically.

Sara paused for a moment, took a deep breath, and she did exactly that. "Dear Lord," she started, "thank you for this wonderful day. And thank you for blessin' me with the best friend I could've ever prayed for." Her voice was low but loud enough to carry over the wind.

Kenny froze, staring at her. Her eyes closed deep in reflection. He couldn't believe it. The sincerity in her words—the way she said them. It left him...breathless, and for a moment, everything else faded, and he was just... watching her.

Her tone was soft, and there was a steadiness in her, a quiet truth. She wasn't pretending. She was standing there in the evening light, high atop Bledsoe Hill, doing something real.

Sara continued. "Thank you for blessin' me and Kenny with your creatures and with this bountiful land. May you watch over us, protect us, and guide us, especially through the hard times we know that will most certainly come," her voice grew steadier with each word. "And may we always appreciate the little things, like this moment right here, together," she continued.

Kenny felt something stir inside him. It struck him like a note held long and low on a fiddle string. The quiet grace in her words left him with a warmth that felt foreign but comforting all at once, like he actually belonged to something, or to someone.

Sara's voice softened as she finished, "And please bless momma frog with a new prince charming. Amen." There was a pause. "Ahem," Sara said, prodding Kenny to snap from his daze.

"Amen," he concurred, shaking his head. He wasn't sure how long he'd been staring at her, but in that brief silence, something had changed in Kenny's world.

On that day, something shifted in the way Kenny saw Sara—it wasn't anything obvious at first, at least not something he could put into words. But in that quiet moment, with a fire crackling between them under the shadows of the old cottonwood tree, Kenny saw his Gracie in a new light.

She wasn't just the girl he'd grown up with, the one who teased him and raced him down to the creek or to the pond. She was something steadier now, like the moon rising over the Bledsoe land.

Yes, something had changed—and Kenny knew he didn't want it to change back.

***

>>>>>

By sunrise, Bledsoe Hill was wrapped in a quiet procession of cars, lined bumper to bumper from top to bottom. Word had spread—through whispers in the halls and murmurs in town—and now, everyone had come for their chance to say goodbye to Caleb.

The autumn morning felt like something sacred, like God Himself had gifted the little town a moment of grace. A light flaking of snow had begun to caress the fields—silent, untouched, and sparkling beneath the soft gaze of the morning sun. As if the earth itself held its breath in reverence.

The trees were bare but beautiful; they stood in solemn stillness, their branches etched in frost like delicate lace. The air was crisp and sharp enough to sting the lungs, yet calm—no bitter wind, no cruel chill. Just a quiet, reverent kind of cold, that wrapped around the town like a gentle embrace.

The sound of the small creek running nearby drifted through the air. A quiet, steady reminder that life carried on, even beneath the veil of grief.

Kenny hadn't planned what he'd say—he only knew that something needed to be said.

He hardly acknowledged the large crowd that had gathered. His focus was on the small group around him—Ma, Pa, Sara,...and Kate, who had silently stepped behind him. Knowing her place wasn't beside Kenny, but wanting him to know she was there, in his peripheral, if he needed her. Pa was beside Ma, standing tall even in his grief, his weather-beaten face set in that quiet way of his, as if holding the whole family steady was something he'd been born knowing how to do.

As Kenny stepped forward—perhaps the single most difficult steps of his life—he reached out his trembling hand and his fingertips brushed the cold, polished surface of the casket.

For a moment, he let his hand linger there. As if hoping to feel...something. Then, gently, he took the folded note his dad had left him all those years ago on his pillow, and he placed it atop the wood. Like an offering to his brother, like a final exchange between him and his father. He stepped back, silent, as the weight of goodbye settled in his chest.

As he tried to address those gathered, the words wouldn't come. Or maybe it was deeper than that. Maybe he couldn't find the strength to speak them.

Whatever the case, Kenny stood frozen like a lone tree in the dead of winter—bare, exposed, and bracing against the cold. As he paused, whether for a few seconds or what felt like a few seasons, his life flickered before his eyes.

He saw it all—his brother Michael, his father, his mother, Ma, Pa, Sara, Kate—and most certainly, Caleb. His brother. His keeper. His mentor. His heart.

But before he knew what was happening, Sara stepped forward and took his hand in hers. Her voice was soft, and though she fought with everything she had to hold back her own sorrow, she spoke with the same quiet grace Kenny had witnessed all those years ago—at a funeral of a different kind, on a much lighter night than this dreadful morning.

Sara took a deep breath, trying to steady herself, but as she began to speak, her voice trembled. "I don't know how to say this...how to say goodbye. So you'll forgive me if I won't."

Her voice dropped to a whisper, like she was afraid if she spoke too loudly, she might completely fall apart. "You were supposed to be around, you know? To grow old and weird and tired like the rest of us. To tease me when I cry at dumb movies. To show up late and still somehow manage to steal the show."

She closed her eyes, trying to steady herself. "You were supposed to be here—with me and Kenny." She squeezed Kenny's hand as tight as she possibly could. "You were supposed to drive us all around God's green earth, me sittin' in the middle, like always. You were supposed to be here to drive me crazy, to keep things loud and funny and complicated. To keep us grounded and spinnin' out of control all at the same time." Her tears started to fall now.

"So no, I won't say goodbye. I'll carry you with me. I'll live louder because you can't, and if you're listening... I hope you know I still love you. We still love you. Always," she finished softly.

That's when it hit Kenny all at once—like the night they gigged that frog all those years ago. He was in love with Sara.

Just thinking the words hit like a slap to his soul, knocking the breath clean out of him. Sara had been part of him all along—her laugh, her big sappy heart, the way she saw the good in everything. She made life feel worth living, even when it didn't make sense.

But loving her came with a weight: sudden, real, and unavoidable. That's what loving Sara felt like. Because in his heart, she would always belong to Caleb. No matter what he felt, that truth wouldn't change.

So he stood there, holding it all in, knowing he loved her—and knowing that loving her would have to be enough. Because that's all it could ever be.

Chapter Twenty-One

By the time the sun clipped the treetops, the people were gone—and so was the snow. It disappeared without fanfare, like it had only come to bear witness and then quietly slipped away. It vanished like the footprints of those who had shown up to say their goodbyes, back to where they came from, back to their lives, back to the rhythm of normal.

Kenny found himself sitting on the steps of the front porch. The whirlwind of the last few days drifted through his mind as he thought about better times, which, as always, led him to remember the worst ones.

As he sat alone on the aged wood, Coach Wills approached him. He lowered his broad frame beside Kenny. He didn't speak at first—there wasn't much to say on a day like today. But as Wills always seemed to do, he spoke in just the right tone at just the right moment.

"I'm gonna tell you somethin' I've never told another soul," he said, dead serious.

Kenny, caught off guard by his words, turned to face Wills, his expression shifted with surprise.

"My wife and I—well, she wasn't my wife yet back then—we had a ba–a little girl." He paused; his voice was quiet but steady as he continued. "We gave her up for adoption. We were young, thought we had it all figured out. When really, we didn't know the half of what we didn't know."

Kenny sat in silence, unsure of what to say.

"I just remember...her eyes," Wills continued. "She was... breathtaking." He let out a small breath, his gaze distant. "Not a day goes by that I don't think about that little girl—what she's doin', if she's...happy," he paused, offering a small, wistful smile. "Does she like basketball?" he added, only half-joking.

Kenny looked at him, still not knowing what words to offer in reply.

"Regret isn't the right word," Wills went on. "Back then, it felt like the right thing to do ya know? We made a choice...but...we were young." He exhaled, shaking his head slightly.

"People like to make excuses," Wills said, his voice steady. "They like to say life's complicated. That there's no absolutes. Shades of gray, they call it. But the truth is, life is simple—it's about choices. There's always a right choice and a wrong one." He paused, his eyes staring off into the fields around the two.

"The part they don't tell you," Wills continued, "is that you have to live with the choice you make. That's the hard part. It's not just about picking what feels easy or comfortable—it's about making the choice you can live with, no matter how it turns out."

He glanced at Kenny as his expression softened. "I'm not making any sense, am I?" he asked.

But before Kenny could reply, Wills continued, frustration creeping into his voice. "I guess what I'm tryin' to say, son, is that there are things in life worth dwelling on—things you replay over and over in your mind, trying to figure out what you could've done differently. What you should've done. But this... this ain't one of those," he said.

He turned to Kenny, his gaze steady. "You hear me?" he questioned. "This ain't your fault, son. And you can't play that game. The 'if I only did this, or if only I said that.'"

He paused for a moment, his voice tightened. "Teenagers are supposed to be bored, not anxious," he muttered, seemingly angry at the world, as the words left his mouth.

Wills dropped his head and shook it for a moment before continuing. "I want you to take some time away from basketball," he said, his tone softer now. "Be with your grandmother. Take all the time you need. And we'll be here if you need us. You understand me?" he asked.

Kenny shook his head slightly. "I don't need time away," he replied quietly. "I just wanna play ball, coach," he said a little louder.

Wills let out a slow breath, his gaze never leaving Kenny. "I get it," he said, his voice firm but kind. "Hell, I get that more than you know. But right now, it's not about some game. It's about you, son. If you don't take care of yourself you're gonna flame out, and that's not gonna help anyone—not our team, not your family, and especially not you," he said firmly.

He paused, studying Kenny's face for a moment, making sure he was hearing him. "You need to step away. Just for a bit. I'm tellin' you, it's not a weakness; it's the strongest thing you can do right now," Wills said.

"Coach, I'm playing," Kenny blurted out, his voice tinged with anger. "I mean, with all due respect, you guys need me. I can handle myself, coach, I swear. Please, I need this." His words filled with conviction, a hint of desperation in his eyes. Kenny wasn't sure what he needed exactly, but the thought of stepping away from basketball felt like losing a part of himself.

Coach Wills knew Kenny was wrong. He understood what might lie ahead if Kenny didn't find some peace before returning to the team. But he couldn't bring himself to tell the boy, who had already lost so much, that he would have to take even more from him.

He sighed with a heavy heart, and nodded. "Okay," he said.

Wills pulled Kenny into a firm hug—rare for a man who wasn't known for showing much emotion—and held on a little longer than expected. Like he was saying something he couldn't quite put into words, before finally letting go.

As he walked away, a quiet ache settled in his chest. He turned his head, stealing one last glance at Kenny—just a boy sitting all alone on those steps. He wanted more than anything to help Kenny through this, to make basketball the thing that would bring him back to himself. But deep down, Wills knew—some battles had to be fought alone.

$$***$$

<<<<<

The air was warm, the kind of late summer day that put everything in slow motion. Like time was dragging its feet. The sun hung low in the sky, tired and tender as soft shadows fell over the wooden steps on Ma and Pa's front porch where Kenny and Caleb were seated together.

They were small then—maybe five and six—too young to understand everything that had happened to their family, but old enough to know when something was missing.

Their mother stood in front of them, her hands shaking. Her eyes cold and distant, as though she hadn't slept in months. The dark rings beneath them stood in solemn contrast to the wild sparkle that once danced there—like dusk where morning used to live.

There was faded warmth in her voice, which trembled as she spoke and tried her best to steady it.

"Listen to me, boys," she began. "There's somethin' I need to explain to you. Momma's not goin' to be around for a little while," she said through a shaky breath.

Kenny's brow furrowed in confusion, his small fingers dug into the wooden steps as he stared up at her. He didn't fully understand the words, but something about the way she was acting, the way her hands fidgeted, told him this wasn't a normal conversation.

"Why?" Caleb asked quietly, "Where are you goin' momma?" His voice was small, but steady.

Their mother's gaze shifted as she tried to bring herself to look at Caleb, but she couldn't. She softened as she turned to Kenny. She took a deep breath.

"Sometimes, grown-ups have to make hard choices," she began.

"And right now, I have to go. But I love you both, more than anything in this world. Always! I need you to be strong. You boys are strong. You're gonna be fine, I promise," she finished, her words falling heavy from her mouth, like hail from a thunderstorm.

And that was that. She turned, got in her car, and slammed the door shut—not just on the vehicle, but on the last fragile breath of her boys' innocence.

Kenny, still trying to understand the magnitude of the moment, turned to Caleb. Like the look on his big brother's face would give him all the answers he was searching for.

As the engine of their mother's car rumbled down the gravel road, a knot formed in Kenny's stomach. He watched, wide-eyed, as it made its slow descent down the hill, each second stretching longer than the last.

Caleb took Kenny's hand in his and squeezed it gently.

As the car neared the edge of the horizon, Kenny stood up and began to chase after it. Caleb, his legs longer and faster, chased after and caught him. He grabbed Kenny by his hand and pulled him to a stop.

The two boys stood there for a moment, silent, like statues frozen in time. Their eyes fixed on the car until it was nothing more than a speck in the distance.

"It's okay, Ken," Caleb said softly, his voice steady despite the tears welling in his own eyes. "We're gonna be okay. We've got each other. Always."

The boys, still standing in the dust of their mother's leaving, didn't know it yet, but high atop Bledsoe Hill that day, they'd already begun to grow old..

Chapter Twenty-Two

As Kenny strode into school, his footsteps echoed down the empty hallways. He was late. The only reason he even bothered to show at all was simple—if he didn't, he couldn't play that night. And right now, basketball was the only thing keeping him moving.

As he walked, his eyes drifted to the row of lockers ahead, and to Caleb's locker. He hadn't meant to stop, but his feet slowed anyway. Flowers, notes, and candles were scattered in front of it—a makeshift memorial. He stared at the locker for a moment as his chest tightened and his knees buckled. The heaviness was too much. He wasn't ready for this. Not here. Not now.

He tried his best to gather his thoughts as he approached Ms. Carter's classroom and peeked through the tall, rectangular window in the door. He pressed his face against the glass, unnoticed by those inside—until, across the room, he caught a glimpse of her. Kate.

For a split second, their eyes locked. In that brief moment, everything felt too real. Before he could process it, he turned and bolted through the hallway. Without a second thought, he veered away from the class-rooms, cutting through the halls until he reached the gymnasium. He headed straight for the locker room. The boys' basketball locker room was empty, quiet, and familiar. There he sank onto a metal chair, resting his elbows on his knees and stared at the scuffed floor.

It was easier there. There, he didn't have to speak. He didn't have to feel the stares of eyes fixed on him. No, for now, he'd stay right there in the in-between where he didn't have to confront the cold reality waiting just beyond those locker room doors.

He sat in front of an old white marker board; his eyes drifted toward the TV and the stack of game DVDs piled on a black cart beside it.

Then it hit him. He didn't want to watch; he could barely stand the thought. But something in him, quiet and stubborn as a mule, told him he had to.

He knew which one he wanted to see. It was the final game from his freshman year. His stat line for the contest wasn't eye-popping, but he remembered it fondly. It was the first time he had been in the starting lineup with his big brother. Kenny had worked his tail off that season to earn more minutes, pushing himself harder than ever before. And despite being one of the more valuable players on the team, the coach had kept him coming off the bench, preferring to start more experienced players.

There were times when Kenny thought about quitting, when the frustration ate at him. But Caleb wouldn't allow it. He always told him the same thing: job's not finished.

That night, that game, was one of the best moments of Kenny's life. Not because they won—no, the Knights won plenty of games—but because he had earned the right to be on the same court as his big brother. To hear a second Bledsoe name announced over the loudspeakers during the starting lineups. Just the thought of that night, the heart of it, curved a smile onto Kenny's face.

As the game played on the old, not-so-flat screen, his eyes darted from one side to another, watching with a sense of pride. But as the moments unfolded, he felt the sting of sorrow welling in the corner of his brown eyes.

It was at that moment, as the tears threatened to spill over, a voice shouted, "What are you doin' in here, boy?!"

Kenny jumped in his seat; his heart raced. He turned quickly, and there was Kate standing in the doorway, doing her best deep-voiced impression.

"I thought I might find you here," she said with a grin. "Ditchin' class today, are we? Bueller? Bueller?" she called out in a teasing voice.

As she walked toward Kenny, he did his best to discreetly dry his eyes. Kate noticed but didn't dare mention it.

"Mind if I sit?" she asked, motioning to a row of chairs behind him. Kenny shook his head, still trying to hide his face somewhat. "Watching the Butler East game, are you? That was the first one you ever started, right?" Kate recalled off the top of her head, like it was nothing. "I remember you had, like, four steals," she added with a knowing smile.

"How do you remember all that?" Kenny asked, his voice tinged with surprise.

"I remember a lot of things, Kenny Bledsoe," she said, a hint of playfulness in her voice. With a shift in tone, she added, "You really don't remember?" she asked.

Kenny looked at her dazed, like his thoughts were still stuck in yesterday.

Kate sighed. "Of course you don't," she muttered, her voice a little less playful. "What are we gonna do with you Kenny Bledsoe?" she teased.

"What are you talkin' about?" Kenny said, searching for a little help.

"I had your number that night, you big dummy!" she said with a grin.

Kenny looked at her, uncertain, still searching.

"Oh my gosh," she continued, as she rolled her eyes. "You're such a butthead."

Kenny shrugged his shoulders and nodded his head slightly in agreement.

"That was the game where all the freshman girls had to wear one of the guys' names and numbers on their shirts. We painted them with big gold letters. I remember a few girls fightin' over Caleb's, but I wanted number twelve. I wanted Kenny Bledsoe," she said with a smile.

"Yeah right, you're full of it, Covington," Kenny smirked.

"No, for real," she said, her tone softening. "I knew you'd be special. I could see it. You just needed some time to find your confidence." She eased in closer and stood behind him now.

"You were like a baby deer out there," she chuckled. "Jumpin' around all high and fast, not quite sure where to go. But you were special, Kenny," she added as she placed her hands gently on his shoulders as he sat in front of her.

"There was no denying it," she continued. Kenny's gaze stayed locked on the TV screen in front of them, but Kate's was on Kenny. He felt her soft touch on his shoulders, like a bolt of lightning, a jolt that made him tense in his seat. "I do remember thinkin' a few other things, too," she teased.

"Oh yeah? Like what?" Kenny asked, with more than a hint of curiosity in his tone.

"Like that I thought you were pretty stinkin' cute out there," she said through a playful grin. "And how I hoped you'd notice me in your number and come talk to me after the game," she said the last part with a pouty face.

She leaned a little further forward, her voice dropping to a quieter tone. "I guess I've always been just waiting for you to notice me," she whispered in his ear.

"Oh come on now," he said, grinning. You say that like every guy in this school doesn't drool all over themselves every stinkin' time you walk down those halls," Kenny said, completley serious.

Kate smiled just a touch. She knew he wasn't telling any lies, but still she continued with her playful game. "Yeah well, I wasn't wearing their number was I?" she whispered as she started to play with the curls in his hair.

As Kenny turned to face her, the room buzzed with an electric charge. He wasn't Romeo, but he was smart enough to know when Juliet was standing in front of him. Slowly, he leaned in, his heart racing, ready to kiss her.

But just as their faces were inches apart, Kate pulled away, with a mischievous grin on her lips. "But...I guess you were too focused on Gracieeee," she teased, stretching out the name.

Kenny caught himself just in time—he'd leaned in too far and nearly tipped forward. Quickly, realizing the error of his ways, he straightened up, a flush of embarrassment crept over him.

"No, no, I was just... young and dumb," he said, a grin tugging at his lips, playful and unhurried.

"Oh, well if that's what happened... then..." Kate said, as she sat beside him and leaned back in towards him.

Kenny, believing he had paid his penance, leaned back in too.

"I guess some things never change," she said, as she pulled away for the second time, her voice full of amusement.

"You're enjoyin' yourself, aren't you?" Kenny asked, completely at Kate's mercy.

"Can't say I hate it," Kate replied, as mischief danced in her eyes like lightning bugs on a Kentucky July night.

It was then that Kate leaned in for a third time, her face inches away from Kenny's. She brushed his curly hair back over his ears. "I've missed you, ya know," she said softly. Her eyes lingered on his face, the faint freckles scattered across his cheeks, the way they deepened when he smiled. She'd never noticed them before, and the thought sent a slow warmth through her, like she was seeing him for the first time all over again.

"You just saw me the other day," Kenny replied.

"I know," Kate pouted, her expression softened. "But...that was so long ago," she teased.

As the two leaned in for a kiss, for real this time, the locker room door burst open with a loud bang.

"Is somebody in here?" a voice jolted out. It was Mr. Johnson, the sixty-year-old PE teacher who moved like a tractor low on gas. "No one's supposed to be in here," he barked again.

At the sound of his voice, Kenny and Kate quickly scrambled to the back of the locker room, ducking into a shower stall, and pulling the curtain shut.

"Hey! Is anyone in here?" Mr. Johnson yelled again, his voice growing louder as he rounded the corner. "Well, don't be if ya are!" he threatened, his eyes scanning the room.

"Hmm..." he muttered, shrugging his shoulders. Kenny and Kate peeked out from behind the curtain, holding their breath.

Mr. Johnson, having clearly had enough excitement for one day, decided to take his leave. As he waddled away, Kenny and Kate couldn't help but snicker watching him walk off in his white tube socks pulled up to his short gym shorts.

As Mr. Johnson exited the locker room, Kenny swished the curtain open and the two shared a quiet laugh. Kate went to step outside the shower, but Kenny pulled her back by the hand, wrapping his arms around her. They stood face-to-face for a moment before Kenny planted a kiss on her lips.

The kiss lingered for a moment and as they pulled away they both attempted to catch their breath.

"I very much enjoy kissin' you," Kenny said with a grin, "Don't pull away," he joked.

"Well, don't be a butthead," Kate teased back, and the two shared another kiss.

When the kiss finally ended, it was indeed Kate who pulled away first, grinning. "Come on," she said, playfully. "I don't kiss boys in the basketball showers. Out you go, mister," she said as she pulled him by the hand.

Kenny, not wanting the moment to end just yet, submitted an alternative option to his diamond eyed damsel. "Well, can't you make an exception for number twelve, Kenny Bledsoe?" he asked.

"To be continued," Kate replied with a playful smile.

Kenny didn't mind the sound of that one bit. With a crooked grin and a heart beating faster than it ought to, he followed Kate out of the locker room. Not knowing what the day held, but sure as hell knowing who he wanted to face it with.

Chapter Twenty-Three

There was something maniacal about the way the sun lingered—hot, relentless, and unwilling to let the day die as it continued its slow descent on Kyrock, casting shadows like bruises along the Bledsoe barn.

The summer air didn't move—it just sat there, thick as molasses, making the whole world feel slow and sticky. As Kenny made his way across the field and down the dirt path, he knew where Caleb would be.

Sure enough, there he was—out by the hoop nailed to the side of the old barn, just outside the shadow of the giant cottonwood tree. He was dribbling in slow, steady beats against the packed earth. His movements sluggish, his shoulders hunched. The usual fire in his game was replaced with something else—something heavier.

Kenny leaned against the barn door, watching for a moment before he spoke up. "You know, most people shower before a first date," he teased.

Caleb didn't stop dribbling, just let out a tired exhale. "Not really in the mood for all that tonight," he gruffed.

Kenny stepped onto the makeshift dirt court, swiping the ball mid-dribble and took a lazy shot. It clanged off the rim; he chased it down and bounced it back to Caleb.

"Come on, man. Gracie's been yappin' about tonight for weeks. You don't wanna leave her hangin'," he said.

Caleb caught the ball and held it for a second, staring down at it like it held answers to questions he wasn't even sure how to ask. "Pfft. Gracie?

131

Sounds like you're the one that should be gettin' ready for a date with her," Caleb said, his tone laced with frustration.

"C'mon man, you know it's not like that." Kenny replied.

"Yeah," Caleb muttered, rolling the ball between his hands. "I know, i'm just..." His words trailed off before Kenny nudged him. "Then let's go, brother! It's the Fourth of July. We're talkin' fireworks, food, and oh yeah—a girl who's crazy about ya. Plus, have you seen Gracie in a sundress and boots? Not too shabby," Kenny said as he wiggled his eyebrows.

For the first time in what felt like weeks, Caleb let a small smile tug at the corner of his mouth. It wasn't much, but it was something. "Alright, whatever," Caleb said, tossing the ball aside. "I'll go."

"Heck yeah!" Kenny cheered, pumping his fist in the air.

As the ball rolled away and disappeared into the dusty shadows beside the barn, the two brothers set off, leaving the shadow of the past few weeks behind them. Then, as if out of thin air, Caleb said something that stopped Kenny stone cold.

"Hey, Ken," Caleb said.

"What's up?" Kenny replied, wiping the sweat from his brow.

Caleb's eyes drifted up to the branches swaying above them. "If somethin' ever happens to me... don't let them put me in some cemetery," he said calmly.

Kenny's face scrunched. "What are you talkin' about, man?"

Caleb's voice was steady, softer than usual. "I mean it, if somethin' ever happens to me, I want you to bury me right here, under this tree. So I can be out here forever."

Kenny swallowed hard, the wind catching in the branches above them as he searched for words that wouldn't come. "Nothin' is gonna happen to you man. C'mon, quit all that silly talk," Kenny said.

"I know," Caleb said. "I'm just sayin."

"Yeah well, I'm just sayin', we need to work on your small talk for this date," Kenny teased. "Now, let's get you cleaned up brother, you smell like you've been shakin' hands with a skunk," Kenny joked as he wrapped an arm around his brother's shoulder.

***

Some places smell like memories, but the Kyrock fairgrounds? It smelled like grease, sugar, and trouble on the way. The night spun like the Ferris wheel—bright, loud, and a little dizzying. Somewhere in the chaos, new stories were being written in real time.

Caleb and Sara sat on a worn-out picnic blanket in the grass, tucked away from the biggest crowds but close enough to hear the distant hum of chatter and carnival rides. Kenny had been right about one thing—Sara lit the night on fire in her yellow sundress and tall Frye boots.

Kenny watched them comfortably from a little ways off. He leaned against a fence with a soda in hand, grinning as he saw Caleb smiling. Sara was talking animatedly, her hands moving with every word. Kenny had always joked that if someone tied her hands up, she wouldn't be able to speak at all.

Then Kenny caught sight of something he hadn't seen in, well, he couldn't say when the last time was—but there it was, plain as day.

Caleb was laughing. A real, true, tilt your head back and shake your belly kind of laugh. His shoulders were loose, and his eyes were bright enough to notice all the way back from where Kenny stood.

As the first firework shot into the sky, a loud boom was followed by an explosion of color. Sara gasped as her eyes went wide with wonder. Caleb soaked it in, completely mesmerized—until he turned and caught sight of his brother across the way. Their eyes met, and Caleb's face lit up. He grinned and shot Kenny a thumbs-up. Then he turned and resumed chatting with Sara.

Kenny exhaled slowly; calmness soothed his soul. He couldn't pin down what had been weighing on Caleb so much lately, but for the first time in a long time, it felt like, at least for tonight, his big brother was okay. And for him, that was good enough.

Chapter Twenty-Four

Ma's radio crackled like burning firewood in the hush of the house. She leaned in, her hands stilled in their work. She listened intently as the announcer's voice rang out with excitement.

"Kenny Bledsoe is playing like a man on fire out there tonight! 17 points, 11 rebounds already in the first half. Kyrock takes a commanding 41-27 lead over their archrival, Grayson County."

In the gym, the crowd erupted with deafening approval as the Grayson County head coach was forced to call a timeout. The energy was palpable with fans on their feet, the student section bounced in unison. In the stands, Kate cheered wildly, clapping and shouting Kenny's name.

Down on the baseline, Sara led the cheerleaders in a booming chant for the Knights, her voice carrying over the noise of the packed gym. The entire place was alive, feeding off the fire burning in Kenny's game.

The radio announcer's voice popped through the speakers of Ma's antique radio with urgency.

"And we're back to live action here as Grayson County inbounds the ball. Wilson brings it up over half court—oh! It's stolen away! Kenny Bledsoe picked his pocket, and he is all alone! He takes off—goes up for a dunk—"

A sharp gasp filled the gym.

"Oh no! Wilson just undercut Bledsoe midair, and he's taken a brutal fall! That was a hard, hard landing! Oh my—Kenny is down. That looked nasty. I just hope he's okay."

In the Bledsoe house Ma's heart hitched like a startled thoroughbred in a summer storm.

Back in the gym, Kenny lay sprawled out on the baseline as pain radiated through his shoulder. Just inches away, Sara stood frozen. Concern etched across her face as she stepped toward him.

Before she could reach him, the Grayson County player hovered over Kenny, extending a hand in what appeared to be an offer to help. But his words landed harder than any fall. "Uh oh! Don't take too many pills now, pretty boy."

Kenny's eyes flickered with fire, the throbbing in his shoulder instantly forgotten. He locked onto the player, his body coiling with tension as he slowly pushed himself off the hardwood. The Grayson County player, still feigning concern, smirked as he leaned in one more time and said. "Don't want you to end up like your brother."

That was it.

Kenny lunged, shoving the kid with everything he had, sending him stumbling backward. The gym erupted. The referees' whistles shrieked from within the chaos, but it was too late. Both benches emptied in an instant. Players from each team rushed the court as coaches and officials scrambled to keep them apart.

Back at home, Ma gripped the arms of her chair as the radio buzzed with urgency.

"Oh my, folks,. It has broken down here! Kenny Bledsoe did not take kindly to that hard foul—he's shoved Wilson from Grayson County, and now it's an all-out mess! Players from both teams are storming the floor, and they are having to be restrained from each other. This has gotten ugly in a hurry!"

Ma let out a slow, tired sigh. The kind worn thin by years of worry and prayers as she reached over and turned the radio off. She didn't need to hear another word. She knew.

Kenny wasn't ready. Not yet.

***

No one said it, but they all felt it. At halftime, the locker room was eerily quiet except for the occasional drip of a leaky faucet in the corner. The silence was the kind that can only come from intense pressure. The air was filled with tension; the energy from the brawl lingering like static.

Coach Wills stood in front of the team, his voice calm but firm. "Is this how you wanna do it?" he asked, scanning the room. "Is this the way you honor Caleb?"

No one answered. A few players lowered their eyes to the floor, silent. Others leaned back against their lockers, arms crossed, waiting for someone to speak first.

Kenny paced furiously near the benches, his fists clenching and unclenching at his sides. His chest rose and fell with every frustrated breath until finally, he snapped. "No one has my back!" he yelled, his voice echoing off the cinder block walls. "None of you! You don't know what Caleb would've wanted! You don't know anything!"

He turned, eyes blazing, as he kicked a metal chair out of his way. "This is all stupid. This whole damn thing is stupid!" he yelled louder.

The room stayed still, the blunt force of his words pressed on everyone. Kenny shook his head, his jaw tight. His vision blurred with frustration. "I quit!" he yelled as he took his jersey off and threw it at Coach Wills. He grabbed his bag and stormed toward the door, kicking it open. As he disappeared into the gym, the door slammed shut behind him.

Chapter Twenty-Five

As Kenny tore through the exit, heads in the crowd turned. Murmurs spread like wildfire through the gym. Noticing the commotion, Kate didn't hesitate. She leapt from her seat and took off after him.

The cold night air hit Kenny like a slap as he stormed into the parking lot, his breaths gasping. His fists clenched. He didn't know where he was going—just away from the gym, the game, away from all of it.

"Kenny!" Kate's voice rang out behind him. He didn't stop, but she was faster, grabbing his arm and forcing him to turn.

"What?" he snapped, yanking his arm away. His eyes were wild, his chest rising and falling like he'd just run sprints.

Kate didn't flinch. "Really? This is your move? You're just gonna walk away?" she asked.

Kenny let out a sharp laugh, shaking his head. "Hmmf, so now everyone is an expert on what I should do? You don't get it, Kate. None of you do," he said as he turned again to walk away. But she stepped in front of him, refusing to let him go.

"Then make me get it," she challenged. Her voice softened as she looked at him, her eyes searching his. "You're right—I can't imagine what you're going through. But don't run. Don't leave. Let me get it with you. Let me help... please," she said with a quiet desperation in her voice.

Kenny exhaled hard through his nose, peering past her, searching for words that wouldn't come. His jaw clenched so tight it ached.

Suddenly, another voice rang out, "Kenny!"

They both turned to see Sara jogging over, her brown hair bounced with each step, her face drawn with concern.

Kate let out a breath. "Of course," she muttered, rolling her eyes.

"Excuse me," Sara said sharply, her voice rising.

Kate couldn't hold back. "Of course, here you come to save the day," she said condescendingly.

"This really doesn't concern you if you wanna know the truth about it," Sara said sharply.

Kate's face flushed slightly, but she stood her ground. A spark of frustration flickered in her eyes. "I'm just trying to help," she said, her voice tight with restraint. "But you're not making it easy, Sara."

Sara's jaw clenched as she stepped toward Kate, the tension between them thickened. "You think you can just swoop in and fix everything? You're not the one who's been here. You have no idea what this is like." Sara retorted. Something in her voice caught Kenny off guard. There was a tone to it he'd never heard before, like a crack in the surface he couldn't quite name. There was a hint of something that sounded more personal than just the hurt from losing Caleb.

Kenny flinched, torn between the two of them. He didn't want them fighting. He didn't want any of this. But he felt helpless to stop it.

"Look, I get it," Kate said, motioning her hands in a gesture of calm. "I know I'm not the one who's been through all of this. But I'm here, okay? I'm here for you, Kenny." She turned to him, her voice softening as she reached out, but Sara interrupted.

"Oh, of course, you think you can just step in and bat your pretty eyes and fix it all," Sara spat, the words laced with bitterness. "You think just because he looks at you like a little puppy that you know what it's like? You don't have the slightest idea!" Sara growled, her voice rising.

Kenny's head pounded. He hated this. He closed his eyes. "Gracie, please—" he pleaded.

"No," Sara cut him off, as she raised her hands and rested them atop her head. "I'm tired, Kenny. I'm tired of everyone acting like they know what's best for me, for us. No one's been through this the way we have.

She doesn't know what it's like to lose him." Her voice cracked on the last words, and for a split second, Kenny saw the pain she was hiding.

Kate, sensing the depth of Sara's hurt, took a step back, her expression softened.

"You're right," she said quietly, her voice tinged with guilt. "I'm not... I shouldn't be here," she hesitated, her words heavy. "This... this isn't my place. I can't...," she cut herself off.

Without another word, she turned and walked away. Kenny stood frozen, watching her go, but he didn't try to stop her.

His gaze didn't linger on Kate. It quickly shifted to Sara. His heart ached at the raw sorrow in her eyes. His chest tightened as he whispered, "Gracie..." the word leaving his lips like a rock dropped in still water.

Her name hung in the air, half admonishment, half acknowledgment, as she too turned and walked away from him.

The silence that remained with Kenny as he stood there all alone was suffocating. No matter how much he didn't want to face the fact—no matter how much he didn't want to believe it—he had no choice. Caleb was gone, and he wasn't coming back.

And now he found himself there without Kate, without Sara, and without basketball.

Kenny's life remained the way it inevitably was without Caleb—alone.

Chapter Twenty-Six

Morning tiptoed in quiet as a prayer. The light seemed to remember everything as it eased gently through the tall kitchen windows, settling on the old table where tired hands had rested and timeless stories had been told.

The wood, once a dark brown, had faded to a shade lighter, as if time itself had worn it with memories. Outside the Bledsoe house the first signs of spring were springing.

On this quiet morning Kenny was seated at the table, the local newspaper spread out before him. His fingers traced the creases of the pages absentmindedly. He sipped his coffee, trying to shake off the fog that had settled in his mind over the past several weeks.

His eyes lingered on a headline that caught his attention: "Kyrock Knights Struggle in Tough Loss against Warren North. Fall to 14-14 on the season."

Kenny felt that familiar knot in his stomach tighten as he carefully placed the paper back on the table.

"Read anything good in there?" Ma asked, her tone a little sharper than usual, knowing full well the state of the team after Kenny's departure.

"Same as always at the Kyrock Gazette," Kenny replied, his voice flat. "More bad news."

"Yeah, well, don't you have some readin' to catch up on for school?" she asked, knowing the answer to that question also.

For the past few weeks, Kenny had been getting his assignments brought to him by Ms. Carter. That is, since he'd decided to take a break from school and from the team, if that's what you'd call it.

"I ain't about to have no dropouts livin' under my roof grandson," Ma said firmly.

"Isn't Pa a dropout?" Kenny joked.

"Yeah, well, if you want to go get a job to support your family of 12 and then go off and enlist in the army to fight for the greatest country that ever existed, then, well, you have my blessin'. But until then, grandson, you will finish your schoolin'," Ma said, her tone firm. "And I assume today's not the day you go back to practice then huh?" she questioned.

"You would assume right," Kenny said quietly under his breath.

"Then I expect you to get your chores done around here, you hear?" she questioned again.

"Yes ma'am," muttered Kenny.

"Coach Wills calls me every day to check on you," Ma said, shaking her head. "And I don't know how many more times I'm gonna have to tell that Covington girl you ain't feelin' well. You better be careful, grandson. A pretty little thing like her? It won't take too long for someone else to snatch her right up," she said as she gave him a sharp look.

"Yeah, well, I'm sure they'll get the hint eventually," Kenny muttered, heading for the door, in for another long, lonely day.

***

Kenny smelled like sawdust, sweat, and chickens—which meant he was off to another tired, dusty day on the Bledsoe property. He wiped his hands on his jeans like that'd fix anything, then stepped out of the coop and back into a day that felt off somehow. Like it was holding its breath, waiting to deliver bad news.

Winter was losing its grip on Kyrock, stubbornly hanging on as spring peeked out like a secret too good to trust.

144

The sharp crunch of gravel made Kenny lift his head. His gut twisted when he saw her—Kate, standing there like she belonged nowhere else.

She strolled up looking as sweet as some of Ma's iced tea. Like she'd walked straight out of a picture-perfect moment Kenny had no business being part of. Her hair was pulled back under an old ball cap, her jeans hugged her just right— tighter than a tick on a hound dog. And that old hoodie she wore made her look like something familiar, like home.

Kenny swallowed. Unsure of what to say, he settled for nothing at all. Instead, he bent down to grab his feed bucket as if she wasn't even there.

Kate scoffed, just enough to make her point, but it was the reaction she'd expected. After all, Kenny hadn't responded to a single text or call of hers in weeks.

She stood there watching him, arms folded softly over the worn boards of the fence that surrounded the coop. A playful smile lingered like a secret on her lips as she waited for his eyes to catch hers.

"I miss you," she said finally, cutting through the silence.

Kenny let out a breath, but still he didn't look up. "Well, I ain't really worth missin'," he replied calmly.

Kate, arms still folded, tilted her head to the side. Curious, much like a chicken sizing up the world, she stared a hole through Kenny, unwilling to waver. "Yeah? Well, unfortunately for you, you don't get to decide that," she said playfully.

Kenny stopped what he was doing and stood up straight, meeting her eyes with his. He exhaled sharply as he adjusted his grip on the bucket and wiped the sweat from his brow. "Come on, if you're just gonna stand there, you might as well work a little," he said like a jerk.

"Oh, these boots ain't made for workin', Bledsoe," Kate teased.

Kenny eyed her shoes, not boots at all, but spotless black and white Chuck Taylors. They looked like she'd pulled them out of the box that morning.

"Well these ain't much for workin' either," he joked, looking down at his flip-flops. "I s'pose we can just walk a little then," he said through a small grin.

"I'd like that," Kate replied with a smile of her own.

As they walked side by side across the property, Kenny couldn't help but realize how good it felt not to be alone.

"I saw in the paper you might get first-team All-State," Kenny said. Kate laughed. "Hold on, you all still get the paper? Ever heard of this fancy new thing called the World Wide Web?" she teased.

"Yeah, well, I think Pa pays more for the paper than we do for the internet," Kenny shot back, laughing. "and stop tryin' to change the subject."

She smiled, tucking a strand of hair behind her ear. "Yeah, well, the season's not over yet," Kate, her own worst critic, replied with a shrug.

"They'd be crazy to leave you off that," Kenny replied. "You're havin' an amazin' season."

Kate looked at him for a beat before she nudged his arm. "You could still have one too, you know," she said softly.

"What's that?" Kenny asked.

"An amazing season," she replied.

Kenny exhaled and looked down at his flip-flops as they walked. "I don't know how to get back there," he muttered under his breath.

Kate stopped and turned to face him. "Just come back," she said.

He let out a dry chuckle. "It's not that easy," he said, shaking his head.

Kenny hesitated for a moment as a flicker of doubt crossed his face. Before he could think any more on it, Kate jogged ahead and scooped up a basketball that had been resting in the shadows as they reached the worn hoop on the side of the old barn.

She grinned as a challenge sparked in her eyes. "Alright, I'll play you for it then," she offered.

Kenny arched an eyebrow. "Play me for what?" he asked.

"If I win...you go back," she said simply.

"And when I win?" Kenny asked confidently.

Kate smirked. "Then, you can keep hidin' out here, playin' farm boy, pretendin' you don't miss me," she said with a wink, her voice soft as whipped cream.

Kenny, well...he did miss her. Of course he did. How could he not when she looked like that?

Clouds had started to cover the sun as Kenny lifted his eyes to the rusted basket, the net tattered and barely hanging on. The hoop was showing signs of age and neglect, but it was still standing. It felt fitting somehow.

He shook his head and let out a small laugh. "You really think you can take me, don't you?" he asked.

"Ain't no think to it!" Kate said with the confidence of a cat on a porch rail.

She dribbled the ball a few times in Kenny's direction. Then, with a quick spin and a smooth step back, she launched a shot that swished right through a net that looked incapable of swishing.

"That's 1-0," she said grinning, clearly pleased with herself.

"Make it take it," she proclaimed, as she dribbled a few more times before stepping back to launch an even longer shot than her first.

Kenny turned his head to watch as the ball sailed through the air and dropped cleanly through the rim, barely even grazing the net this time.

"That's 2-0," she said, shaking her head side to side while holding her follow-through in the air with a triumphant swagger.

Small drops of rain began to fall from the clouds. Soft and steady at first,, but quickly gaining momentum.

Kenny snapped into it. "What are we playing to?" he asked.

"First to 3," she said with a wink, ready to take her next shot.

"Hey, wait just a dang minute," Kenny said.

Just as Kate was about to fire the ball for the third time, Kenny launched his long arm toward her.

In the blink of an eye, she pulled the ball down with an incredible pump fake as she expertly dribbled past him. Kate made a move toward the old hoop, going for the winning layup off the backboard. But out of nowhere, Kenny soared in— all six foot three inches of him— and swatted her shot away with a fierce block.

He scooped the ball away in mid-air and dribbled it back out across the dusty ground.

"Not so fast," he said with a crooked grin. Kenny pulled up and sank a long jump shot.

"Lucky shot," Kate teased, tossing the ball back to him.

Kenny waited for Kate to close the distance; his eyes locked on hers. He faked left, then right, before bursting past her with lightning speed. He cruised toward the basket and, with a smooth motion, dunked the ball in easily.

"I believe that's 2-2," he said, standing tall and holding the ball with a swagger of his own. He smirked like he'd just gotten away with something.

"Just imagine how bad it'd be for you if I had shoes on," Kenny joked, looking down at his flip-flops.

"Boy you sure are full of excuses today," Kate teased.

As she checked the ball back to him, she guarded him tighter now. Kate hated how much she liked it, how tall he was, how he could look down at her with that half-smirk like he already knew her next move. She'd never admit it though, not even if hiding it meant stumbling over her own heart. Kenny turned his body and began to back her down as he dribbled toward the hoop.

"You didn't think I was just gonna let you win just because you're so dang...pretty?" Kenny asked, as he spun around her quickly and fired up a shot. They both watched as the ball spun high through the air.

"That's ball game!" Kenny gloated triumphantly. But as the words left his mouth, the ball bounced hard off the rim and ricocheted right into Kate's hands. She dribbled back outside as Kenny, realizing what had happened, sped over to her and closed in tight.

As he leaned into her and she backed against him, the moment became tense. A sense of enjoyment came over Kenny as he pressed close and caught the faint scent of her perfume.

Kate saw the look of enjoyment on Kenny's face and gave a sly grin. "Don't get too comfortable now, Bledsoe," she said confidently.

Kenny raised an eyebrow. "Why's that–?" he asked. Before he could finish the question, Kate spun around him and quickly dribbled toward the old hoop.

Kenny chased her, leaping high into the air to block her shot. But Kate, with a slick, graceful move, scooped under the basket. With impeccable backspin, she kissed the ball off the backboard and into the hoop.

"And that...is game!" Kate exclaimed, raising her arms in victory as she taunted Kenny, pushing her face close to his.

Kenny shook his head and grinned.

"No fair! I was...," he trailed off, his words slipping away as Kate's face left him speechless. "Distracted," he finished. But he couldn't help the way his eyes lingered on Kate. She was indeed, as Kenny put it best, pretty.

"So whatta you say, Bledsoe?" Kate asked, stepping even closer to him, her voice dropping just a hint. "Are you gonna finish what you started, or what?" she whispered with curiosity in her eyes.

Kenny paused, unsure if she was still talking about basketball or the two of them. The way she looked at him, the tension in the air—it felt like the lines between the two blurred in that moment. Maybe Kate didn't know what she meant either.

As they stood there face to face, the rain picked up, falling heavier. The sky darkened quickly. A sudden flash of lightning cracked through the air, followed by a strong ripple of thunder that startled them both. Without flinching, Kenny grabbed Kate's hand and the two began to run.

Chapter Twenty-Seven

"Come on!" Kenny shouted, his voice urgent against the rising storm.

The two continued running through the heavy rain, the droplets hitting their skin like tiny pinpricks as they dashed toward the barn for shelter.

The moment felt surreal, caught between playful competition and the undeniable pull of being together in the midst of the chaos.

As the two sought refuge in the tired red barn, rain rattled on the tin roof like loose change in a jar. The wind howled through the cracks in the wood. The wind chimes could be heard in the distance as they sang with the gusts, adding to the symphony of the storm.

As they stood there catching their breath, drenched but perfectly content, Kenny spoke first.

"I've missed you too, ya know," he said softly, pulling Kate in close, his face inches from hers. He grabbed her hat, flipped it backward, and settled it atop his tangled curls.

Kate paused, a spark of amusement lighting up her smile.

"Well," she said, her voice light,. "I most certainly am worth missin'."

Their shadows twisted with each other, as if the space between them couldn't decide who it belonged to.

"You sure are somethin' Kenny Bledsoe," she whispered, as she wiped drops of rain from his face.

There was a pause before Kate whispered, "This is where you say something cute back."

"Oh, right. Let's see," Kenny paused to think on the matter.

"How 'bout I think you're hotter than a billy goat in a pepper patch?" he winked, clearly pleased with himself.

Kate tilted her head back and laughed.

"Hey now, that was a pretty dang good line, huh?" Kenny joked.

"Yeah...it was...pretty good...but not good enough to get–"

Before Kate could finish, he pulled her in for a kiss.

Her soft lips washed away the roughness of his world. It was as if everything else disappeared, and for that moment, nothing mattered but her.

He didn't want to stop kissing her, not even to come up for air. It felt like the rain, the storm, everything faded into the background as their connection grew stronger with every breathless second.

But such are spring storms in Kentucky—as quickly as they come, they're gone.

The rain tapered off, and the barn was quiet. Kenny felt his hands running along Kate's back, her skin soft beneath his touch. Her breath came a little faster now. Then she pulled away.

"We gotta stop meetin' like this," Kate teased.

"Yeah...I don't know if I agree with ya there, Covington," Kenny joked.

Kate's cheeks were flushed; she took a small step back, clearly torn in the moment.

"I need to go," she said, blushing. Her words lingered in the air between them. "But I have somethin' for you," she added.

"Come with me," she said quickly, brushing her hair back, catching her breath as she steadied herself.

With fingers intertwined, they made their way across the Bledsoe property. Ma and Pa's blue house stood off in the distance.

The ground was softer now, much like Kenny's disposition. Though it wasn't quite spring yet, the air had the promise of it—a hint of something new on the way.

As they walked Kate glanced at Kenny with a playful smile.

"Well, that was embarrassing, huh?" she asked.

Kenny looked at her, confused.

"Whatta you mean?" he asked.

"Getting beat by a girl," she said with a grin as she laughed, light and carefree.

Kenny chuckled, squeezing her into his side.

"I'm pretty sure I just let you win," he said.

"Pa–lease!" Kate exclaimed. "I had you beggin' for mercy out there."

Kenny shook his head, but one thing was for sure. Kate did have him at her mercy.

The two walked for a while until they reached her car. Kate swung open the driver's side door and rummaged through the console for a moment. When she reappeared, she handed Kenny something wrapped in old newspaper.

"Don't open it until later. Promise me?" she commanded.

"You and all these promises," Kenny replied, his voice soft but sincere as he took the mystery package.

Kate gave him a look that lingered.

"Okay...okay, I promise," he said.

"I've gotta go to practice, but think about what I said, okay?" Kate asked.

Kenny nodded, "I will," he replied. Though he wasn't entirely sure if he wanted to.

Kate paused for a moment, before she added, "And hurry up, would ya? A girl misses seein' you around, ya know?"

She removed her hat from Kenny's head and held it in her hands, perhaps the same place that held his heart.

As the two leaned in for a goodbye kiss, Kate suddenly shrieked and threw her hands in the air.

"Ahhhh—sshhiii-!"

A bee had buzzed its way into the proximity of her golden strands of hair.

Now, as tough as Kate liked to think she was—and truth be told, she was pretty dang tough—her Achilles' heel was bugs. Big or small, flying or crawling, didn't matter. The tiniest unknown insect could make Big Brave Kate leap like she'd seen a ghost with a chainsaw.

Kenny nearly doubled over laughing at the sight of Kate flailing around like she was under attack.

"It's just an ol' wood bee!" he called out between chuckles. "Harmless!" he laughed.

"You don't know that!" Kate yelped, still swatting the air.

"That thing was coming right for me!" she gasped.

Kenny grinned wider.

"You sure are somethin', Kate Covington," he said with a smile.

Kate, still glancing around for the killer bee, finally straightened up, smoothed her hair, and gave him a look. Calm and collected.

"Yeah," she said, "and don't you forget it." She leaned in and planted a soft kiss on Kenny's cheek.

And with that, she climbed into her car and was gone.

As she drove off, the dust from her tires swirled like smoke in a fading fire, lingering in the air before slowly settling back to earth.

Kenny stood there, watching the car disappear like a fading dream. He couldn't help but think about everything she'd said.

A quiet doubt crept in—maybe Kate had a point.

Maybe it was time to get back to things left undone.

To a job not finished.

Chapter Twenty-Eight

<<<<<

If joy had a smell, it'd be Ma's famous Christmas ham and whatever magic she put in the air that made you forget the world was falling apart outside.

But it wasn't just the ham, or the cinnamon, or even the warmth of the fire crackling. It was the way Ma made a house feel like it remembered you.

The wood-burning fireplace popped, casting a warm glow that danced along the walls. A thick needled tree was perched in the corner, draped in lights and mismatched ornaments, some older than Kenny himself. A string of popcorn wrapped around it; a tradition Pa had insisted on keeping alive, even though Ma swore it was too much work.

Caleb sat cross-legged on the floor, shaking a present in his hands. His face was lit up like a little kid.

"C'mon, Ma," he pleaded, shifting his gaze from her to Pa, who was doing a poor job of hiding a grin behind the rustle of his newspaper.

Each of the brothers had only one small gift under the tree—money had never spread far in the Bledsoe house. But as the warmth of Ma's cooking filled the air and Pa's laughter rumbled through the room, it was clear they had more than enough.

"Now, you know the rules," Ma said, a softness in her voice. Caleb was convinced she'd cave soon enough.

Kenny stretched out on the couch as he lazily tossed a single popcorn in the air and caught it with his tongue.

"Give it up, Caleb. Every year she says she's gonna make us wait, and every year you fall for it," he said.

Caleb rolled his eyes and tossed a kernel at Kenny. "You ain't got any Christmas spirit, little bro."

"And you ain't got any patience," Kenny shot back, dodging the popcorn with a smirk.

Pa folded his newspaper and rested it on his lap as he shook his head with a chuckle. "I swear boys, if that tree ends up on the floor again like last year, there ain't gonna be no presents."

Caleb smirked. "Well, that was Kenny's fault."

"Oh yeah, because I just threw myself into it like some kind of idiot," Kenny shot back.

"Sounds like somethin' you'd do," Caleb teased.

"Enough of that," Ma said, shaking her head, but unable to hide her excitement as she reached under the tree and pulled out two small packages wrapped in newspaper. "Here, somethin' special for each of ya."

Kenny took his package and ran his fingers over the clean wrapping job. He glanced over at Caleb, who was already tearing into his with joy written all over his face.

Inside was a brand-new basketball jersey—blue and white, just like the ones the Kentucky Wildcats wore. Caleb lifted it, eyes wide with surprise. "No way," he breathed.

Kenny opened his and then flipped it around, the bold white letters on the back spelled out **Bledsoe.**

"No way!" he exclaimed, mimicking his brother—some habits didn't fade, even as they grew older.

Ma smiled at them both. "Figured you'd each want somethin' to remind everyone of who you are."

Caleb was speechless as he ran his fingers over the jersey, then he looked at his grandmother with something soft in his eyes.

"Thanks, Ma. This is—this is perfect," he said.

"Well, it'll have to do 'til you get the real thing one day," she replied with a smile. And she meant it.

Kenny, still holding his jersey in his hands, nodded as he struggled to find the right words. "Yeah...thanks, Ma," he finally mustered.

But Ma wasn't done just yet. With a smile she reached behind her and pulled out two small boxes, placing them in front of the boys.

"One more," she said beaming, full of pride.

Pa sat up straighter in his recliner. A smile stretched across his face.

Caleb and Kenny exchanged a glance before they carefully opened the boxes simultaneously.

Inside each was a blue basketball pendant on a silver necklace resting against the fabric lining.

"It's so you'll always have a piece of the game," Ma said softly. "And a piece of each other," she added.

Caleb swallowed hard, running his thumb over the pendant before slipping the necklace over his head. Kenny did the same, his chest tightening in a way he hadn't expected.

Both boys stood and hugged their grandmother.

"Thanks Ma, they're just like...they're...perfect," Kenny whispered and Caleb nodded in agreement.

It's hard to say if it was the warmth of the stove, the echo of holiday music playing from Ma's old radio, or the scent of Christmas in the air that night in Kyrock. But on that chilly December evening, it felt like the kind of night that belonged to forever.

***

\>\>\>\>\>\>

Kenny sat on the edge of the windowsill in his bedroom, right where Ma used to perch and sing to him when he'd have a long, sleepless night. Memories wrapped around him like the old handmade quilt resting atop his bed.

How much is that doggy in the window... The one with the waggly tail?

Ma would sing that song to him over and over, her voice soft and steady—a gentle lullaby meant to soothe his restless heart.

Tonight, a different kind of nervous energy pulsed through him.

He turned Kate's gift over and over in his hands. The old newspaper wrapping crinkled beneath his fingers as he hesitated, staring at it. For some reason opening it felt bigger than it should—like once he did, there'd be no going back.

As he peeled the paper away, a laugh escaped him. In his hands was a CD, the words *Listen to me* scrawled across it in black Sharpie. He shook his head as a smile crept onto his face. Kate had a knack of making him do that—it was starting to become a trend.

As he looked around the house for a way to play the outdated compact disc, he finally spotted an old CD player tucked away on a shelf near Ma's sewing kit. Dusting it off, he popped the CD in and pressed play.

At first, there was only static and the faint crackle of a microphone being adjusted. Until finally—Kate's voice.

"Alright, Bledsoe, if you're listenin' to this, that means you actually opened it—took you long enough."

Kenny let out a laugh, shaking his head as her vibrant voice filled the quiet bedroom.

"I didn't really know what to say, but... I just wanted you to know, you're not as alone as you think you are. And you don't have to figure everything out by yourself; we can figure it out together. So... just let me know when you wanna start?"

"Oh, and—will you go to homecoming with me?"

There was a pause, and another pop from the microphone. Then Kate's voice again, a little rushed now.

"You should totally say yes, by the way. Because now this is just awkward if you don't... This is Kate, by the way... okay, bye."

Kenny let out a real, full-bodied laugh—the kind he hadn't laughed in... hell, he couldn't remember how long. There was a pause, followed by the sound of Kate taking a breath.

"Oh, and one more thing—I picked out some songs for you. Hope you like 'em. And if you're sittin' there laughin' at me, you should definitely not do that because my momma died and all that…I mean it's a really sad story, Bledsoe. Okay, bye!" she finished cheerfully.

And with that, the first song started to play.

I Wanna Dance with Somebody by Whitney Houston

Kenny leaned back against the window, his eyes tracing the cracks in the ceiling. The music curled around him like a memory he couldn't quite let go of. Thoughts of Kate stirred something in his chest—a slow ache and a quiet pull.

His whole life had been one uncertain step after the next, never sure of the ground beneath him. And even though he still didn't know where he was going…maybe, just maybe, Kate was the closest he'd come to figuring it out.

Chapter Twenty-Nine

That night, Kenny climbed into the Tundra with his heart pounding. He was ready to face Kate and give her the answer she deserved in person. The winding back roads of Kyrock stretched out like a gauntlet, each turn flooded his mind with memories—flashes from his past that seemed to echo in the quiet of the truck. He popped the CD Kate had made for him into the truck's player and skipped ahead a few tracks.

Gypsy by Fleetwood Mac filled the truck's speakers. For a moment, Kenny was lost in the sound. The melody brought back pieces of the past he hadn't even realized he'd tucked away. Memories of his mother dancing in the kitchen, her laughter mixing with the music as she cooked dinner.

This was the same song that had played in the background of their small house during the good times—the happy times, before everything changed.

His throat tightened and a tear, small and stubborn, welled in his eye as he found himself singing low and soft. The words rose from some tender place he thought he'd forgotten. It was as if the music had unlocked a part of him he had kept buried for far too long.

It was at that moment that Kenny knew exactly what he needed to do.

He pressed the gas pedal harder as the truck tore through the crooked roads, as if the drive itself was urging him on.

When he finally pulled into the driveway and threw the truck in park, his heart raced. He sat there for a moment, gathering the courage to say the words he had been holding onto. But this time, he wasn't going to run away.

As Kenny knocked on the door, his heart fluttered in his throat. And when the green door swung open, he was greeted warmly. "Kenny Bledsoe, oh my goodness! Come in" Coach Wills' wife said as she pulled him inside their home with a big smile and an even bigger hug.

"Jackson! Look who's here!" she called out.

Kenny crept through the hallway and sheepishly entered the kitchen, where Coach Wills and his three kids were seated eating dinner. An awkward tension settled into the room; Kenny's cheeks flushed from the uneasiness of the moment.

"Let me fix you a plate," Wills' wife said with a warm smile. "Sit down and eat, honey."

"Oh, I really can't," Kenny stammered, his words stumbling over each other. "I don't want to be a bother."

"Sit down, son," Coach Wills demanded, his voice firm but kind. "My wife wants you to eat, so you're gonna sit and eat with us," he said, settling things.

Kenny sat at the table, not quite sure how to start or what to say next. He pushed his food around the plate, losing his appetite as the discomfort settled in deeper with every passing second. The silence stretched like a rubber band about to snap. Coach Wills and his family carried on with some of their conversations, but there was a noticeable tension in the room. Kenny could sense the pressure of it; his shoulders stiffened as his mind raced.

Without warning, Coach's youngest daughter Bianca, no older than eight, looked at Kenny with wide, innocent eyes. "So...are you gonna come back to the team?" she asked, her voice cutting through the silence like a tiny splinter of glass.

Kenny froze as the question hung in the air. He glanced over at Coach Wills, then back at the little girl. "Well, that's what I wanted to talk to Coach—uh, your dad—about," Kenny said, his voice uncertain.

The youngest Wills girl nodded sagely, as if she'd been waiting for that answer all along.

"Oh, we don't talk about basketball at the table son," Wills said matter-of-factly before going back to his mashed potatoes.

Deron let out a quiet chuckle, smirking as he caught Kenny's eyes across the table.

Coach Wills' wife, sensing the discomfort, tried to lighten the mood. "So, how is your grandmother, dear?" she asked warmly.

Kenny's shoulders relaxed a little, grateful for the change in topic. He glanced at her and back at his coach, offering a small smile. "She's... she's doing alright," he said, trying to shake off the nerves clinging to him. "She's keeping up with everything at home."

Mrs. Wills nodded. "That's good to hear," she said kindly, offering him a reassuring smile.

As silence started to settle over the room, Bianca piped in again, "Well, I heard that Kate Covington loves Kenny and she wants to marry him!"

The tension at the table snapped instantly as everyone burst into laughter, the awkwardness lifting like fog in the morning sun. Even Coach Wills chuckled, shaking his head with a smile. "Well, I don't know about all that, but I do say this is a darn good meatloaf," Wills said.

And with that Kenny was off the hook, at least for now.

***

Time stumbled forward. Kenny pushed his chair back from the table. He gathered his plate and silverware as he glanced at Mrs. Wills.

"Let me help you with that," he offered.

"Oh, sweetheart, you don't have to—" she started, but Kenny was already stacking plates, as he followed her towards the kitchen sink.

Coach Wills raised an eyebrow but didn't say anything as Kenny set the dishes by the sink and rolled up his sleeves.

"I'll wash and you can dry," Kenny said with a grin, reaching for the sponge.

Mrs. Wills chuckled, shaking her head. "Well, aren't you somethin'?" she marveled, handing him a plate.

As the warm water ran over his hands, the kitchen filled with the gentle clatter of dishes and the hum of quiet conversation. The awkwardness from earlier had faded, replaced by something calmer—something nearly normal.

When the last dish was put away, Kenny dried his hands on a towel and turned to Coach Wills, who was leaning against the counter watching him.

"I wanna come back," Kenny said abruptly, his voice steady but uncertain. "To the team," he continued.

Wills studied him for a beat before letting out a slow sigh. "You haven't earned that right," he said plainly.

Kenny felt his stomach drop.

"At least... not yet," Wills continued. He crossed his arms, his expression unreadable. "If you're serious, you'll have to put in the work. Not just show up and come back—but work for it."

Kenny nodded, absorbing the meaning of his words.

"I won't stand in your way," Wills said. "But I won't make it easy," he added.

Kenny swallowed hard and gave a single, determined nod. "I wouldn't expect anything less," he said. Coach Wills smirked, patting him on the shoulder. "Good. I'll see you at practice at 6 a.m.—if you're up for it."

Kenny turned, grabbing his jacket from the chair before heading to the door. As he stepped onto the porch, the crisp, night air filled his lungs with something that felt a little like hope.

It wasn't the answer he'd hoped for, but it was the one he knew he deserved.

Chapter Thirty

The stars were scattered like spilled seeds, and the crescent moon was sawed off in the Kentucky night sky as Kenny perched on the tailgate, the cold metal sharp against the fire of his thoughts. He fished his phone from his jeans, fingers hesitating, knowing his feisty blonde foe was going to be the one reading whatever he sent.

This CD is pretty good. Come listen with me.

In no time at all, the front door of the Covington house creaked open and Kate stepped out. Her arms crossed against the chill as her hair cascaded perfectly over her shoulders. She smirked as she walked toward him barefoot, somehow making a baggy sweatshirt and gym shorts look effortlessly perfect.

"You admittin' I have good taste, Bledsoe?" she teased as she climbed beside him on the tailgate.

Kenny chuckled, shaking his head. "Well, you definitely have good taste in guys," he joked.

The two sat there for a moment as the soft strumming of an old REO Speedwagon song drifted from the truck's speakers. The silence between them wasn't awkward—it was easy, natural.

Kenny removed his jacket and placed it around Kate's shoulders.

"I talked to Coach Wills," Kenny said.

Kate turned to him, her eyes searching his, "And?" she asked.

"He said I haven't earned it yet. But if I want to put in the work, I can earn my way back."

Kate let out a breath and before he could react, she threw her arms around his neck, pulling him into a tight hug.

"Kenny, I'm really proud of you," she whispered against his shoulder.

He felt himself relax into her, his arms wrapped around her waist. It felt...nice.

After a beat, she leaned back just enough to look at him. "So," she said, tilting her head. "You never gave me an answer."

Kenny furled his brow, "About what?" he teased with his crooked smile.

Kate jabbed him playfully on the shoulder.

Kenny smirked. "Oh, the Homecoming Dance, right...yeah, I'd love to, but I have plans that night."

Kate's mouth dropped open.

"Yeah, I've got a hot date that night," Kenny teased as Kate cocked her head to the side.

"Yeah, she's smart and funny and really good at basketball. And really," he paused for a moment. "Pretty," he finished with a grin.

Kate stared at him, pretending to be unimpressed by his witty banter, but the corners of her mouth betrayed her, curling into a smile she couldn't quite hide.

Kenny grinned. "Of course, I'll go to Homecomin' with you Kate Covington," he said.

"Good, because I can't wait to dance with you Kenny Bledsoe," Kate replied.

Kenny rolled his eyes, but he couldn't deny it. He was looking forward to dancing with Kate, too.

She reached for him, her fingers curled around the collar of his hoodie. He met her halfway, their faces drawing close together with nothing left between them but the beat of their young hearts.

"Can I ask you a question?" Kenny said out of the corner of his mouth.

"Of course," Kate replied quickly.

"So, like...what's the deal with the CDs? I mean... how do you even..." He trailed off, trying to pin down exactly what he was asking. "You do know about cell phones, right?"

Kate laughed and Kenny smiled with her.

"Yeah, I'll admit it's not the most convenient way to go about it," she said as sincerity flickered in her eyes.

"But I don't know...I guess when my mom was... going through it all... I'd make them for her—she used to have a big collection. I just, I dunno...it was kinda like I wanted to give her these little trinkets of normal or something...ya know, just to take her mind off...all of it," she paused, her gaze growing solemn, as if lost in thought about her mother.

"Then, after she died, it just kind of became my thing. Like... somethin that, I guess, brought me peace. You know? Like I could still be with her somehow... I know it sounds stupid," she whispered.

"No, it doesn't," Kenny chimed in. "It doesn't sound stupid. It sou nds... real." His eyes locked on hers, filled with awe—at her beauty, her heart, her vulnerability.

The two sat there, enjoying the quiet of the night for a moment before Kenny finally spoke again.

"So... what was it even like out in California?" he asked. "Was it really all beaches and sunshine like folks say, or is that just TV talk?"

Kate laughed, nudging him with her shoulder. "You're such a dork, TV talk," she mimicked in an exaggerated country drawl. Kenny grinned.

"I mean... it wasn't 'California' to me," she said, as her voice softened. "To me it was... home." Kenny raised his eyebrows and nodded, listening intently. "You know, when you're young, you think not having the newest phone is the end of the world. Or not getting enough attention from the cute boy at school is the worst thing that could ever happen."

Kenny pointed at himself. "You talkin' bout me?" he asked.

"Shut up," Kate teased, giving his arm a light punch. Then her smile faded into something more thoughtful.

"But then one day life gets real. And your innocence," she paused, searching for the right words, "it just goes. And you don't even realize that today is the day it's gonna leave you."

She let out a soft laugh, shaking her head like she didn't want to step too far into that kind of truth.

"So...can I ask you a dumb question?" Kate said, her eyes narrowing.

"Shoot," Kenny replied softly.

"Are you okay? And before you answer, I know you're gonna say you're fine, and I know I used to hate it when people asked me that after my mom died... like, no, dude, I'm not okay, my freakin' mom just died." The words fell from her mouth half a laugh, half a wound still healing.

"So just level with me," she said. "Say anything you want. Tell me everything sucks and that you want me to shut up. Tell me that I'm stupid for even asking. I can take it," she said through a wince.

Kenny looked at her, a smile danced on his lips. "Honestly?" he said. "Right this second, right here with you..." he paused, gently taking her hand in his, "I'm good." And for the first time in what felt like forever, he actually meant it.

"Okay, I've got a serious question for you now," Kenny said, grinning.

"Oh gosh," Kate sighed, rolling her eyes playfully.

"It's a doozy." Kenny teased.

Kate scrunched up her face. "All right, hit me."

"What's your all-time favorite song?" he asked, leaning in like it was the most important question he'd ever asked.

"Ahh, now you're speakin' my language," Kate laughed, smiling wide. "Okay, so play track twelve."

"Hey, I like that number already," Kenny joked.

"Why do you think I put it in that spot, genius?" Kate teased.

Kenny hopped down from the tailgate and skipped ahead to track twelve, just like she asked. *Lights* by Journey started to play through the truck's speakers, filling the night with its soft, familiar sound.

"If I'm ever mad at you, just play this song and dance with me, and all will be forgiven," Kate said.

"Man, that's it? That's the key to peeling back the layers of the mysterious Kate Covington?" Kenny grinned, slipping his arm around her waist and pulling her in close, hugging her tight as the music wrapped around them.

The two shared the chill of the night as the music floated softly around them; stars tossed across the sky like dreams yet to be dreamt. In that moment, Kenny felt something he hadn't in a while—the fragile hope of belonging.

***

The old Tundra hummed along the back roads of Kyrock, windows cracked, night air whistling in like an old friend. The moon lit up the fields with a butter-colored glow, and Stevie's voice floated through the cab like a memory.

Kenny felt lighter than he had in months—maybe even years. Like for the first time in a long time, things were starting to make sense.

That's when his phone rang. He glanced down at the screen, and his eyebrows pulled together when he saw Gracie's name. He answered.

"Kenny," her voice came through the line, shaky, broken—nothing like the Sara he knew.

He sat up straighter. "Gracie? What's wrong?"

A choked sob came through the speaker, and that was all it took for his stomach to drop. "It's my daddy," she managed. "He—he had a heart attack. We're at the hospital."

Kenny's grip on the wheel tightened.

"I didn't know who else to call," she admitted, her voice barely above a whisper.

He didn't hesitate. "Which hospital?" he asked.

She sniffled, trying to steady herself. "Med Center. They just took him back."

Kenny swallowed hard, nodding even if she wasn't there to see it. "I'm on my way," he said.

He didn't think; he didn't question it. He turned the truck around and pressed hard on the gas pedal.

***

As Kenny stepped into the emergency room, the sterile smell of antiseptic hit him immediately, grounding him in the harsh reality of it all.

His heart pounded as he scanned the room searching for Sara when his eyes finally landed on her. She was sitting on a chair, her hands tightly gripping the edges, her face pale and streaked with tears. Her usual composure was gone, and the hurt in her eyes made Kenny's stomach twist.

As soon as she saw him, her tears that had been threatening to fall broke free. She stood quickly, her knees nearly buckled as she took a shaky step toward him. Without a word, Kenny was there. He wrapped her in his arms, holding her tight as if he could somehow make everything okay.

"I'm here," he murmured, his voice steady even though everything inside of him felt chaotic.

Sara buried her face in his chest, crying harder.

Kenny didn't know what to say, so he just held her, letting her lean into him as he tried with all his soul to steady the earth for her.

She didn't speak; she didn't have to say anything. Kenny felt her pain settle deep in his bones, knowing how much she needed someone—not just anyone, but someone who truly understood.

In that instant, like the hush before a summer storm, it came to him—clear and whole—he was the one she needed now. With Caleb gone, it fell to Kenny to be her protector. And deep down, something in him wanted to step into that role, even if he didn't quite know how.

Chapter Thirty-One

Kyrock gym echoed with the rhythmic sound of sneakers squeaking against the freshly swept floor and the sharp bounce of basketballs. Kenny could barely focus on anything except the exhaustion weighing on him.

He had been at the hospital with Sara all night, barely catching a few hours of sleep before having to wake up to make the 6 a.m. practice. But he wasn't about to let anyone know just how tired he was. Kenny knew he had to keep moving.

"Hey, Bledsoe!" Coach Wills shouted from the court, pointing at him. "You're on water duty today. Keep the guys hydrated!"

Kenny nodded and moved to the sidelines, prepping the water bottles and towels for the team, making sure each guy had what they needed. As he passed out the towels, his legs ached and his head felt like it was full of cotton, but he didn't slow down.

His breath was ragged, his legs felt like lead, and the gym lights were blinding. But he kept moving, every step a reminder of the night he'd just spent in that hospital room with Sara— her father barely clinging to life after his heart attack.

It had been a long, long night. But he couldn't let it show. Not here. Not now.

Coach blew the whistle. "Alright, guys! Full-court sprints! Let's go!"

Kenny's stomach dropped, but he didn't have a choice. He took his place alongside the rest of the team, standing shoulder to shoulder, his body screaming in protest.

He wanted nothing more than to collapse onto the floor and sleep for a week. But as the whistle blew again, he took off, pushing himself harder than he thought he could.

His body felt like it was on autopilot, moving without any real thought. Sweat dripped down his forehead, stinging his eyes. His legs wobbled like jello, but he didn't stop. He couldn't.

As the whistle to stop echoed throughout the gym Kenny made his way over to the sidelines, his chest heaved, and sweat slid down his skin like rain off a tin roof.

"Bledsoe, you good?" Coach Wills called out. "You look like you're running on fumes, son."

"I'm fine, Coach."

Kenny didn't look up, trying to keep his voice even.

"That's good," Coach Wills said, as he crossed his arms. "Because here's the options I'm gonna give you. Either the whole team can run six more sprints, or you can run three by yourself."

It didn't seem like much of an option to Kenny as his legs shook with exhaustion. He staggered back to the baseline as sweat beaded into his eyes; he nodded in silent agreement. The decision had already been made.

His teammates, however, weren't about to let him do this alone. As Kenny took his place at the starting line, they stood from their bent-over stances, hands on hips, and started to cheer him on.

"Come on, Bledsoe! You got this!" they shouted from the sideline.

Kenny took a deep breath. His body ached, but he started his first sprint. Every step felt like a battle, but with the sound of his teammates' cheers behind him, something shifted. His legs burned, but the support from his team kept him moving.

And just when he thought he had nothing left, a voice cut through the exhaustion—one he hadn't expected. He could hear Caleb's voice in his head, clear as day.

"Keep going, Ken. Job not finished."

The words were like fuel to his fire, pushing him forward, one step at a time. And even though Caleb wasn't there, the flame that burned inside Kenny matched the one his brother had always carried on the court.

As Kenny finished the third sprint, his feet pounded hard against the court before he slammed into the padded wall at the end of the gym. His chest heaved, and he barely had time to catch his breath before Coach Wills called him over.

"Bledsoe, about the homecoming game," Coach started.

Kenny's posture straightened his tired eyes wide with anticipation.

"We're gonna need you on the bench, son," he said, expressionless.

Kenny's heart leaped—until Coach finished his sentence. "We're gonna need someone to keep track of stats for us."

The excitement drained from Kenny's face, replaced by a dull ache worse than any sprint. But he swallowed it down; he had to fight through.

He nodded, his voice heavy with exhaustion. "Yes sir. I'll be there." He gritted his teeth and with a steady resolve as he reminded himself: Job not finished.

***

<<<<<

Kenny's heart was pounding loud enough to scare off the crickets as he knocked on Sara's front door, bracing himself for whatever might come. When the door eased open, whatever words he'd planned to say scattered like leaves in a breeze. The porch light haloed around her, and her dress shimmered like creek water catching the last kiss of daylight.

The way she looked at him, the soft curve of her smile, was breathtaking. But the second her eyes landed on him the excitement in her face wavered.

"Hey Kenny," Sara said, peeking past him. "Where's Caleb?"

Kenny flinched. "He's...on his way," he said not so smoothly. "He said he had to head into town to grab something special for you."

Sara blinked, surprised. "Oh,...okay."

Kenny nodded as he stuffed his hands in his pockets. "Yeah. You know Caleb—always big plans, that one. But he'll be here soon." The words fumbled from his mouth.

Truth be told, that was a lie and a clumsy one. Caleb was nowhere to be found. Kenny had checked the usual spots—and nothing. And now he was left standing here alone buying time for a brother who might not even show.

Sara hesitated and smiled softly. "That's sweet of him."

Kenny forced a chuckle. "Yeah...he's the sweetest."

As the minutes melted into each other, Sara anxiously checked her phone. Her fingers fidgeted at the hem of her dress. Kenny knew he couldn't stall forever.

He made his best attempt at non-chalance as he stepped outside and dialed Caleb's number for what felt like the fiftieth time that evening. Still, there was no answer. His grip tightened around his phone as he exhaled sharply.

The sound of the door opening behind him made him turn. Sara stepped out onto the wide, polished front porch of the Whitmore house, her expression growing more concerned by the minute.

"Is everything okay?" she asked.

Kenny forced a nod, swallowing the unease rising in his chest. "Yeah," he lied, "just a small change of plans."

Which, to be fair, wasn't technically a lie. Sara didn't look convinced.

Kenny cleared his throat, scrambling for something—anything—to say. "We're gonna pick Caleb up at our house. It's takin' a little longer than he thought to...uhh...grab the thing he got for you."

Another lie.

"He got me somethin'? Oh, tell me, what is it Kenny?" Sara asked.

He felt the tingle of sweat beading at the back of his neck. *My gosh this girl and her 21 questions!* Kenny thought.

This was the first time he'd ever lied to Sara. He hated how easily it rolled off his tongue, but for Caleb? He'd do it. "Uhm...I have no idea what it is," Kenny said, the truth of that one tasted good on his lips.

***

As the two pulled up to Ma and Pa's house, Kenny barely had Betty Lou's old car in park before he jumped out springing to his grandmother, filling her in on the night's chaos in a hushed voice. He asked for her help stalling—just long enough for him to find Caleb.

Ma's sharp eyes studied him for a moment, then she nodded.

"Go on grandson, I'll keep her occupied," she said, stepping off the porch to greet Sara with a warm smile and warmer hug.

Kenny took off toward the barn, toward the cottonwood tree, his heart hammering.

"Come on, Caleb," he muttered under his breath, scanning the trees. Nothing. No footsteps, no silhouette in the moonlight, just silence.

By the time he circled back to the house, his insides were coiled like a spring. He had no choice. Caleb wasn't here, and Sara was inside waiting to go to prom. He had to fix this. A wild, last-ditch plan formed in his head. It wasn't perfect—not even close—but it was something.

Kenny slipped in through the back door, moving quickly down the hall to Pa's room. He yanked open the closet, his fingers pushing through flannels and worn-out jackets until he found what he was looking for—a suit. It was old and a tad musty, but it would do.

He stripped out of his clothes in record time, stretching into the too small dress shirt and adjusting the cuffs. The pants were loose around the waist, so he grabbed a worn belt from the dresser to keep them from falling. He found a pair of scuffed dress shoes that were a little too big, but with thick socks, they'd work. And finally, he donned the jacket.

Kenny's arms were too long for the sleeves, but they weren't farm strong in the biceps like Pa's. The jacket swallowed him in places and inched short in others, a double dose of ridiculous.

Taking a deep breath, Kenny stood in front of the mirror. He couldn't help but laugh at himself. Pa's clothes seemed to wear him more than the other way around. And to top it off, the icing on the cake of his preposterousness, his tie was crooked.

But on the bright side, at least he could say he somewhat resembled a prom-goer.

He ran a hand through his curly hair, took one last breath, and turned toward the door. If Caleb wasn't going to show, he would. He didn't feel like a worthy replacement, but Sara deserved the effort. Gracie deserved the world.

His heart pounded as he made the long walk down the hallway to step into the living room where Sara was waiting. But as he did so, the front door swung open.

And there he was.

Caleb, slightly disheveled, was fully dressed in his well-fitting jacket and perfect bow tie, grinning ear to ear. He walked in like he hadn't just sent the whole night spiraling.

Somehow, he made the look work for him. He could always pull it off; it was his superpower.

"There you are!" Sara beamed, her face alight with excitement. Her eyes fixed on Caleb, not noticing Kenny on the opposite side of the room. "Caleb Bledsoe, I was gettin' ready to pitch a fit," she teased. "Where have you been?"

Kenny could see where this was headed, so before Caleb could fumble for an excuse, he bolted to his room. His hands shook slightly as he grabbed his blue charm basketball necklace from his dresser—the one Ma had given him all those years ago. Still in its box, untouched, because he'd been too afraid of losing it. But right now, Caleb needed it more than he did.

Kenny quickly removed his oversized jacket and slipped back into the living room. He greeted Caleb with a hug. "There you are brother. We were starting to get a little worried something had happened," Kenny said as he discreetly pressed the small box into Caleb's hand.

"You didn't want her to know, but you had to pick this up for her," he whispered in his ear.

Caleb's eyes flickered with understanding. He nodded and turned to Sara, presenting the box.

She gasped softly as she opened it, her fingers brushing over the small charm. "Caleb... It's perfect. Now we match. Now we're together," she said gleefully.

Without hesitation, Sara turned and lifted her hair as Caleb fastened the necklace around her neck. Caleb glanced at Kenny, his mouth was unmoving, but his eyes, wide, said everything: Thank you, brother. And just like that, they were gone, stepping out into the night. Off to prom happy, whole, and together.

Ma sensing the emptiness left in the room moved to Kenny's side. She wrapped her arm around his waist, and whispered in a soft, warm voice, "Well done, grandson. Well done."

Chapter Thirty-Two

Kenny caught his reflection in the mirror, pausing as his hand swept through the tangle of his curls, trying to tame them but failing, as always. A flicker of something—nervous excitement, maybe—stirred in his chest, an unfamiliar guest he didn't send away.

He swung open his closet door and pulled out a crisp dress shirt, the fabric cool against his palms. His eyes drifted to the two ties hanging there, swaying slightly—a black one that felt heavy with memory, and a blue one, borrowed from Pa's closet, frayed at the edges but still holding strong.

His fingers hesitated over them; his throat tightened as his thoughts drifted to his brother.

What would Caleb have to say about tonight? About the fact that Kenny felt excitement, real genuine excitement, about seeing Kate?

And, like a ton of bricks, the thought hit him. The pendant. A sharp pain shot through his chest. It was in Caleb's room.

Kenny hadn't stepped foot in there since the night everything fell apart. He hadn't even let himself glance at the door in passing. Just the thought of it made his stomach churn.

But if he wanted the pendant, if he wanted to carry a piece of his brother with him, he was going to have to walk through that door.

Kenny stood frozen just outside Caleb's room, staring. It was just a door—plain wood, chipped at the edges, nothing special. But in some ways, it was more than that. It was a barrier, a thin piece of space and silence that had kept out the pain and misery of that awful night.

His hand hovered over the doorknob, his pulse thrumming in his ears. Crossing that threshold meant facing everything he'd been trying to outrun. It meant stepping into a room frozen in time, untouched, as if Caleb might walk through it at any second.

But Caleb wasn't coming back.

As Kenny entered, the air inside felt heavier, thicker. Like the room had been holding its breath since the night Caleb left. Everything was exactly as Caleb had left it. The unmade bed, the basketball jersey draped over the chair, the pair of muddy boots kicked off by the door.

It was like stepping into a memory. One that hadn't yet faded, one that still carried his brother's presence in every corner.

His eyes scanned the room then dropped to the worn wooden floor—the very spot where he saw his brother that awful night. A sharp, searing pain shot through him, like a wound being torn open all over again. Kenny flinched at the thought; it was the kind of pain that settled into the soul and never truly left.

He lifted his eyes to an old wooden desk and there it was—the small black box. He spotted it from where he stood, untouched, waiting. Kenny had never questioned why Caleb stopped wearing it. Never asked, never thought to. But now, standing in this room weighted with memories, he wished he had.

As he lifted the box and opened it, Kenny found something inside he hadn't expected—a letter. It was folded neatly, the word *Kenny* scrawled on the exposed paper in Caleb's handwriting. The sight of it left Kenny devastated.

He felt the blood rush to his head; his heart pounded in his chest. He didn't know what to do. His fingers hovered for a moment, unsure whether he was ready to face whatever Caleb had written. But something inside him urged him to open it. So, with a shaky breath, he unfolded the paper.

The handwriting was familiar, the way Caleb always wrote—neat but rushed, as if he had something to say and no time to say it. Kenny's eyes scanned the words, each one sinking deeper than the last.

Ken,

I knew you'd come looking for this soon enough. Guess I owe you one, huh?

I know you love her. I've always known it, and to tell you the truth, she loves you too, even if she doesn't realize it yet. Promise me you'll take care of her. You've got the kind of heart that can love fully, without holding back.

You two have always been on a collision course for each other. And that brings me peace.

I love you brother. Always.

Job not finished.

Kenny finished reading the letter and his heart shattered.

Seeing his brother's words on the page, hearing his voice in his head… it felt like losing him all over again. Tears broke from his eyes like tired stars falling from the sky, softly staining the paper as he sat, head in hands, reeling from the words Caleb had left behind.

Just as he'd managed to lay one note to rest, another had found a way to breathe itself back into his life.

***

The mood inside the truck as Kenny drove to pick up Kate was somber, to say the least. He didn't sing songs; he hardly even breathed the air in the cab. He was numb, the spark he had felt earlier about taking Kate to the homecoming dance was dissipating like air slowly leaking out of an old bicycle tire.

He thought about texting her, saying he couldn't make it. Thought about claiming he was sick. Thought of plenty of excuses—some true, some not so much.

But then, he thought about Kate—about the way she'd been looking forward to tonight. The way her face lit up when she talked about it. He

181

thought about how she'd showed up for him, even when he didn't totally deserve it. So with a deep breath, he tightened his grip on the steering wheel. He couldn't do that to her—not tonight.

As he pulled into the driveway of the Covington's modest ranch-style home, his phone rang. Gracie's name lit up the screen. Kenny stared at it, his thumb hovering over the decline button. He considered ignoring it, but then he thought about Caleb's letter.

With a heavy breath, he answered. The moment he put the phone to his ear, he could hear Sara's sobs echoing through the line.

"They don't think he's gonna make it, Kenny," she choked out. "It's bad."

Kenny's stomach twisted. "Gracie," he said, his voice steadier than he felt. "Take a breath. Just breathe." Kenny's voice was gentle but firm. "It's gonna be okay." But even as the words left his mouth, he knew how hollow they sounded. Nothing about this felt okay.

"He's dying, Kenny," Sara choked out. "My daddy is dying." Her voice broke, shattering like glass. "Caleb left us... and now my daddy is dying, too."

Her cries tore through Kenny, splintering the pieces of his broken heart, fractured earlier by Caleb's letter. Kenny gripped the steering wheel tighter, trying to ground himself. He didn't know what to do, didn't know what to say.

He thought about the letter—Caleb's words still echoing in the corners of his mind. He thought about his life, about Sara, about Kate... about all of it. How everything seemed to constantly change and yet somehow stay heartbreakingly familiar.

How love and loss had a way of weaving themselves together within his world until you couldn't tell where one ended and the other began.

He thought about his brother Michael, his father, his mother....and Caleb again. And for a moment—maybe for the first time he could ever remember—Kenny felt something unfamiliar toward his brother.

He felt anger.

Anger that Caleb had left him. Anger that his brother hadn't stayed to hold tight to the people who loved him. Why hadn't he stayed to love Sara himself? Anger that even in death, Caleb had decided how Kenny should live his life... who he should love.

Sure, Kenny loved Sara and he was in love with her—always had been. But that love felt more like a truth he buried quietly in his chest, not some grand gesture meant to win her over. It wasn't a choice to love Sara. It just was.

So in that moment a flicker of a thought crossed his mind—quiet but sharp.

Had he ever really decided anything for himself?

Or had he always been chasing shadows, loving things he couldn't hold, living in the eclipse of someone else's sun—of Caleb's life, Caleb's losses, and now Caleb's absence?

And so, for the first time in a long, long time, Kenny made a choice—a selfish one, a human one.

He chose Kate.

"Gracie, listen to me," he said, his tone stronger now, steadier. "Gracie, I love you," he said softly into the phone.

He heard her breath hitch on the other end, a quiet pause stretching between them. "I love you too, Kenny," she whispered back.

But before he could stop himself, before he could think better of it, he kept going, his voice stronger than he expected.

"You know I love you, Gracie. But the truth is, I guess, well, I'm in love with you. Always have been, I s'pose. I guess part of me has always known it. But if I'm being completely honest, I was okay with never saying it. I was content just bein' the brother of the guy you were in love with. And that would've been enough for me—just existing in your orbit. Because whether you know it or not, Gracie, you are the sun. You're my sun."

His throat tightened as he thought about Caleb's letter, about the consequences of what his brother had left behind.

"But I've been thinking," he continued, exhaling slowly. "And... well, I just thought you should know. You'll always have my heart, Sara Grace

Whitmore. Always. But right now, it's not yours to carry. So no matter what happens, no matter where life takes us, you'll never have to be afraid of being alone, because you'll always have me," he paused briefly before finishing. "But right now, I just wanna dance with Kate."

Chapter Thirty-Three

Sara was silent, so silent it was as if the world had hit pause. Her sobs had quieted—hell, for a moment, Kenny wondered if she was even breathing.

Just as Sara finally found her voice, "Kenny..." she began.

A sudden THUD, THUD, THUD against his truck window startled him. Kenny jolted, the phone slipped from his grasp, dropped to the floor and vanished under the passenger seat with a hollow CLUNK.

He looked up, and there she was—Kate, standing outside the truck, her face lit by the glow of the breaking sun. He rolled the window down.

"Dang, keep a girl waiting much, Bledsoe?" Kate teased with a smirk. "So much for chivalry."

"Sorry," Kenny said, his voice apologetic. "I got an emergency call...that I...uhh... I needed to answer."

"Oh gosh, is everything all right?" Kate asked, her brow furrowing in concern.

"Yeah, yeah," Kenny replied quickly, slightly dismissive. "You look... you look...pretty," he added, his words catching slightly as his eyes fell over her.

And look pretty, she truly did—her blue dress seemed to glow against the soft pink haze of the setting sun. It hugged her just enough to make him forget what he was about to say.

Her blonde hair cascaded along her shoulders in soft waves, catching the light and sending a warm glow around her. Her every movement seemed to make the strands shimmer. For a moment, Kenny felt a flutter in his chest—like the world had paused just to highlight how beautiful she was.

Kate smiled, a soft laugh escaping her glossy lips as she stepped closer to the door. "Don't gawk Bledsoe, you're gonna make a girl blush," she joked. "You look pretty good yourself, ya know," she said with a wink, her tone light and warm.

As she climbed into the truck, Kate noticed Kenny's phone on the floor. She picked it up, and the screen lit up with Gracie's name.

"Hold on," Kenny said quickly, reaching for it, but before he could stop her, Kate brought the phone to her ear.

"Hello?" she asked, her tone sharp, a hint of anger in her voice. There was a pause on the other end, and the call ended abruptly. Kate looked down at the screen, her expression shifting into something uncertain, her eyes flicking to meet Kenny's.

"Is everything okay?" she asked, concern creeping in her voice. Her gaze was wide, searching his.

"Yeah," Kenny said quietly, his voice barely above a whisper, "It's just... Gracie... Sara's dad," he corrected himself quickly. "He's in bad shape. She just called to let me know."

Kate sat there for a moment, staring at Kenny as if she were trying to process his words. After a beat, she turned and stared straight ahead, her hands resting in her lap.

"Oh, gosh...well..." she started, her voice more neutral now, "Do you need to go or something?" Before Kenny could respond, she added, "I mean, it's fine if you do. I completely understand."

Her tone, however, didn't match her words, making it perfectly clear it wasn't fine.

"She'll be fine," Kenny said at first, before second guessing himself. "Well... I don't know," he admitted, running a hand through his hair. "She was pretty upset. I don't really know everything that's goin' on." He let out a breath, glancing at his phone before looking back at Kate. "I'm sorry."

"You don't have anything to be sorry for, Kenny," Kate said, her voice even. "But if you need to go, you should probably figure that out now... right?" she asked.

Kenny hesitated for half a second before shaking his head. "No, it's fine," he said, forcing a small smile. "Let's just go."

***

As they pulled into the school parking lot, the truck was quiet—much like the ride over. Not much was said, aside from some small talk about Kenny's earlier stint as the team's unofficial stat keeper, watching from the sidelines as the team dominated an overmatched Warren North.

When they'd parked, Kenny hopped out of the truck and quickly moved around to open the door for Kate. She smiled, but it didn't land quite right—something was off.

As they walked toward the entrance, the music from inside spilled out into the cool night air. Kate stopped abruptly.

She took a deep breath and turned to face Kenny.

"Just go," she said softly.

Kenny squinted. "Go...where? What are you talkin' about?" he asked, a puzzled look on his face.

She forced another smile, but it wavered. "Kenny. You don't have to pretend with me," she said.

"I'm not pretendin'," he said, perplexed.

The line of students waiting to enter the gymnasium had started to grow; the energy buzzed with anticipation. From inside, music echoed off the walls, muffled but alive, like the heartbeat of something about to begin. Kenny and Kate quietly stepped aside, moving out of the way of the crowd gathering at the entrance.

Kate took a break from biting on her bottom lip. "Ya know," she said, "I'm not this girl."

Kenny glanced at her, his eyes tight. "What do you mean?" he asked.

She gave a humorless laugh. "I'm not the girl who makes a scene at homecoming over a boy choosing someone else." Her words tasted like irony as she stood in line outside the dance.

"I just... I like you, Kenny," she continued. "A lot, and for better or worse, I—" she paused, her words catching somewhere between hope and disappointment. "I just thought tonight might be special," she said softly, her tone flat—like the magic she'd imagined had slipped away.

Kenny, lost, wasn't sure what to say. He opened his mouth then shut it, trying to gather his thoughts. But again, he tried. "I like you too, Kate. I just —" He exhaled, shaking his head. "I'm not sure what's going on here," he said in reference to the current conversation, not their relationship.

Kate paused, taking a moment to steady herself. "I just think this thing is doomed," she admitted, her voice quiet but sure. "I can't compete with...with all of it." She didn't say Sara's name. She didn't have to.

"I mean, sure, part of me likes a challenge," she said with a shrug. "And if I'm being completely honest, I don't mind a little competition. Kinda enjoy it—you know, all's fair in love and war... that whole thing." She let out a quiet sigh, her gaze dropping for a second before meeting his again. "But no matter what I do, it just feels like fate is always pushing you two together... and pulling us apart." Her words hung there for a moment, heavy but calm. She wasn't mad, she wasn't angry, just...disappointed.

She continued. "Oh, God, it's all so dramatic, talkin' about fate...uh hh!...And here I am, soundin' like the biggest ass, mad someone's in the hospital over a stupid high school dance," she said, shaking her head with a hollow laugh. "But it's not just tonight. It's not just that you need to be with her for her dad or that she needs to be there for you because of Caleb. That's not it at all."

Kenny interrupted. "Kate, I don't know what you think is going on but it's not like that with me and Gracie. I just wanna go to the dance with you," he said, nearly pleading.

Kate took a breath. "That's the point, the fact that you don't even see it. The fact that no matter what happens, you two are always gonna need each other. And you're never gonna need me like that. Like you need her," she said, her voice softer than before.

She offered the last part with a small, sad smile, like she had already made peace with it. "We both know it. So... let's just call this thing before a girl gets hurt," she said, trying to joke, but the sadness in her eyes was there, as if they were just waiting on her heart to catch up.

"Wait," Kenny said, "Are you... are you breaking up with me?" he asked, finally starting to understand.

Kate let out a frustrated laugh, "That right there...that's what I'm talking about," she said, her voice tight. "I can't even break up with you, Kenny Bledsoe; you were never really mine to begin with. You're always somewhere else, waiting for someone else, always."

Kate shook her head, her frustration blending with hurt. "And in case you didn't notice, you can't break up with someone you never really dated in the first place." She let out a frustrated sigh, running a hand through her hair.

"God," she muttered, "This isn't me. I'm not this girl." She took a deep breath, trying to steady herself. "I know you've had an impossible few months, and I'm not faulting you for that. It's not your fault... I just... I just can't do this. You should just go."

Her words hit Kenny sharp like a dagger. Kenny's heart clenched and he took a step forward, desperate. "I don't want to be with Sara. I want to be with you," he tried to reason.

Kate looked at him, her eyes searching his face, but her voice was charged with something unspoken. "You don't know how much I wish you actually meant that," she said.

"I can't be the girl who throws herself in the middle of unstoppable forces...you know what happens to that girl, right?" she paused before continuing. "She gets absolutely crushed. So, I'm letting you off the hook. Just go," she pleaded.

"No, Kate... please..." Kenny said in a voice on the verge of breaking.

He took another step forward, but Kate stepped back and put her hand out as if to keep him at arm's length. Her eyes glistened with unshed tears, but there was no turning back now.

"I do hope I get that dance one day, Bledsoe," she said. Her words felt unfinished as she turned and walked away. But the moment, their moment, was most certainly over.

Kenny stood outside the old gymnasium and watched as Kate walked away. He didn't bother to chase her. He knew she didn't want to be chased. What Kate wanted, more than anything, was to be caught by someone who only wanted her.

Chapter Thirty-Four

<<<<<

Kenny stood at the edge of the gym. The music was loud, too loud, as colorful balloons bounced under flashing lights. Kids scurried around in their little dress shirts tucked into their blue jeans and their frilly little dresses complete with matching hair bows.

The air smelled like punch and hairspray, and the floor was covered in skids from little shoes that couldn't quite keep time with the beat. Somewhere in the heart of Kyrock the school's annual elementary school dance was in full swing.

Kenny and his friends were huddled together, laughing and tossing playful jabs at each other. They talked about the "gross" girls who were trying to get them to dance.

Kenny was pretending not to care, but a part of him couldn't help but be a little nervous. He didn't understand what it meant to dance with a girl; he hadn't really thought about it before. But the more he thought about it, dancing with a girl, that is, the more the whole idea was starting to seem... less gross.

"Girls have cooties," one of his friends, Bobby, said, scrunching his face like it was worse than the worst thing in the world. "And if they kiss you, you get infected. You start getting pimples all over your face, and sometimes you even die!"

Bobby was serious, and so everyone else was too. They all nodded, agreeing like it was a universal truth. As if the very idea of a girl's kiss could bring about a catastrophic fate.

Kenny, still trying to figure out what it all meant, didn't question it. If Bobby said it, it must be true right? I mean, why would Bobby lie?

Across the room, he spotted her. Sara Grace.

She was standing by the punch bowl, which sat atop a card table that was directly underneath an old white basketball hoop. She was chatting with a couple of the other girls, but when she noticed him looking, her eyes met his and she smiled. A bright, soft smile that made everything around Kenny seem stiller— like the entire world paused for just a moment.

His heart skipped.

Kenny wasn't sure what was happening, but something tugged at him as he watched Sara Grace walk toward him.

She wore a little pink dress and a matching bow that held up her trademark ponytail, which bounced with each tiny step she took. His friends noticed her walking over too, and they all started making "oooooh" sounds, nudging him playfully.

Sara Grace stopped in front of him with her wide, hazel eyes. "Dance with me, Kenny?" she asked, her voice sweet and sure.

Kenny felt light in his head, like an afternoon ride on the merry-go-round spinning too fast, but in a way that made him want to go again.

She smiled as she took his hand and gently led him to the middle of the gym. The music shifted to something slower, something softer. For a moment, he was too scared to move. But without notice Sara Grace stood on her tippy toes, and in an instant quicker than a hiccup, she kissed him gently on his cheek.

It was just a soft peck, innocent and fleeting. It didn't even leave a mark, but it left an imprint on his heart that would never fully disappear.

As the song finished Sara Grace leaned in and whispered, "Thanks for the dance, Kenny." Her perfect smile lit up the moment.

Kenny remained frozen as Sara Grace walked back to her friends, his face a mix of confusion and excitement. He didn't know what it all meant, or why she had made him feel like his whole world had just shifted slightly. But for the first time, he realized that maybe, just maybe, some cooties weren't so bad after all.

***

>>>>>

The high beams of the old Tundra carved tunnels of light into the Kentucky country night. Fields blurred past in yellowish waves as moonlight caught on dew-slick grass. Kenny mouthed along to some twangy old country song on a forgotten radio station—something about "she broke my heart and took the dog"—which, in its sad, pitiful way, was almost comforting.

Maybe I should get a dog, he thought.

Time slipped in the country night; could've been an hour, could've been three. Out there, with the stars overhead and the winding road beneath him, time felt like it was holding its breath, waiting for whatever came next and Kenny took a breath to replay what had transpired.

He wasn't sure why Kate had made the choice she did—why she let him go so easily, or why it hurt so much that she had. But in the quiet that followed, in the ache of it all, Kenny had done the only thing he knew how to do. He called Sara. There was no answer.

And in that moment, everything Kate had said felt true—painfully, unmistakably true.

Be that as it may, he wanted to find Sara—needed to. He wanted to hear her voice, to know she was okay, or maybe just to let her know he wasn't. He wanted to hold on to something familiar in a world that had shifted too fast beneath his feet that night—something steady, something that made sense.

His mind kept replaying the conversation with Sara from earlier that day—the way he had unloaded everything on her and vanished, much like how Kate had done to him.

It felt like he was constantly caught in the pattern of being the one left behind, always the one left to deal with the fallout.

Why today, of all days, did he have to find Caleb's letter? If he hadn't, would he have told Sara how he felt? He certainly hadn't meant to; he definitely didn't plan on it. The words had just sort of slipped out, messy and unfiltered.

Oh, God! Would Gracie even wanna be around him now? Was everything between them about to shift, about to become weird?

Sara had always been his constant. The thought of life without her made him feel like he would spontaneously float away.

He dialed her number again, the rings filling his ear, each one taking longer than the last. Like watching paint dry on a cold day. Just as he was about to hang up and toss the phone onto the dash, she answered.

"Hello?" Her voice seemed different, unfocused, the background full of music and muffled chatter.

"Gracie?" Kenny asked, his voice curious.

"Kenny, Kenny Bledsoe?" she responded. Her tone was casual, slightly mocking, and it was clear she wasn't quite herself.

"Where are you?" he asked.

She didn't hesitate. "I'm having a party," she replied, her laugh a little high-pitched. "Come celebrate with me, Kenny. It'll be fun," her voice wavered, a little slurred. It was clear she wasn't sober. "Come celebrate all the good things in our lives, my Kenny!"

Kenny's stomach dropped. "A party? Gracie are you—" he started, but she interrupted him.

"Just come, I want you...here Kenny. I want to see you," she said, her words thick with alcohol and something else—something Kenny couldn't quite place.

He could hear music blasting, voices laughing, and the sound of bass thumping in the background. The whole thing sounded like a hot mess.

"Hellooooo...hello, Mr. Kenny, are you there?" she slurred, her voice exaggerated.

"I'm on my way, Gracie," Kenny muttered, trying to steady his nerves.

"Oh, I'm on my way!" she mocked in a deep, manly voice. "Always so serious, my knight in shining armor. Coming to save me. Hahahaha, Knight—get it?" she cracked herself up.

"Gracie," he said quietly, trying to interrupt the horrible standup comedy routine. But Sara wasn't having it.

"Oh! Just get to me Kenny Bledsoe! Get to me, or I shall perish!" And with that, she ended the call.

***

As Kenny pulled into the driveway of the Whitmore house a gathering of cars had filled the large circle driveway. The lights from the house flickered through the curtains and music pulsed from inside. It was obvious this wasn't just a casual hangout—it was a full-on party.

As Kenny slowly made his way inside, the space was crowded with people. Some he recognized from school, others who were strangers to him, all chatting, laughing, and losing themselves in the chaos. The air was thick with beer, Axe body spray, and the wild, restless buzz of a small-town party that had gone a little too far.

As Kenny walked through the kitchen, a friend from school shouted, "Bledsoe!"

He nodded absently as his eyes scanned the room. When he rounded the corner, his gaze immediately locked onto the family room.

Standing near the back wall was Sara. The first thing he noticed wasn't just Sara, though. She was standing out amongst the sea of people—but he couldn't help but notice the guy standing to her left, a little too close to her. His arm was casually draped around her waist as they both stood watching some others crowded around a pool table engaged in a game of beer pong.

Kenny's stomach twisted. He wasn't sure what it was about the sight—was it the casual intimacy of the gesture, or the way Sara seemed perfectly at ease with it—but it hit him like a punch to the gut. Seeing that guy's arm around her made Kenny's heart ache in a way he wasn't prepared for.

Before he even realized it, he was cutting through the crowd heading straight for her. The music, the voices, the buzz of the party seemed to fade as he got closer. All that mattered was reaching Sara. When he made his way to her he noticed her eyes were a little glossy, their normal beam a tad duller.

"There you are! You made it!" she called out when she saw him, her voice louder than the music. "This is my friend, Kenny," she said, gesturing his way as she introduced him to the group. The others nodded in his direction, offering polite smiles.

Kenny wasn't sure what bothered him more—the glaze in her eyes, or the way she casually referred to him as *friend*. The word felt like a cold slap, and for a moment, it was all he could focus on. *Friend?*

Was referring to him as a *friend* just a pretext? A way of signaling to someone else in the group that he was no threat—that he was just... Kenny? Her way of making it clear that he wasn't anything more, that he never would be. And more importantly, if this guy—whoever the hell he might be—was more than just a friend.

A fire burned in Kenny's chest, an unfamiliar heat that made his breath shallow.

"Play with us, Kenny!" she shouted, pulling him into the group. As he joined the table his eyes were fixed on Sara, on Sara and this guy.

Who was this doofus? The flame in his chest intensified. How dare she do this to Caleb!

Would you look at this idiot? he thought as he sized the guy up, trying to swallow the rising anger bubbling inside of him.

And why wouldn't he just take his damn hand off of her? Kenny's blood began to boil as his thoughts spun out of control.

"I need to talk to you!" Kenny yelled, trying to make himself heard over the pounding music.

"Hold on, it's my turn," Sara said, as she effortlessly sank a ping pong ball into a red solo cup. The others cheered and simultaneously took a drink from their matching cups.

Sara, a little too drunk to remember the rules, took a drink too, her eyes glancing at Kenny over her cup. "Okay, let's go chitty chat now," she said, her words fuzzy.

The two made their way through the chaos and stepped out onto the back porch, which was a little quieter, though the party had spilled out into the back yard. A few kids were in the hot tub laughing and shouting. Kenny glanced around, trying to steady his thoughts.

Sara did her best impression of someone sober as she stood on the porch and looked at him with glossy eyes, her focus on the middle Kenny in her sights.

"Well, let's talk, Mr. Talky," she said, her voice slurred, clearly several drinks in already. "Give me those woooorrrds," she drawled, her mouth slipping and tripping over her own as she swayed slightly, to the left and back to the right again.

"What's going on, Gracie? What are you doin'?" he asked, concerned.

"I'm celebrating," she replied, her words slow and unsteady. "Shouldn't we celebrate all we have to be thankful for? All that God has given us?" she stumbled over her words, her speech thick with spirits. "You're just... un...grateful," she slurred, pausing mid-sentence, as if trying to collect her thoughts like they were loose change she'd dropped on the ground. "Un-graaaate-ful," she repeated, her words jumbled, her mind clouded.

Kenny gently took her by the hand and looked at her, really looked at her. "Gracie," he said, his voice soft but firm. "I know it hurts, believe me, I know. But this aint'...," he paused, looking around at the mess of a party, the noise, the chaos. "This ain't you," he said.

He was about to say more, but before he could finish his thought, the guy from before appeared, sliding onto the back porch with a smirk.

"Hey, there you are," the dude said, his voice too casual for Kenny's liking, as he moved in close to Sara once again. He slipped his arm around her waist for the third time that night like it was nothing.

Fueled by the day from hell and a rush of jealousy that had been simmering since he laid eyes on the guy, Kenny finally snapped. "Hey, man, this doesn't concern you," Kenny said, his voice sharp.

The guy, clearly surprised, took a step back. "Woah, bro, what's the problem?" he asked.

"I don't have a problem, but I can think of a few for you," Kenny shot back, his fists clenched at his sides.

The guy laughed, trying to shrug it off. "Hey, man, I'm just having a good time with Sara Grace. Isn't that right?" he asked, tightening his grip on her waist.

That was the final straw for Kenny. Sara's middle name coming off this jabroni's tongue might as well have been accompanied by a French kiss.

WHAM! Kenny's fist connected with the guy's cheek, knocking him back a couple of steps. The guy stumbled, cursing as he clutched his face.

"Ah, hell, bro, what's your problem?" he grumbled, rubbing his face.

Sara's face was a mixture of shock and concern as she leaned over to check on him. "Kenny, why did you do that?" she asked, disbelief clear in her voice.

The guy staggered and sneered at Kenny. "Hey man, don't be a jealous little bitch just because she ain't interested in you."

WHAM! Kenny hit him again, this time harder, sending him down to the porch with a thud. Kenny stood over him, his chest heaving, his anger not yet spent. "And get your damn hand off of her!" he growled.

Sara's eyes had cleared a little, but the confusion was still there. "Kenny, what the hell is wrong with you?" she shouted, trying to push him back.

Kenny stood there for a moment looking at her. There were too many answers to give, too many emotions tangled inside him to respond to that one simple question. So, instead of answering, he let out a breath and said, "Enjoy your party."

And for the first time in his life, he turned his back on Sara and he walked away.

Chapter Thirty-Five

Before the sun could drag itself over the hills of Kyrock, Kenny found himself inside the boys' locker room. The lights above buzzed like a hive as he stood there, alone and awake when no sane person should be.

It wasn't even 5:30 a.m. and he was folding jerseys, stacking them neatly in piles. The smell of sweat and cleaning supplies lingered in the air. A reminder of the games, the practices, and the grind of it all. He missed it, every part of it.

His hands moved methodically; he had a rhythm down. And despite the time, the smell, and the monotony, he didn't mind. It felt like the only thing in his life that had any sense of order at the moment.

The scene shifted and Kenny was on the gym floor alone, except for Coach Wills, who sat on the sidelines in a chair reading from his morning paper with a whistle dangling from his neck.

Wills checked his phone; it was 6:00 a.m. Time to begin. With a fluid motion Wills blew his whistle, signaling Kenny to begin, before letting it fall and hang loose once more. Kenny's shoes slapped against the hardwood as he sprinted from one end to the other. The sound of his breath echoed in his ears. Coach Wills didn't speak much, if he spoke at all. The only sounds bouncing off the walls of the empty gym were the occasional sharp blasts from his whistle to signal when Kenny had reached the next starting point.

Kenny's muscles burned, but he didn't stop. The rest of the world seemed somewhere far away. Each blow of the whistle, each sprint, was a reminder, a quiet command to push harder, to prove something. Kenny was determined to do just that. After all, the job was not finished.

Next in Kenny's day was the library. It was 7:00 a.m. sharp as the tall grandfather clock chimed out 7 times. The light of day was just starting to break through the old rectangular glass windows filling the otherwise dark space with an eerie sense of focus.

Kenny sat at a desk in a far corner, working on something he'd been looking into for a while now. He had some papers in front of him as he scanned the computer screen, typing something. His fingers moved over the keys in sharp, deliberate motions.

His eyes darted back and forth between the monitor and the sheet of paper beside him. He wrote something down, underlining it twice. Whatever it was seemed important—a few scribbles in his notebook that seemed paramount, urgent even.

He paused for a moment as he stared at the paper in front of him— as if something had clicked, he smiled.

Suddenly, the first bell of the morning cut through the air, sharp and loud, slicing through the quiet of the space. Kenny stood quickly, grabbed his backpack, and made his way out of the library, heading off to class without looking back.

The halls were starting to fill with students and the world was moving fast, however, for a moment, Kenny's thoughts stayed locked on whatever he had just uncovered inside that room.

Ms. Lillian Carter was at her desk, sipping coffee and grading a stack of quizzes when she checked the time on her laptop. At exactly 7:26 a.m. Ms. Lilly looked over her computer and saw Kenny slip into her classroom, the final bell for the morning still a few minutes away. Her room was still quiet, bathed in soft morning light that had spilled through its low, aged windows.

"Kenny Bledsoe," she said with a curious smile, resting her mug on the desk. "What a pleasant surprise to see you here early."

He nodded, closing the door behind him as he glanced toward the hallway to make sure no one had seen him come in. "Can I talk to you about somethin'?" he asked, his voice low.

"Of course," she said, motioning to the seat in front of her desk. "Is everything okay?" she questioned.

"I need your help," he said, sitting in front of her. "With somethin' I've been working on. I was searching in the library this morning and well...I'm pretty sure I've got somethin'. But you've got to promise me first—whatever I tell you...stays between us."

Her eyes narrowed slightly, sensing the seriousness in his tone. She nodded slowly. "You have my word, Kenny," she said.

Kenny reached into his backpack and pulled out the paper he'd been scribbling notes on just a few minutes before. His hand trembled slightly as he unfolded it. "I found somethin'. I just need to know what to do next," he admitted.

Ms. Carter leaned forward, her expression shifted between curious and concerned. "Alright," she said softly. "Let's see what we can figure out."

***

The circular wall clock read 8:11 a.m. After the usual morning proceedings had wrapped, Ms. Carter stood at the front of the classroom and cleared her throat, calling the room to attention.

"Alright, listen up," she said, holding a stack of papers in one hand. "Part of your final grade this semester will be dependent on your participation in a group project. This won't be just any group project—it's a three-person assignment. And before you ask, no, you don't get to choose your groups. I've already assigned them."

Groans rippled across the room, followed by a few dramatic sighs.

"This project is called *Stories That Shaped Us*," she continued. "You and your group will choose a local figure, someone who has made a lasting impact on our community—someone who changed things, who left behind a story worth telling. You'll research them, interview people if possible, and present your findings creatively. That can mean a presentation or a short video—whatever format you feel best tells their story," she said to the class.

As Ms. Carter continued through the list of students, Kenny felt a slow, creeping dread in his chest. She was naming off group after group, and his name still hadn't come up. He was beginning to brace for the worst.

"And lastly," she said, looking up from her clipboard, "we have Sara Whitmore, Kate Covington, and Kenny Bledsoe."

Kenny died a little inside.

The room didn't go silent, but it might as well have. His heart thudded in his ears. A few students turned in their seats, some exchanged amused glances. Kenny wanted to sink into his desk and never crawl out.

Sara, as always, was seated across the room. She didn't look at him. She stared straight ahead, jaw clenched, lips pressed into a tight line. They hadn't spoken since the party.

Kate, two rows over, let out a short, bitter laugh under her breath. They hadn't spoken since, well, the same night—but you already know that.

Ms. Carter continued. "So I want you all to break off into your groups and start discussing who you might choose and why. You're going to be doing research together from here on out. If you don't do the work together, you will not pass. I hope I'm making myself clear?"

Somehow Kenny had managed to pull it off. The daily drama doubled. Somehow he had ended up stuck with two different girls, with two different unresolved messes of which he had zero ideas how to clean up.

The time on the giant clock was now 8:20 a.m. or maybe it was 8:21. Whichever it was, Kenny was ready for this day to be over.

Chapter Thirty-Six

After the final bell had rung releasing the students of Kyrock High for the day, Kenny checked his watch in the parking lot and stood by, full of melancholy. He watched as the crowd of students thinned, his eyes scanning until he finally spotted Kate heading toward her car.

He stepped forward, voice barely above a mumble. "Hey… when's a good time for us to work on the project?" he asked. As if they hadn't just tripped all over whatever they were a few days ago.

Without breaking stride, Kate brushed past him. "Any time before practice," she said, eyes locked on her car as she walked away.

Just then, as if on cue, Sara strolled by, earbuds in and her backpack snug over both shoulders.

Kate, catching sight of her, couldn't help herself. She turned her head and called out. "Hey, Whitmore! You got any big plans today?" she shouted, her voice soaked with piss and vinegar.

Sara paused and removed one of her buds. "No, I don't guess. Why?" she replied.

Kate smirked. "Whatta ya say we knock this stupid project out now?" she asked Sara, leaving Kenny out completely.

Kenny, in a moment of blind optimism or possibly temporary insanity, spoke up. "Ya'll wanna ride with me?" he asked.

Sara glanced around for a second and shrugged. "Sure, why not," she said.

Kate lifted her brows, her tone sugary-sweet. "Oh, I'd love to ride with you two," she quipped, letting the sarcasm hang in the air.

And somehow—with minimal discussion—it was settled; the group project would start today.

***

You could've cut the awkward in that Tundra with a butter knife—though silence was doing a darn fine job whittling away at the three of them. It wasn't like the old days when Kenny would third-wheel with Caleb and Sara with ease. This was something else entirely—something colder, tighter, a full country mile from comfortable. As the three traveled down the road in silence, it was Sara, never one to sit quiet for long—who finally broke it.

"So..." she started, looking between Kate and Kenny, "what were you guys thinking? As far as a person we could use for the project?"

"I gu....." Kenny started to speak but Sara quickly interrupted.

"What were you thinking, Kate?" she asked as she whipped her head around in Kate's direction. Her ponytail swished in Kenny's face as she did.

"Why don't we interview Mrs. Bledsoe," Kate said emphatically. "I mean, she was a state champion."

Kenny leaned forward in the driver's seat, glancing over at her. "I thi..."

Kate cut him off now. "What do you think, Sara?" Kate asked.

"I like the idea of a little woman power," Sara said with a smirk.

Kate continued, "Yeah, too much testosterone in Kyrock if you ask me"

"I couldn't agree more," Sara said with a mischievous grin.

Kenny sat quietly like a scolded pup eyeing a rolled-up newspaper—knowing better than to bark back. He'd met his match with these two, and the grin tugging at his lips revealed it.

Sara was in the middle between Kenny and Kate when she leaned forward and asked, "Hey, what's this?"

She picked up a CD from Kenny's console, one that Kate had recently made for him.

"Let's listen to it," she said.

Kenny tensed. "No, no, let's not," he urged.

Kate, always the antagonist, shot a glance over at him. "Yeah, let's listen to it, Kenny. What's wrong with a little music?" she prodded, the challenge evident in her eyes.

"Sure, why not... I guess this is what we're doin'," Kenny agreed.

Sara pushed the CD into the player. The first song that began to play was, *Jolene* by Dolly Parton.

Quickly, Kenny reached across Sara and hit the skip button. "Nah, I'm not really in a Dolly mood," he muttered.

Sara smacked his hand away from the buttons. "Hands off, mister," she said mischievously.

As the next track started to play, *Back to December* by Taylor Swift, Kenny's eyes widened.

He thought it was a little too on the nose for this particular truck, and he reached for the skip button again.

Sara however, stopped him in his tracks. "Don't you dare change Tay-Tay, Kenny," she threatened with a smile on her face. "I freakin' love this song!" she exclaimed.

"I love it too," Kate said, nodding in agreement as she stared a hole through Kenny.

Kenny swallowed hard.

As the lyrics of *Back to December* echoed through the truck, Sara softly sang along with the chorus, her voice light and carefree. *"So this is me swallowing my pride, standing in front of you saying I'm sorry for that niiiiight,"* she sang along, lost in the music.

Kate couldn't help but join in. *"Turns out freedom ain't nothin' but missing you,"* they both sang in unison, their voice's blending, their words filling the truck with teenage heartbreak energy.

Kenny sat in silence, his hands gripping the steering wheel tight. He couldn't help but wish he could go back to December—or honestly just any time before this one. That's when he got a big-brained idea to make them stop.

"Dang it!" he hollered, reaching down under the steering wheel and grabbing at his foot.

"Oh my gosh! Don't start with this," Sara groaned, shaking her head like she'd seen this act before.

"My gas toe!" Kenny cried out. "It's so... itchy!"

"You're just... sad, honestly," Sara said, though a smile had started to sneak across her face.

"Uh, hold up, did you just say—and I quote—'my gas toe is itchy'?" Kate asked, staring like she'd just witnessed a car crash in slow motion.

"Oh, he does...whatever this is... whenever he gets nervous," Sara explained, shaking her hand in Kenny's direction. "He says he can't drive with an itchy—"

"Gas toe!" Kenny cut in, still awkwardly scratching at his foot with theatrical intensity.

Kate blinked at the curly-haired cutie in the driver's seat. "Is he... for real right now?"

Sara rolled her eyes. "I'm afraid so...I'm afraid so," she said exasperatedly.

"Ahhhhh," Kenny sighed, exaggerated and dramatic like he'd just found salvation.

Sara and Kate burst into laughter. As ridiculous as this whole situation was, Kenny had somehow managed to outdo it—turning absurd into downright preposterous.

But Kenny could always do that—lighten the heavy, patch the broken. Whether he knew it or not, he had a knack for those types of moments.

He had a certain pull about him—something easy and quiet—that made folks want to be near him, especially the two lovely ladies riding in that truck. Funny thing was, the only one who couldn't see it was Kenny himself.

***

When they stepped into the Bledsoe house and wandered toward the kitchen, the green glow of the oven clock greeted them like a quiet witness. Kenny had been expecting to find Ma, but she wasn't there.

"She must be out with the chickens. I'll go look for her," he said eagerly, trying to put a little distance between him and his two waiting adversaries.

But before he could, Pa stepped out from his bedroom, maybe stirred by all the ruckus, or maybe sent as Kenny's guardian angel.

Leaning on his walker, he slowly but steadily made his way into the kitchen and took a seat at the table with a little help from his grandson.

As Henry took a second to catch his breath, he glanced up at both ladies and with a playful twinkle in his eye. "Well, well, you two must be lost. I know two sweethearts like y'all wouldn't be here with Kenny," he teased, his voice warm, but with a hint of mischief that only Pa could manage.

The sparkle in Henry's eyes was unmistakable, a sign that he was himself today, fully present. Which was enough to spark a smile from Kenny.

Kenny whipped open the fridge and pulled out a carton of milk and poured a tall glass worth into a mason jar. Then he added four ice cubes, carefully dropping them in one at a time and passed it to Pa. It was Henry's favorite drink. Simple and cool, just like the old days.

"So, how's the season going, Kenny?" Pa asked, his voice calm and curious. Maybe he remembered that Kenny had quit the team, maybe he didn't. But Kenny didn't want to bring it up—not when Pa was in a good place.

Sensing the lifeline Kenny needed, Kate stepped in, eager to fill the silence.

"Well, our season's going great," Kate said with a smile. "We're first in the region, and we're just startin' to play our best ball."

Pa's eyes lit up and he chuckled. "Ahh, you're the Covington girl, aren't you? Oh my, we're in the presence of a heck of a ball player!" he said. "Maybe we can get you to teach Kenny a thing or two," he teased.

Kate grinned. "I'm gonna need a little more help with that one," she joked back.

"Haha," Henry laughed. "Oh, I like you, sis," he declared.

"And Sara Grace Whitmore," he said, looking her way. "If you get any prettier, Betty Lou's flowers out front are gonna get jealous," he beamed, his smile wide and infectious.

When he was on, Henry could light up a room. It was easy to see where the Bledsoe boys had gotten their charm.

As the confidence in his eyes grew, Pa got an idea of his own. "Let me tell y'all a little story," he said.

"Pa, they probably need to get goin'," Kenny cut in.

"Let the man talk!" Sara exclaimed.

"Yeah, Bledsoe, we wanna hear a story," Kate said in agreement.

Pa smiled as he launched into a tale, his voice rich with experience. His storytelling skills were so sharp they could put Whitman to shame. He began to weave an account from a time long, long ago—back during the war.

Time seemed to slip away unnoticed as Pa continued to tell his tale. The three youngins sat there, entranced, caught up in the world he painted with his words. Minutes crept toward an hour, and they hardly even noticed.

As Pa finished, he leaned back with a satisfied grin. "And that's how I convinced your grandmother to marry me," he said, the pride in his voice clear. The three laughed, each of them wearing huge smiles.

The back door flung open.

"Speaking of the devil," Henry muttered. They all shared a laugh as Ma stepped inside with a basket full of chicken eggs in hand.

"Well, as much of a pleasure it is to have you ladies with us, Ms. Covington, Ms. Whitmore," Ma nodded in their direction. "According to that sunlight, I'd say it's around 4:15. Don't y'all have a couple of practices to be at?"

"Oh crap," Kate said, glancing at the clock. "Yeah, we've gotta' go."

She stood up quickly and Sara followed close behind her.

Both girls hugged Ma and Pa goodbye. As they did, something unspoken passed between them all—an understanding that, without needing words, Henry Bledsoe was their hometown hero. The man who had helped shape their world years before they were ever even in it. The person who had made a difference simply by being who he was: a good man that loved his wife, his family, and his country.

Chapter Thirty-Seven

At practice that day, Kenny was a new man. Reenergized by Pa's stories, he moved with purpose, filling in wherever Coach Wills needed him—here, there, everywhere. His energy was infectious.

Kenny was so sharp, so focused, that during the scrimmage, the second team, with him leading it, demolished the starters. He was flying all around the court, back to his old self, back to the fire that once burned inside him.

Coach Wills' final whistle pierced the air, calling an end to practice. As always, Kenny moved to the baseline, ready for the runs that had become his ritual since coming back. But today, something changed.

As Kenny toed the line, every member of the team stepped in front of him lining up to run themselves. Coach Wills' back was to them as he blew the whistle expecting Kenny to run alone. But instead, the whole team took off together, side by side, every last one of them running with Kenny.

Wills turned as he heard the noise of the collection of sneakers echoing throughout the gym.

Kenny's heart swelled. For the first time since he'd come back, he wasn't alone out there.

Wills blew the whistle again, then again, and again. Still, the team ran together, in an unspoken tribute to their teammate.

Finally, Wills blew the whistle one last time. "Okay, Bledsoe," he called out, "time for yours."

But that's when it happened. Deron, one of the captains and the coach's son, stepped forward. "No, sir," he said. "If Bledsoe runs, we run."

Another player spoke up. "No Coach, if Bledsoe runs, we all run."

Wills had seen enough, he called the team over. He pulled Kenny closer, bringing him in front of the group.

"Well, I guess ya'll leave me no choice then," he said, his voice low but firm.

With that, he handed Kenny his game jersey and the team roared in approval.

Kenny, overcome with emotion, did his best to hide it. He clapped hands and dapped up his teammates. Then he turned to Wills.

"Thank you, Coach," he said, his voice barely above a whisper.

"Don't thank me," Coach Wills said, his voice rough. "You earned it."

The team roared again, their voices a powerful, unified chorus.

"Bledsoe, break us down," Coach Wills called out.

Kenny's chest swelled as he looked around at his team, the air humming with the promise of what was ahead.

"Alright," he said, "a little change-up before we go win this whole dang thing."

He lifted his hand, eyes sharp. "On three—job not finished. One, two, three—job not finished!" the team roared back, the words echoing through the gym.

The guys erupted in cheers running off the court together.

***

<<<<<

It was spring—more or less. In Kentucky it could be hard to tell. The air hung with the smell of fresh earth and something barely blooming, like a promise half kept.

Kenny and Caleb sat side by side in a porch swing, their little legs dangled as the rusty metal chains creaked in rhythm. They gently pushed themselves back and then swung forward.

Out in the gravel driveway, their brother Michael and their father were shooting baskets. The thud of the ball against the old backboard and the rustling of sneakers in the gravel carried softly through the evening air. Just across from the boys, their mother sat in her favorite rocking chair, a blanket draped across her lap and a worn notebook in her hands.

"Oh, I love spring in Kentucky," she said, breathing in deep, her eyes half-closed like she could taste it. "It comes on like something wild and new, something free from all worry."

Kenny always remembered the way his mother loved the smell of the spring air. It was the way her eyes would light up when she talked about it—like it carried magic. Like she believed the season itself was a story waiting to be told.

As she rocked, slow and steady, their mother opened her notebook in her lap. She had always read to the boys, her voice a constant in their lives. Though Kenny couldn't recall most of the stories now—not the words or the plots—he could still remember the way her voice filled the air: soft and warm, a steady comfort.

But this night, this memory...he never forgot.

It wasn't just that this would be the last time she would ever read to them. It was what she told them before she began.

"Boys," she said, glancing up with a smile that glowed from somewhere deep inside, "I have some exciting news."

Both brothers looked over, their curiosity piqued.

"I've just about finished my book," she said full of pride.

"Your book?" Caleb questioned, tilting his tiny head.

"Yes, sir," she said proudly as she tapped her fingers across the cover of her notebook. "I wrote every word in this right here."

"So, like... you wrote it? All of it?" Caleb asked again, his voice filled with awe.

"I did indeed," she beamed as her eyes sparkled.

Little Kenny perked up too, scooting forward on the swing. "Can we hear it, momma? What you wrote?" his voice was small and sweet.

"I was hoping you'd ask that," she said as she opened to a dog-eared page. "After all, it's about you boys,"she proclaimed with a smile.

"About us? Really?" Caleb asked, a spark jumped in his eyes as he leaned forward.

"Of course, honey," she nodded, "It's about you boys, your brother, your father, Ma and Pa... it's about this land, this little town... it's about my heart," she said to her sons.

"What's it called, momma?" Kenny asked, his eyes wide behind strands of his curly brown hair.

She paused, smiled, and shook her head. "That part I don't know yet," she answered.

"Well, what are you thinkin'?" Caleb asked, still leaning forward in the swing.

"I think... it's just one of those things," she said thoughtfully, tapping her chin, "that when I know, I'll just... know."

The boys didn't quite understand what she meant—but they believed her.

She began to read to them and to the Kentucky spring day. The sounds of the rusty swing and a bouncing basketball faded behind her words. And in that moment—between the light in her eyes, the rhythm of her voice, and the peace that wrapped around them like the blanket across her lap—Kenny knew what heaven must feel like.

This had to be it.

Chapter Thirty-Eight

The air wasn't warm, but it was warming—just enough to hint at what was coming. Kenny stepped out of the Tundra atop Bledsoe Hill that night after practice and inhaled deeply. He could smell it, spring. Which, as always, made him reminisce on his mother.

The air was charged, alive, on the edge of better days. Like the world was holding its breath, waiting for the next thing to come.

Kenny felt that way too—reenergized, like something lost inside him had finally returned. He was back on the team, really back. And he couldn't wait to tell Ma and Pa.

He stepped inside the house, expecting the familiar sound of the television and Ma calling out her guesses to Wheel of Fortune. But the house was quiet and still.

"Ma?" he called out, nothing. "Pa?" Again, no answer.

He made his way into the kitchen, hoping to find them there. It was empty—except for a plate on the counter, covered neatly with foil and a note propped beside it.

Me and your grandfather decided to have a date night. Love you, grandson. —Ma

Kenny smiled to himself. The simple words warmed him deeper than the meal ever could, and Ma could cook the hell out of some food.

He sat at the table and peeled back the foil: fried pork chops, green beans, mashed potatoes—his grandmother's version of love on a plate.

As he ate, something stirred in him. Maybe it was the quiet, or the scent of spring air drifting through the cracked window. Maybe it was the fact that his grandparents had gone out, living and loving in their own small way. Whatever it was, it made Kenny reach for the folder he'd been keeping tucked inside his backpack. The secret he'd been working on.

Ms. Carter had helped him look into it—encouraged him, even—but he hadn't been sure. He still wasn't. But something about tonight... something about this early spring night made him want to put it into words.

He retrieved a sheet of paper from Ma's desk and sat at the kitchen table chewing the end of his pen like he always did when he was deep in thought. He started writing. Not just about basketball or school—but about everything: about what he'd been through, about where he was headed, about Caleb, about hope, and about forgiveness.

When he finished, he folded the letter carefully and slid it into an envelope. He scrawled the address across the front in his messy, hopeful handwriting, licked the stamp, and placed it on the corner. All that was left was to mail it.

And on this night, Kenny felt ready.

***

As Kenny climbed into the truck, the letter in his hand felt heavier than just paper—it felt like possibility. When he reached the bottom of the hill, he pulled up beside the old black mailbox. The paint had faded over the years, but the little red flag still worked just fine.

He sat there for a second as the engine idled low, the envelope resting in his hand. With a steady breath, he slipped the letter inside, raised the flag, and slammed the cover shut.

It was a small thing—barely took a flick of the wrist—but it felt like moving forward and letting go of one thing and reaching for something...new.

As he pulled away, he still had an anxious energy that made him want to talk and to celebrate. His phone rested in the console. He picked it up and scrolled through his recent messages.

Two names stared back at him at the top of the list: Gracie and Kate.

He hesitated for a second—maybe longer. He didn't know who he wanted to text. The truth was, part of him wanted to tell them both. They each held a different piece of his story, but telling them both somehow felt...selfish.

Finally, his fingers hovered over Gracie's thread and he started typing.

Hey, I have some exciting news. Send.

A soft ding let him know the message had gone through. *Message read* his phone displayed beneath her name. Moments later, her reply buzzed through.

Interesting. Tell me more.

Before he could start typing again, another message lit up the screen.

I'm at the pond. Tell me in person.

Chapter Thirty-Nine

Kenny stared at her message for a beat, his thumb hovering.

The pond. Their pond, he thought to himself.

He dropped his phone back in the console, shifted the truck into drive, and turned toward the familiar road that led to water.

Some things you couldn't say in words on a screen. Some things had to be felt in the air, spoken face-to-face. And tonight, under a blue Kentucky moon, Kenny knew this was one of those things.

As he pulled up, his headlights spilled into the clearing and landed softly on the dock. There she was—sitting alone, her legs dangling just above the water. Her dark hair was pulled back into a ponytail. He was excited to tell Sara his news—but truthfully, he was just excited to see her.

Even though they hadn't talked about that night—her party from hell—things between them always found a way of working themselves out somehow, some way.

Kenny parked the truck and made his way down to the dock. He didn't say anything, just eased down beside her like he'd done dozens—maybe hundreds—of times before. The boards creaked beneath them, the air alive with the quiet hum of night and the chorus of frogs calling out from the dark.

They sat in easy silence, side by side, with their feet swinging over the edge as the cool night air brushed against them like a quiet grace. It was peaceful. And for the first time in a long time, Kenny felt it, too. Peace.

Sara turned to him, her voice soft, breaking the stillness. "So... what's this exciting news?"she asked anxiously.

Kenny looked over, and for a moment, he couldn't speak. Her face, lit by the soft glow of moonlight, seemed dreamlike. Her eyes sparkled, kind and familiar.

"I got back on the team," he said.

"Oh my gosh, Kenny, that's amazing!" Sara's face lit up. She leaned into him and wrapped her arm around his shoulder and pulled him close in a quick, tight hug. I knew you would. They need you; honestly, they ain't winnin' nothin' without ya."

Kenny laughed and shook his head. "I don't know 'bout that," he said quietly.

Silence settled back in, not uncomfortable, but the kind that rested easily between people who knew each other well. A frog croaked somewhere near the shore. The water lapped softly beneath them.

"I'm sorry about the other night," Sara spoke, quieter this time.

Kenny's eyes dropped, nodding. "Yeah... well...me too." He paused before adding, "I was just... I don't know. I was havin' a bad day, and I...I wanted to see you. I thought maybe..." he trailed off, the right words not quite forming.

Sara finished the thought for him. "You thought maybe I'd be there for you," she said.

He nodded. "It's fine, seriously," he replied.

"It wasn't," she said. "I know that. I don't even know what I was thinking. I guess, honestly, I just... didn't wanna think for a while. So, I invited some people over, and well, one thing led to another... and before I knew it...it just got outta hand."

"Yeah? What were you thinkin'?" Kenny asked, his tone laced with just enough sarcasm to land somewhere between teasing and truth.

Sara looked at him, puzzled. "What's that supposed to mean?"

"Who was that guy?" Kenny asked, raising an eyebrow.

Sara blinked. "Which guy?" she asked sincerely.

"The guy who couldn't keep his hands off you," Kenny said, cocking his head to the side.

Sara let out a groan. "Oh my gosh—Mark? That's Mark Green. He's a family friend from church."

Kenny gave her a cynical look. "Well...he didn't seem very...churchy."

She nudged him on the shoulder, half laughing. "Shut up. It's not like that, seriously."

"Well," Kenny smirked, "you might wanna let Clark Green know that."

Sara rolled her eyes. "Mark Green, and please." Her voice dropped a little. "No one in their right mind would want me. I'm a freakin' mess," she sighed and looked away from him, out over the water.

Kenny didn't let the silence settle. "Yeah, and you snore like a freight train," he teased.

Her head snapped back toward him. "Oh my gosh—you shut up. I do not!" she said as she laughed a real laugh, full and genuine.

"Give me a break," Kenny said. "Every guy in our school—and I'm sure in *Maaark's* school—would give anything for a little attention from Sara Grace Whitmore," he said confidently.

Sara shook her head. "Yeah, well... they shouldn't," she said, quieter now.

Kenny didn't say anything for a second. He just looked at her. He loved the way she tried to play tough. He loved a lot of things about Sara, but what he loved the most was how she'd let her guard down with him. No walls, no faking, just...Gracie.

"Too late for that," he finally said.

"Well, I don't want to be a party pooper," Sara said, her voice hesitant, "but... I kinda have some news too."

Kenny sensed the shift in her tone. "What's up?" he asked, concern in his eyes.

She took a breath. "I... I...kind of quit cheer," she muttered.

"You what?" Kenny said, shocked. "You quit?"

"Yeah," she said quickly. "I wasn't gonna say anything tonight—you're in such a good mood—but, I just...I mean we had that fight the other night...and it's just been killin' me... and if there's anyone in the world I want to talk about it with... it's you," she said in the way only Gracie could.

She didn't mean for that last line to hit so hard, but it landed like a hammer on a fence post. Kenny felt it in his gut because he knew she meant it. Sara didn't say things she didn't mean.

It was quiet again before Kenny finally asked incredulously, "Why?"

Sara looked at her hand in her lap as she fidgeted with the hem of her sleeve. "I don't know," she said softly. "My whole life has been so... clean, so neat, so perfect. And I'm not asking for sympathy for that—oh, poor little Ms. Whitmore with the perfect life—that's not what I mean."

She paused, looking out over the still water. "I just... when Caleb died, that was the first time I'd ever really lost someone. The first time I'd ever truly hurt. And it broke me into a million little pieces. It shattered something in me that I didn't even know I had. And truthfully, I didn't know how I was gonna keep goin'."

She stopped again, gathering her thoughts. "And then I thought about you..." she said softly.

Her eyes found his. "I look at you and how strong you are. How no matter what, you've always put me first. And I just—I feel like a fraud. Like... straight A's, cheer captain, preacher's daughter... but I didn't earn any of that. Not really," she sighed, brushing a strand of hair behind her ear.

"I just—I want to do something real, something genuine. For once in my life, I want to feel like me. Not some version of me watching myself live my life... I just want to do something different," she said, her voice soft but certain. "Change it up. Feel excited." She sighed. "I know this doesn't make any sense."

Kenny knew exactly what she meant. After all, he felt the same way about his own life sometimes. "Gracie," he said softly, "look at me." She lifted her eyes to meet him, hesitant but open.

"You're the most amazing person I've ever met," he said, full of fire. He paused, letting the words land then took a breath and continued. "You're kind—even when kindness doesn't seem like an option. You're sweet and corny in the best way imaginable. And no one, no one, has a bigger heart than you."

She smiled just a little as he continued. "You make me laugh like you've got some secret code that only you know. You make a small town country boy wanna grow up to be a man that can give you the whole world. Because that's what you deserve."

Sara looked at him, but she didn't speak, she couldn't. His words—and the heart behind them—made her blush, a warmth rising in her cheeks she couldn't hide. Kenny didn't notice he just kept going.

"And yeah, sure, you've got good things in your life—but that doesn't mean you didn't earn em or that you don't deserve em. Hell, the fact that you feel guilty about that proves my whole point, ya know?"

She shook her head slightly, her eyes still locked on his.

"Because shitty people don't feel guilt; that's what makes them shitty." He took another breath, his voice low but steady. "And just because bad things have happened to me…that doesn't mean you're some terrible person. If anything, it means that I wouldn't have made it through all those awful things without you."

He stopped to take a breath but his eyes, never leaving hers, could not have been steadier. For a moment neither of them said a word. The pond below them shimmered under the moonlight.

"How do you do that?" she asked.

"What?" Kenny replied.

"Make me…feel like that," she said. Their faces pulled close together before Kenny dropped his eyes and turned his head.

"You know, people always tell you to move on with your life, to live. But what they don't tell you," Sara said, "is that moving on isn't something you do just once. It's something you have to choose—every single day."

Her words landed like a truth dropped from the sky. Kenny felt them deep in his chest. She was right. "After Caleb died..." she continued, barely above a whisper, "I didn't want to move on. It felt like...like forgetting him."

She turned to Kenny, her eyes soft and honest. "But, every day since then... there you are." She smiled faintly. "And somehow, you make it seem possible. Because you...you've always been..." her words trailed off quietly as the two sat there on the dock face to face.

For a moment, they just sat there in the quiet, looking at each other under the moonlight. When something shifted in Kenny's eyes—like a spark catching fire.

"Well," he said with a grin tugging at his lips, "if you really wanna do somethin' crazy..."

He stood up quickly, removing his shirt and flinging off his flip-flops.

Gracie looked at him, immediately suspicious. "Whatcha doin' there, sport?" she asked.

Kenny backed up a few steps with a mischievous look.

"We could always just..."

He stopped his words midthought and took off running toward the edge of the dock. He launched himself into the air with a loud, exaggerated jump.

SPLASH! Water exploded up into the air as Kenny disappeared into the pond.

Sara's eyes widened as her jaw dropped. "Kenny!" she shouted, half-scolding, half-laughing, both hands covering her mouth.

A second later, his head popped up above the surface, his hair slicked back, laughing.

"You're insane!" she yelled, laughing now too.

"Come on, Gracie," Kenny called out, kicking his legs beneath the water, floating just above the surface with a carefree grin.

She sat at the edge of the dock, hugging her knees. "Isn't it cold?"

"Nah," he said, shaking his head, droplets flying from his hair. "Feels great."

"Kenny, I can't," she said with a nervous laugh.

"Oh, come on, Gracie! You just said you wanted to do somethin' exciting for a change," he reminded her.

"Yeah, well, gettin' hypothermia wasn't exactly what I had in mind," she teased.

He grinned and sent a small splash her way. "You baby—it's perfectly fine in here. Warm even! Unless of course... you're too afwaaaid," he added, exaggerating the word with a mocking tone and a sly smile.

Her eyes narrowed playfully. "Oh, you think you can bully me into jumping in? What am I, eight? You think you're sooo cute, huh?"

He shrugged, floating backwards, smirking. He was cute, maybe the cutest.

Sara stood up slowly, brushing off her jeans and kicking off her shoes. "Well then, Mr. Cutie," she said, backing up a step. "How do you like this?"

And with that, she ran forward and leapt off the edge of the dock, arms outstretched like the young girl that gigged frogs all those years ago.

Splash! Water exploded around them as Kenny laughed and covered his face from the wave she created. She surfaced quickly, pushing her wet hair from her face, gasping from the cold.

"Oh my gosh, it's freezing!" she shouted, half-laughing, half-shivering. "You lied!!!" she yelled.

"Yeah, about that..." Kenny said, a sheepish grin spreading across his face. "I may or may not have been completely honest about said temperature," he teased.

Sara's eyes narrowed. She splashed water in his direction. "Kenny! I'm gonna kill you!" she shouted.

He laughed, ducking under the water. "Come on now, Gracie, it's not that bad."

The two floated face to face, the coolness of the water making their skin tingle. Sara wrapped her arms around Kenny's shoulders.

"It's sooo cold," Sara said, her lips pouting. Her teeth chattered just slightly.

"Yeah... okay, you're right. It's pretty dang cold," he caved with a chuckle as the two began swimming back toward the dock.

As they climbed out, the night air sliced against their soaked skin like the world's way of saying, spring's not here yet— not so fast, my friends.

"You liar!" Gracie yelled through a laugh. "We're gonna freeze!" she said as they stood there close together.

Kenny rubbed her arms and grinned. "Hey! I've got some towels in the back of the truck." He took off running barefoot through the grass, his silhouette raced across the moonlight.

Sara stood shivering on the dock watching him. Moments later he returned, slightly out of breath.

"Well," he said, holding up a towel, "bad news. Looks like I've only got one. So... guess you'll have to tough it out."

"Oh no, you jerk!" she said, playfully lunging at him to grab it.

"Okay, okay," Kenny laughed. "I suppose you can have it," he said as he tossed it her way.

She wrapped herself in it, still shivering, but her smile remained warm. She looked over at Kenny, standing there, dripping, shirt clinging to him. His hair was glistening in the moonlight, his lean body shivering from the cold.

"Hey," she said, "Come here. I suppose I can share."

"Nah, it's okay," Kenny said, trying to play it cool. "I'll live," as he continued to shake.

Sara took a few steps closer to him, opening the towel wide. "I'm serious. Come here," she said.

Kenny hesitated—but only for a moment. He didn't want to fight it. I mean, he was really freaking cold.

He stepped in close to her side, but Sara grabbed his waist and pulled him in front of her, face to face. She wrapped the towel around them both, pulling him in tight. The cold disappeared, replaced with the warmth of her body pressed to his. It felt electric.

It was a little awkward at first, maybe for the first time ever between the two.

Their breathing grew heavier in the hollow of the night. Kenny didn't know what to say.

Until Sara looked up at him. "Did you mean what you said the other night on the phone?" she asked.

The subject hadn't come up since then. Not until now, wrapped in a single bath towel.

"Remind me again which part? Maybe you've had too much to drink since then?" Kenny said, trying to tease.

"That you're in love with me?" she asked, her voice sharp but barely above a whisper.

There was a long pause before he could bring himself to answer her. "You know I am, Gracie... but... I can't be. I know that," he said, turning his head to the side just a little.

"Yeah, well..." she whispered, as she took his chin in her hand and turned his face to meet hers again. "Then I can't be in love with you either," she said.

Her words hung in the air, delicate and dangerous.

Kenny stared at her, unsure of what to say. The smile she gave him next was soft and honest. Full of the love he never let himself believe he deserved.

"I'm your sunshine?" she asked, her voice like something out of a dream.

Kenny's reply came like a breath. "Gracie... you're my world."

And with that, she leaned in and they kissed.

For the first time ever—on the dock, by the old pond, under the Kentucky night—they kissed.

Chapter Forty

Kenny sat at Ma's breakfast table, the one with nicks and stories carved into its surface. Morning light slid through the windowpanes and dragged gold across the wood like God Himself was finger painting.

A newspaper sat open in front of him—a ritual he'd fallen into lately, somewhere between the coffee steam and the sizzle of Ma making bacon. Something that had surprisingly become his favorite part of the day over the past few weeks.

Mostly because of who was sitting across from him. Sara Grace Whitmore, hair still damp from her morning shower, was perched in her usual spot with a cup of coffee wrapped in her hands and one of Kenny's sweatshirts worn loose over her shoulders. Kenny stole a glance at her and smiled.

Even though her presence had relegated Kenny to sleeping on the couch, somehow she managed to make mornings resemble something to look forward to for a change. His eyes drifted back to a headline on the paper.

KYROCK GIRLS WIN REGIONAL TOURNAMENT Fueled by a dominant performance from Kate Covington, the Kyrock Lady Knights won their first regional championship in nearly 25 years with a 63–49 win over Bowling Green.

Kenny let out a small smile and shook his head. "Atta girl, Kate," he whispered under his breath. Kate deserved it. All of it. His gaze moved to the next story.

KYROCK BOYS SET FOR REGIONAL TITLE SHOWDOWN WITH BUTLER WEST The underdog Knights, propelled by returning super-junior Kenny Bledsoe, scored two early-round upsets in the 4th Regional Tournament. The team remains undefeated since Bledsoe's return to the team later in the season. Can the Knights pull off one more miracle and return to the state tournament?

Kenny stared at the paragraph for a moment before folding the paper and setting it aside. "Geez, this Bledsoe guy, he must be pretty good," he said, with a grin.

Behind him Ma stood at the stove, humming to herself as she flipped an omelet with practiced ease. "I've heard he's got a shaky jumpshot," she said without missing a beat.

Sara chuckled behind her coffee. "Oh, he just likes seeing his name in print," she said.

"Kenny," Ma said, not turning from the stove as she flipped another egg, "you've played hard, grandson, real hard. But if you're gonna beat those boys from Butler, you're gonna have to go to another level tonight." Her voice was firm as she spoke.

From across the table, Sara nodded in agreement, her eyes serious. "She's right, ya know," she said, shrugging her shoulders.

Kenny groaned as he leaned back in his chair and rubbed his face. "You two," he muttered, shaking his head with a half-smile. "Can't a guy just enjoy his mornin' comics in peace?" he teased.

Sara sat her mug on the table with a gentle clink and gave Kenny a look. "Yeah, well, you're not gonna enjoy it once you see who Butler's starting point guard is."

Kenny raised an eyebrow, intrigued. "Who?" he asked.

Sara tried to hide her smirk, but it broke through. "You remember Mark? From the party?"

Kenny's eyes widened in disbelief. "Oh my God—"

"Gosh," Ma corrected automatically, still tending to her skillet.

"Mark Greeeeen," Kenny said, teasing. "That doofus is their point guard?" Kenny asked nearly laughing. "This is gonna be fun."

"Just go easy on him, would ya?" Sara said with a teasing grin. "We don't need you fouling out over some bruised ego," she finished.

Kenny leaned forward, a playful glint in his eyes. "Oh, Mr. Grabby Hands is mine," he said in a low, calm voice.

Sara shook her head. "You're impossible," she said through a smile.

"And undefeated since my comeback," Kenny added, picking up his fork with dramatic flair.

Ma set a plate in front of him and gave him a pointed look. "All the more reason not to let some boy from Butler get under your skin, grandson," she leveled as only Ma could.

Kenny grinned. "Yes, ma'am," he said.

"Hey, I've got good news!" Sara exclaimed. "My daddy gets to come home today." She said with joy.

"Oh that's just wonderful sweetheart," Ma said from behind her cast iron throne. "Our Lord is plentiful in his mercy," she added, unironically.

"Yes Ma'am, he is," Sara replied.

Kenny scoffed, almost choking on his bacon.

"Oh! Grandson," Ma exclaimed, jerking up from the stove. "I forgot—a letter came for you the other day. Let me grab it for you, dear."

Kenny's eyes perked up. "A letter?" he questioned.

"Ooh, who's it from?" Sara chimed in quickly, her voice a little too curious as she was close to rising from her seat.

Kenny noticed and grinned. "Don't be jealous," he teased. "It's probably just from one of my many girlfriends across the country."

Sara didn't find that nearly as funny as Kenny did. Her smile faltered.

"Please," she said, rolling her eyes. "You can't even handle one girl-fr—"

She stopped herself mid-word, the sound hanging awkwardly in the air. She hadn't meant to say it, at least not like that. The truth was, they hadn't really talked about things—whatever this was—between them. No titles or labels, just a closeness that had grown so naturally it didn't need an explanation, at least not yet.

Somehow, they'd managed to keep "it" under wraps at school. Maybe no one was paying enough attention to notice, or maybe no one cared. Either way they played the part, going on as if nothing had changed—despite the fact they'd spent nearly every free second together over the last few weeks.

Even at Ma's house they kept up the charade. But Ma was no spring chicken. She wasn't nearly as clueless as they assumed. She let them believe they had her fooled, but she knew what was happening.

And more importantly she knew they needed each other. So she let them be, at least under her watchful eye. Quiet as a shadow, always watching, but never in the way.

Ma returned from the other room waving an envelope in her hand. "Didn't see a return address," she said, setting it on the table in front of Kenny.

Before he could reach for it, Sara snatched it up with a playful grin. "Let's just see which fan club is writing you now," she said with a shaky breath.

"Hey, gimme!" Kenny proclaimed, circling around to her side of the table.

Sara held the letter just out of his reach, teasing, "Who would've guessed the great Kenny Bledsoe has groupies?"

"Oh, that's it," Kenny said seriously as he leaned down and started to tickle her.

"Okay, okay! Take it!" she said laughing, pulling away and handing over the letter. "If some poor girl wants you that bad, she can have you," she joked.

Kenny smirked as he tore open the envelope, but the humor quickly faded from his face. His eyes moved across the lines, growing wider with each word. By the time he finished reading his expression had shifted—part surprise, part confusion, and part something else entirely.

He rested the letter on the table, blinking down at it like it might explain itself.

"Well?" Sara asked, watching him. "What does it say?"

Without a word, Kenny slid the letter across the table. Sara picked it up and began to read it carefully. When she finally looked back up at him, her eyes were wide.

"Are you serious?" she asked.

"I guess so," Kenny replied, voice still incredulous.

"Well... that's...unexpected," she said, resting her hand on the letter.

"To say the least," Kenny muttered.

Sara studied his face, her expression shifting to concern. "Are you sure this is a good idea?" she questioned.

Kenny let out a breath and shook his head. "I don't know. But I guess we're gonna find out," he said, shrugging his shoulders. "Looks like tonight just got a whole lot more interesting," he said as he leaned back in his chair and gave her a sideways glance.

***

The scene inside the Kyrock gym that night was electric—raucous in all the best ways. As fate would have it, the regional tournament was always hosted by random draw and wouldn't you know it? This year, the school that was pulled at random: Kyrock High School.

The old gym buzzed with anticipation. The bleachers were filled half an hour before tip-off, the band was warming up, and tattered banners from past glories hung high in the rafters, quietly waiting, hoping for company.

Back in the locker room, the energy was different: calmer, but tense. The kind of charged stillness that comes just before the storm.

Kenny moved with purpose through the space, his heart pounding in his chest—not from nerves, but from something else. He needed to talk to Coach Wills, now.

He poked his head into Wills' office, but his chair was empty.

"Coach?" he called out, nothing. "Hey, Deron, you seen Coach?" he asked.

Deron shook his head. "Nah, man," he replied.

Kenny was about to check the hallway when the locker room door burst open.

Coach Wills came charging in, composed, a large cardboard box in his arms. "Alright, gentlemen, listen up!" he barked, his voice cutting through the chatter like a whistle.

"Coach, I—" Kenny started, stepping forward, but Coach shut him down.

"It'll have to wait, Bledsoe. Sit down for a second," he demanded.

Kenny hesitated before dropping back onto the seat at his locker. His eyes drifted like they always did to the locker beside his, Caleb's locker. Still untouched, still his, no one had bothered it. No one had even dared to lean against it. The team kept it just the way he left it. A tribute to his brother, to their brother.

Coach Wills placed the box on a bench in front of him, his hand resting on top of the box like it held something sacred.

"First, I just want to tell you boys how proud I am," Coach Wills said, his voice steady with emotion. "Proud of all the hard work you've put in this year. Proud of how you've come together... and stayed together." A hint of a smile ghosted his lips. "You know I'm not much of a rah-rah guy," he added.

"That's the understatement of the year," one of the players joked, drawing a round of light laughter from the room.

Wills cracked a smile but didn't lose focus. "Be that as it may," he continued, "we've been given a gift. Somethin' special donated by an anonymous supporter of this team. And I think you're all gonna like it."

With that, he reached inside the large box and pulled out a brand new jersey—jet black with bold white lettering. The front read "KYROCK," and stitched on the shoulder was a gold patch with the number 21 in black.

Caleb's number. Wills turned the jersey around slowly. Across the back, it didn't read a player's last name. It simply read:

BLEDSOE.

A hush fell over the room. Coach pulled out another, and another. All of them read the same.

BLEDSOE.

On this night they weren't just teammates. They were brothers. They were all Bledsoes. And tonight, they'd take the court not for the name on the front of the jersey... but for the one on the back.

Chapter Forty-One

As the team charged out of the locker room and onto the court, the roar of the crowd crashed over them like a wave—loud, electric, and alive. The entire town had waited for this moment, for this team. And no matter how broken the season had gotten, here they were. Against all odds, they'd found their way to this night. In this gym, with a shot at a regional championship and a spot in the State tournament on the line.

Kenny's eyes scanned the crowd trying to take in every face and every scream.

Sara bounced in the stands, clapping and yelling with a smile so wide it could've lit the place on its own. A few rows over he saw Ms. Carter. Her eyes locked on him with the quiet, steady encouragement she always gave. Next to her was Kate, proudly wearing her regional championship medal, still fresh off her own big win.

And then...he spotted them, Ma and Pa. They were there.

Kenny's heart swelled at the sight. He hadn't even thought of the chance of them coming. But there they were, side by side, in their old seats like nothing had ever changed—and yet everything had. He let the moment sink in, soaking in the noise, the lights and the energy. He wanted to remember it forever.

After a powerful rendition of the national anthem sung by a Ky-rock student whose voice seemed to hush even the rafters, Coach Wills stepped onto the court holding a microphone. The gym fell to a hush.

"Tonight," he said, his voice echoing throughout the rafters, "before we tip off, we honor someone who should be here with us. Someone who will always be a part of this team, this school, and this town."

He turned and raised his hand toward the rafters and nodded. From above the basket a banner unfurled slowly revealing a jersey, Caleb Bledsoe's jersey, number 21, now retired forever.

Gasps, then cheers, filled the gym. Kenny stood motionless, eyes lifted, breath caught in his throat. There it was, his brother, eternal.

And just when he thought it couldn't get any heavier, the student section, led by Sara, raised an enormous sign propped up by dozens of students holding it piece by piece. It unfolded across the entire section like a flag.

JOB NOT FINISHED, it read.

The same words Caleb had left for him. The same words Kenny had repeated to himself every single day since.

Tears welled in his eyes, but he didn't let them fall. He nodded, took a deep breath, and turned to his teammates. He was ready. They were ready. It was time.

From the opening tip, the boys from Kyrock took control. Kenny soared in from out of nowhere and sent Butler's first shot attempt into the stands with a thunderous block. The crowd exploded. Before the Butler boys could recover, Deron stole the ball on the next play and sprinted down court. Kenny was ahead of him, streaking like a thoroughbred. With a perfect lob pass, Kenny rose up and slammed it home: an alley-oop, a message, a moment.

From that point on, the game was never really in doubt. The Bulldogs from Butler and Mark Green never stood a chance. Maybe on paper, maybe in some other gym, maybe in a different story—but not here. Not tonight. Not in Kyrock.

The town, the players, the people in the stands—they were all one. Every bucket was met with a roar. Every defensive stop met with a stomp of approval from the bleachers. This team wasn't just playing for a regional title. They were playing for something bigger. They were playing for Caleb.

By the time the final buzzer sounded, the scoreboard was all but irrelevant—Kyrock: a lot. Butler: not nearly enough.

Confetti rained down from the rafters as people rushed the floor. Kenny stood in the middle of it all, his teammates swarming him. Slapping his back, hugging one another, shouting to the heavens.

He looked up at Caleb's jersey in the rafters and smiled.

Sara made her way to him first, pushing through the chaos with a wide grin on her face and tears in her eyes. "You did it," she said.

"No," Kenny shook his head, pulling her into an embrace. "We did," he said, pointing up at his brother's jersey.

"Did you like the jersey idea?" Sara asked.

"That was you?" Kenny asked, shocked.

"Well, it was my idea, but my daddy wanted to do something nice for you guys," she replied.

"Gracie," he smiled. "You're...unbelievable."

"Ahh, I have my good days," she grinned as the two came together for a tight hug.

Ms. Carter stood watching it all at the edge of the court, clapping and cheering with pride. Ma and Pa waved their arms and shouted from their seats.

Coach Wills found Kenny in the chaos and pulled him in for a long, firm hug. "We've got one more job left, son," he said, his voice true. "But tonight... tonight, you enjoy this."

And at that moment, for the first time in a long time, Kenny did.

Kenny closed his eyes, letting the sound of his town, his family, and his team wash over him. Somewhere, somehow, he knew Caleb could hear it, too.

In a quieter aftermath of the madness, with the roar of the crowd now just a memory and confetti scattered across the hardwood floor, Kenny stood with his arm around Sara, still riding the high of it all.

Ma and Pa made their way over, arms wide, faces beaming.

"Well," Ma said, wrapping her tiny frame around him into a hug, "I reckon those boys from Butler got themselves a butt whoopin'," she said enthusiastically.

"You played like a man on fire," Pa added, pride thick in his voice. "I ain't seen a performance like that since... well, ever," he said.

Kenny laughed. "Thanks, y'all. I couldn't have done it without ya."

As they chatted soaking in the moment, Kenny felt a light tap on his shoulder. He turned, and there she was—Kate, hair pulled back, cheeks flushed from it all. She gave him that perfect smile of hers. "Congrats Bledsoe," she said softly. "You deserve it, Kenny."

He pulled her into a warm hug. "Let's go get two state titles," he whispered in her ear.

"You read my mind," she replied, grinning.

As the group began to leave the court, Kenny noticed Ms. Carter walking toward him through the lingering crowd. She wasn't alone.

Beside her walked a tall young woman— maybe early twenties, long dark hair, a little nervous in her step. Ms. Carter placed a comforting hand on her back as they approached. The woman looked up at Kenny like she'd been waiting for this moment.

"Kenny?" she said, her voice soft but sure. "Hi... it's me. Josie."

Chapter Forty-Two

"Josie!" Kenny replied with wide eyes, full of excitement. He stepped forward, stunned, and broke into a wide smile. "Oh my gosh—how are you?"

He pulled her into a hug, lifting her slightly off the ground in excitement. "It's a pleasure to finally meet you".

Ms. Carter smiled warmly, giving Kenny a small wink before slipping quietly back into the crowd.

Kenny turned to Sara, still holding Josie's hand. "Sara, this is Josie. She's... she's...well, Josie...from the letters," he said excitedly.

At that moment, Sara understood all of it. She smiled genuinely, wrapping Josie in a hug. "It's so nice to finally meet you," she said. "We've been so excited."

Josie laughed nervously. "Awe, you're too sweet, but thank you."

Kenny looked at Josie and his heart raced. "So... should we do this?" he asked.

Josie nodded, eyes misty. "I guess it's now or never."

Together, they walked toward the far corner of the gym where Coach Wills stood alone. His arms were crossed, surveying the court like a general after battle.

"Coach," Kenny said, his voice steady but quiet. "There's someone I want you to meet," he said.

Wills turned and lifted his eyebrows. He looked at the young woman beside Kenny and back to him.

"This is Josie," Kenny said slowly. "She's... well..." he paused.

"I'm your daughter, sir," Josie spoke up.

For a moment, Wills said nothing. The world around them seemed to pause. He looked at Josie—and the tone shifted in his eyes to something deep, something quiet and broken.

"Josie," he said, in nothing more than a whisper. "It's...it's an honor to meet you."

Josie smiled, eyes brimming. "Hi," she whispered.

Coach Wills stepped closer to her, reaching out as if afraid she might vanish. "You look... just like your mother," he said, his voice tender.

They embraced, gently at first, then tighter—as if trying to make up for a lifetime in a single moment.

"I've wanted this moment for a long time," Josie said into his muscular shoulder as Wills held her tight.

Kenny and Sara stepped back, giving them space as if watching something sacred unfold.

***

The Kyrock High parking lot had emptied and traded the last whispers of daylight for the amber glow of tired lampposts. Kenny leaned against the old truck, arms folded tight, eyes locked on Sara as she made her way toward him like she was the only thing left worth watching.

Kenny smiled as he watched her. She had that way about her, like the last light of a sunset, impossible to ignore.

"You ready for your surprise?" Kenny asked, his voice low and teasing.

Sara tilted her head. "A surprise? Don't you wanna go celebrate?" she asked.

"The only person I wanna celebrate with is you, Gracie," he said grinning, and he meant it. He reached behind his back and pulled out a blindfold. "Do you trust me?" he asked.

Sara laughed, shaking her head. "I'm afraid me and you've got different ideas of trust," she replied.

"I promise," he said, stepping closer and gently brushing a strand of hair behind her ear, "it'll be worth it."

She gave him a mock-suspicious look but turned around anyway, letting him tie the blindfold around her eyes. "If I end up in a ditch somewhere, I swear I'm comin' back and hauntin' you," she teased.

"The ghost version of you can't be any chattier," Kenny quipped.

"Hey!" she said with a smile. She tried to smack him on the arm but missed.

Kenny guided her carefully as they loaded into the truck and the engine rumbled to life. He kept the windows down as they drove, letting the cool Kentucky night wash over them. The wind danced across her face. Every now and again, she reached out like she was trying to guess where they were, laughing when she guessed wrong.

Kenny didn't say much, just held her hand across the bench seat, his thumb softly brushing over her fingers. The drive was long enough to build mystery but short enough to keep her antsy. When they finally pulled to a stop, he killed the engine.

Kenny climbed out and jogged around to her side. "Don't take it off yet," he said.

She stumbled out playfully as he helped her down and took her hand, leading her carefully across soft grass and patches of gravel. She gripped his arm, giggling as they walked. "This better not be some kind of prank," she sassed.

"It's not," he whispered. "Just trust me." They stopped. "Alright," Kenny said, squeezing her hand. "You can take it off now," he said.

Sara pulled the blindfold from her eyes and blinked against the glow of the streetlamp above them. Her eyes widened as she realized where they were: Kyrock Elementary School. Confused, she turned to Kenny. "Hmm...can't say I was expecting this, so, if you were goin' for surprise, I guess you win," she joked.

He didn't answer her right away—just took her hand again and led her a few more steps around the side of the old brick building. When they turned the corner and stepped onto the blacktop, she stopped in her tracks.

There, sitting under the glow of a lone light pole near the playground, was a bicycle. Blue and slightly scuffed, training wheels bolted tightly on the sides.

Sara gasped. "Kenny Bledsoe...what have you done?" she asked intrigued.

"I know you said you never learned how," he said, rubbing the back of his neck. "So... I figured we could fix that."

She turned to him slowly, eyes glassy, a smile tugging at her lips. "You're ridiculous," she whispered, trying not to cry.

He took a step closer. "What better place than where I first fell in love with you all those years ago?" he said.

Sara looked at the bike, then at Kenny, overwhelmed. "How did you...I can't believe you remembered that I even said that!" she said, shaking her head.

"How could I not?" he smiled. "I mean, it's a little embarrassing," he teased.

She stared at him, her voice caught in her throat. She reached for his face and kissed him soft and slow, like a promise. Kenny kissed her back, wrapping his arms around her as the wind whistled through the old swing set and merry-go-round.

Breaking the kiss, he grinned. "C'mon now, we've got a lot of work to do," he joked.

She laughed through her tears, wiping at her eyes. "If I fall, I'm suing," she chuckled.

"I'll catch you," Kenny said, and he meant it.

She climbed onto the bike, a little wobbly, but trusting as Kenny stood beside her, steadying the handlebars. He paused as his voice took a serious turn—his hand resting gently on hers. "Look...this is very important," he said seriously. "If you get in trouble out there, just—"

Ding. Ding. He smirked as he rang the tiny silver bell attached to the front handles.

She stared at him trying to keep a straight face. She wanted to be mad—wanted to say something snarky—but the whole thing was just too precious.With a shake of her head and a soft smile, she leaned forward, closed her eyes, and kissed him again—longer this time.

When they broke apart, she whispered against his cheek, "Okay… let's do this." Kenny knew she meant the bike riding—but in his heart, he couldn't help but hear something more, like maybe she was talking about the two of them.

As the night trailed on beneath the stars, they laughed like little kids again—lost in the moment, surrounded by memories both fresh and faded. Joyful for the ones they had yet to make, because they both knew sometimes the greatest rush is not having to rush at all.

Chapter Forty-Three

<<<<<

It felt like they had been driving for days, though in reality, it had only been a few hours. Kenny and Caleb sat in the back seat of the truck, their legs swinging, too small to reach the floor. Pa was driving with Ma in the passenger seat, her eyes fixed ahead as her hands twisted a worn tissue in her lap.

Kenny didn't know where they were going. He was too young to understand distance or direction, but he remembered the way the world looked out the window. The fields and trees of Kyrock had given way to something else entirely—buildings that scraped the sky, glass and steel towering in ways Kenny never knew was possible.

Back home, the second story was usually where everything ended. But here in this strange place it felt like that's where the stories were just beginning. From his seat, peeking out the truck window, it felt like the sky had been lifted higher—just to make room for all these new things.

He pressed his face against the glass. His eyes were wide with wonder, trying to count the floors on a building that climbed into the clouds. Caleb sat across from him, quieter than usual, maybe even a little scared. Kenny could feel it, the way his brother's foot tapped restlessly against the floorboard.

When they finally arrived there—wherever there was—Ma turned around to face them. Something in her eyes made Kenny sit up straighter. Something heavy, something important.

"Boys," she said gently, her voice calm but steady. "You listen to me when I tell you this—you are both loved. We love you more than anything in the whole wide world. You hear me?" she asked, full throated.

Kenny nodded, but Ma didn't settle for that. "Did you hear me?" she asked again, her voice soft but firm.

"Yes, ma'am," Kenny and Caleb said in unison, their voices small but certain.

The seriousness on Ma's face, the way Pa's jaw was set, the long drive that felt like a lifetime—it all told Kenny, even at his young age, that something about this moment mattered in a way he didn't yet comprehend. But as it turns out, he would remember it, always.

The tubed lights buzzed softly overhead as the boys followed close behind Ma down a long, clean hallway. The place looked like a doctor's office—neat, quiet, and the air too still.

There was something different here. Something that made Kenny's stomach twist. The people didn't seem sick, but they didn't seem much like people either.

They passed by rooms with large windows, some with people in regular clothes, some moved slowly, and others just sat staring. Kenny didn't understand it, but Caleb, walking with his head held just a little higher, seemed to have at least some sense of what this place truly was.

At the end of the hall a nurse opened a door for them as she nodded at Ma.

"She's ready," the lady dressed in blue scrubs said softly.

The room had two chairs on each side of a small table, like one of those waiting rooms the boys would sit in when Ma went to talk to their teachers. Except this room had a thick pane of glass inside and a strange, sterile coldness to it.

Then she was there, their mother.

She stood as they entered, her eyes lighting up with something that looked like joy—but fragile, like it might break at any second.

"My babies," she whispered.

Kenny rushed forward first, wrapping his little arms around her waist. Caleb hung back, uncertain, half-hiding behind Ma's leg. Their mom bent down to hold Kenny tightly, closing her eyes as she breathed him in.

"You're getting so big, Mister Man," she said, brushing his curls back. "What grade are you in now, sweetheart?"

"First grade, Momma," Kenny said proudly.

She smiled, looking past him to Caleb. "And you, Caleb? What about you, baby?"

Caleb looked away, hiding his eyes from hers. He didn't answer.

Ma rested a hand gently on his shoulder. "It's alright," she said to him quietly.

Their mother held out her hand. "You don't have to be afraid. Momma's gettin' better now," she said through a shaky breath.

With some hesitation, Caleb stepped forward and reached his tiny hand into his pocket. He pulled out a folded paper, handing it to her. "We made you somethin'," he said.

Kenny handed his over too—crayon drawings, bent at the corners, full of wobbly stick figures and hearts.

"That's all of us Momma," Caleb said with his small voice. "And that's Michael with his wings," he said, timid but proud.

She took them like they were precious. Her hands shook as she ran her fingers over them like she could touch the good in them. And just as quickly as her smile had come, her face crumpled.

"I miss him so much," she whispered. "I miss my Michael," she muttered. A silence filled the room, stealing the breath right out of it.

Ma moved forward, her voice calm. "Now, hun, let's not go down that road right now. The boys are just here to see you," she reasoned. But their mother didn't heed Ma's plea.

"He should still be here. He should still be here," their mother repeated, her voice cracking. "If it wasn't for you—" she said as she turned sharply, eyes wild, staring at Caleb. "It's all your fault!" she yelled. "He's gone because of you! It's all your fault!" As she yelled louder, her voice frothed with anger.

Caleb froze. His mouth fell open, but no sound found its way through. He turned to look at Kenny, and then—a drop, then another—blood began to slip from his nose. Crimson and sure, a harsh bloom against the pale hush of his innocence.

"Stop it right now," Ma said firmly, moving fast, wrapping her arms around both boys. "That's enough, April!" she exclaimed.

"I didn't mean—" their mother sobbed, collapsing to her chair. "I didn't mean—I'm sorry—I just—my babies..." Her cries drowned out the rest of her words as the nurse reentered the room and began to tend to her.

Ma ushered the boys out of the room quickly, trying to shield them from the sound of their mother's sobs as she continued to wail.

Kenny looked back just before the nurse closed the door and saw his mother curled up in her chair, holding their drawings like they were all she had left.

Neither brother said a word as they walked through the hallway and out of the building. Caleb's face was pale. Kenny offered his brother a tissue he had saved in his pocket for when Caleb got his nosebleeds. Then he reached over, grabbed his brother's hand, and held it tight.

The drive home was different that day—it was quiet and heavy. Something in Caleb had shifted, like a flame inside him had been snuffed out, one that never truly sparked back to life.

***

>>>>>

The hum of the highway rumbled beneath the tires of the team bus as it rolled steadily toward Lexington, Kentucky, toward the state tournament.

Most of the players were dozing off or quietly going over their game plans as music leaked from their earbuds. Through the tint of the windows, the hills of Northern Kentucky blurred past in streaks of early spring green. Hills dotted with other places, full of their own stories, their own love and loss.

Kenny sat alone near the back, his hood pulled up over his head, headphones on as he stared out the window with his cheek resting against the cool glass. He wasn't thinking about basketball, not really. His thoughts were wandering through all the things: Caleb, Rupp Arena, Sara's laugh, all of it.

A shadow crossed over him. Kenny looked up and pulled his headphones down. Coach Wills stood beside his seat, motioning to him.

"Mind if I sit for a bit?" Wills asked.

Kenny nodded his head. "Please," he replied.

Wills eased into the seat beside him, letting out a quiet groan as his knees cracked on the way down. "Lord, these bus seats weren't made for old men," he joked.

Kenny gave a small smirk. "Come on, Coach, you're not that old. You're only like what, Sixty, seventy?" Kenny teased.

Wills raised an eyebrow. "Don't make an old man kick you off this bus, Bledsoe," he smiled.

They both chuckled. Then Wills looked forward, nodding slowly. "I've been meaning to talk to you," he said finally, his voice low, "just you and me."

Kenny turned, giving him his full attention.

Wills rubbed his hands together like he was trying to find the right words. "I just wanted to say thank you. For doing what I didn't have the courage to do, son," he said.

Kenny's brow furrowed. "Whaddaya mean?" he asked.

Wills' eyes stayed on the aisle ahead. "For taking the chance to find Josie," he said quietly. "I know that must've been hard. But I'm so glad you did," he said as he patted Kenny on his hand.

Kenny gave a small smile. "Can't say it was the easiest thing I've ever done," he joked.

Coach chuckled softly. "No, I bet it wasn't."

Kenny hesitated, then asked, "What's she like?" as he looked at his coach with wide eyes.

Wills paused, shifting his weight as he exhaled slowly, his gaze softened. "She's..." He took a breath. "She's incredible."

He didn't elaborate but he didn't need to, his smile said it all. Kenny nodded, returning the smile. After all, Kenny knew what it meant to have someone incredible in your life. His thoughts drifted to Sara for a moment.

But Wills continued. "When Caleb passed... I let you down, son. I didn't know how to talk about it. Not to the team, not to you, not even to myself. And I was just...tryin' to make sure you dealt with it," he trailed off a bit before continuing. "I just didn't handle things the way they should've been and... for that I'm sorry."

"Don't sweat it, Coach. I don't guess there's a right way to handle somethin' like that," Kenny said calmly.

Wills grinned. "See, then you do that," his voice genuine. He turned and looked Kenny square in the eye. "You're the strongest person I've ever known, Kenny. And I've known a lot of good people. But none like you," he finished.

Kenny didn't say anything for a moment as his throat tightened. "I didn't feel very strong for a long time," Kenny finally said, his voice barely above a whisper. "Guess I still don't."

"Let me tell you somethin'," Wills said, his voice a low whisper. "The difference between you and the rest of the world, son, is that you don't go lookin' for excuses. You don't wait around for someone else to fix somethin', you just finish it."

They sat in silence again, the hum of the engine swallowing them.

Wills gave Kenny a pat on the back, firm and steady. "Now...let's go finish this thing, for all of us... and for him," he said with a smile.

Kenny nodded, taking a quick glance back out the window. This time not to escape, but to reflect. Then he turned and looked at Wills dead in his eyes. "Yeah," Kenny said quietly. "Job not finished."

Chapter Forty-Four

As the boys filed off the bus and into the bright lights of Downtown Lexington, Rupp Arena stood like a cathedral of Kentucky basketball history. Its glass reflected the cloudless sky; its name a testament to legends from times before.

The girls' state tournament was underway and the Kyrock boys were here to show their support.

Inside the crowd was buzzing, the air electric with high school dreams and school colors. Kenny walked with purpose, his warm-up jacket zipped to the collar, his headphones slung around his neck. But he wasn't locked into his usual pregame zone, not tonight.

He made his way courtside and found his spot near the baseline as the Kyrock girls took the court. He spotted her immediately—number 23, her bright hair pulled back. Confidence was radiating off her as she stepped onto the hardwood: Kate Covington.

Kenny raised his hand and gave her a wave.

She glanced over mid-stretch and when she saw him, her expression softened into a grin. That grin—the one that said, "I got this."

Kenny smiled back.

The game started off strong. The Kyrock girls played with rhythm, poise, and energy. Kate was everywhere: grabbing rebounds, sinking jumpers, leading fast breaks. By the end of the first quarter, they had a modest lead and the crowd was behind them.

But midway through the second quarter, it happened.

Kate caught the ball on the wing, juked her defender, and exploded toward the basket. She cut hard, planting her right foot—and out of nowhere, she crumpled to the floor.

Gasps echoed through the arena like a wave. Kate grabbed her knee instantly; her face twisted in pain. She didn't scream, but the agony was written all over her. The game stopped as the officials motioned for the trainer. The gym went quiet.

Kenny sat frozen in his seat; his breath was caught in his throat.

"Get up, Kate, get up," he murmured under his breath.

But Kate didn't get up. With tears in her eyes, she was helped off the floor by the team trainer.

The rest of the game blurred after that. The Kyrock girls tried to hold on, but their leader was gone. The fight was still there, but their hearts had cracked.

The girls lost.

After the game, deep in the tunnels beneath Rupp Arena, Kenny waited outside the girls' locker room. His hands were in his warm up jacket pockets as he paced slowly, his eyes down. Finally, the door creaked open, and Kate emerged walking gingerly with a crutch under one arm. Her knee was wrapped tight, her face pale and streaked from crying.

When she saw him her composure collapsed. Kenny stepped forward and pulled her into his chest without a word.

Kate buried her face into him and sobbed. Not the kind of cry that needed fixing, just the kind that needed holding. Kenny didn't say a word. He just held her tight and pressed his cheek to her hair, rubbing small circles on her back.

She shook her head against him. "I just... I just wanted to finish it," she choked out the words.

"I know," he said, holding her tight. Perhaps no one in Kate's world could truly understand quite like Kenny.

They stood there embracing, unhurried in that quiet hallway as echoes from the crowd spilled in from the arena against the backdrop of cheers, whistles, and the thump of warm-up music for the next game of the tournament. Signs that life was moving on.

Kate leaned into Kenny further, her face buried in his shoulder. Her breath was hitching as she tried to hold back another wave of tears like she was on the cusp of spilling over, trembling at the edge of something she wasn't ready to admit.

She knew it though, and Kenny knew it too. Her season—her dreams, at least for now—were over.

Chapter Forty-Five

The night air was cold—sharper than usual—even inside the house. Kenny sat on the edge of his bed, his small feet dangling just above the wooden floor. The quiet wrapped around him like the quilt Ma had stitched for him. Small and unsure, he clutched his stuffed wolf to his chest.

The house—like it had been every day since that dreadful day—was quiet, too quiet, until it wasn't. A sound like thunder cracked from the back room, followed by silence. Then he heard his mother's scream.

It shattered through the stillness and pierced him to his core. Moments later she came stumbling out, her eyes wild, her breath heaving. She collapsed to her knees in Kenny's bedroom, clutching Kenny tightly while sobbing into his tiny shoulder. He didn't know what had happened—not really—but he knew something terrible had changed the world forever.

He sat frozen, too small to understand, but old enough to know it would never be the same again.

"Michael!" his mother sobbed again and again, clutching Kenny so tight it made his skin ache.

Kenny never did come to know if his mother was calling out for his father or for his brother.

Later when the ambulance came, when the red and blue lights spun outside his window and the house filled with strange men in uniforms, Kenny sat quietly on the edge of his small bed.

He didn't cry. He reached into the pocket of his pajama pants and pulled out a folded piece of paper.

It had been placed gently on his pillow that night, as if it had been set there with purpose. Like a secret waiting to be uncovered, a riddle waiting to be solved.

The edges were worn, softened from the way he'd gripped it. A note written in his father's sharp, rushed handwriting, folded in half.

On the front side it simply read: Kenny

He recognized all the words on the inside, but he didn't understand what they meant. He stared at it for a long time as the wail of sirens fell faint in the distance. His mother's sobs also faded as she left to follow the people that had taken his father away.

A strange man dressed like a police officer came into his room that night and gently lifted him from his bed. Kenny didn't resist, but he did manage to wiggle himself free from the man's tight grip just long enough to sprint to his bed. He snatched the note in his small hands and placed it in the pocket of his pajamas where he could store it away from everyone.

He didn't show it to anyone. Not then, not ever.

He kept it sealed away like the brokenness, like the pain from losing Michael and from losing his father. Caleb wouldn't need to know. The burden of it was his, and it would be his alone to carry.

***

>>>>>

Kenny sat alone in the giant fancy locker room, his elbows resting on his knees with a folded newspaper spread across his lap. The headline in bold print read:

Can "Cinderella Knights" Win One More, Take State Championship?

He half-smiled at it as he shook his head.

Much like Kenny had been his entire life, it seemed this team had been counted out too—too small, too young, too broken. But here they were,

Rupp Arena. The final game of the season with a chance to do something unforgettable. To be remembered forever as State Champions.

No one had given them a chance in the first few rounds of the tournament, so why should this game be any different? It certainly wasn't lost on Kenny how much today meant to Coach Wills and to Deron—a win over their former team would be more than just a victory; it would be a statement.

As the countdown clock in the locker room hit 25 minutes, Coach Wills gathered his team. He didn't have some big, fancy pregame speech. No, his words—much like his underdog team from Kyrock itself—were small, but proud.

"Gentlemen, I've only got three words," he declared, his voice low but firm. "Job. Not. Finished," he paused slightly between each word, letting them sink in.

"Let's go win the whole damn thing!" someone shouted. The team roared in approval.

With that, they were off.

The crowd was ready for the game. It was what the state championship in Kentucky basketball is all about—a David vs. Goliath showdown. A powerhouse, big-city school against the small-town, blue-collar underdogs.

It was why some folks had fought so hard to preserve the tournament the way it had always been. No classes or school sizes, just every team for itself. A memorandum to days gone by when the little guy could, in the end, get one over on the man.

The rendition of *My Old Kentucky Home* was powerful. The singer's voice echoed throughout the arena, stirring something deep in the air. But unlike the singer's key, the Kyrock boys came out flat.

As the game started, nothing about it felt like a storybook ending. Something was off. Maybe they were smaller, a step slower, not able to leap quite as high as the undefeated Louisville Christian squad. Maybe, tonight wouldn't be Kyrock's night.

Coach Wills' old team, the aforementioned Louisville Christian—the perennial powerhouse from the big city—was a team built on discipline, size, and legacy. And right now, they were showcasing all that and more.

Kenny couldn't get in rhythm. His shots clanked off the rim and his passes missed their mark. Every time Kyrock got something going, it was answered with a run in the other direction. The first half went about as bad as it could've for the boys in black, and the scoreboard didn't sugar coat it: Down seventeen at halftime.

Inside the locker room, the energy was drained. Most of the boys sat quietly with their heads bowed, breathing hard. Some stared at the floor, too exhausted to even speak.

Kenny sank into the locker behind him, staring straight ahead—not at the floor, but somewhere else. As horrible as the first half had been, he'd seen worse.

Chapter Forty-Six

<<<<<

Fleetwood Mac's *Gypsy* played softly over the car speakers as the melody drifted through the open windows like a breeze. Their mother was singing along, tapping the wheel with her fingers as she navigated the winding back roads. She always liked to drive. She said it helped her with writing.

Kenny sat in the back seat wedged between Caleb and Michael, dressed in his best dress pants and a little button-down shirt. Caleb kept adjusting his collar like it was choking him, and Michael had unbuttoned and rolled up the sleeves of his shirt, too.

They were on their way to celebrate their mother—a special dinner, just the five of them. It was one of those perfect spring evenings when the sky blushed as the sun spilled itself over the fields below and a warm, honeyed glow covered everything it touched.

But like spring does, it quickly shifted.

Raindrops began to splatter the windshield—slow at first, then faster. The wipers squeaked as they did their best to keep up.

Before Stevie Nicks could belt the chorus of *Gypsy*, out of nowhere a deer, tall and wide-eyed, appeared standing square in the road.

"Hold on!" their mother shouted, as she gripped the wheel with all her might and jerked the car to the right.

The tires screeched as the sedan fishtailed, spinning out across the wet pavement. Kenny felt his stomach rise in his chest as the world outside blurred in motion. The car finally came to a jarring stop on the shoulder, angled into a ditch.

There was silence as everyone sat frozen for a moment.

"You boys okay?" their dad asked, turning around from the passenger seat.

They all nodded, wide-eyed.

As the tension eased, their eyes were drawn to the road behind them. Maybe a dozen yards back, another car had pulled off to the opposite side. Its front end was crumpled, steam hissing from the engine. It appeared as if it hadn't been as lucky.

Their father opened his door and stepped out of the car. "Oh man, looks like we've got a flat," he muttered, crouching low to inspect it. "I'm gonna need a minute to fix it," he said.

Their mother pulled the car a little farther into the grass and turned on the hazard lights. The blinking ticked like a metronome as the rain started to fall a little heavier, tapping the roof above them.

"Let me get the jack. Pop the trunk, April!" their dad shouted calmly, hustling to try and beat the rain.

The boys sat in the car, peeking out through the windows. Caleb craned his neck to watch as their father struggled with the lug nuts. Another car came around the turn and sped past—fast and loud, spraying up water as it flew by.

Their mother worried under her breath. "These people drive like they've got nothin' to lose," she whispered. She opened her door. "I'm going to try to wave folks around before someone gets hurt," she said.

"Babe, be careful," their father called out, doing his best to tend to the flat tire as the rain picked up.

Their mother stood at the edge of the road with arms raised high, trying to wave down passing drivers as the sky darkened with rain clouds.

Inside the car, Kenny watched her—hair soaked, heart set—doing the only thing she knew to keep her family safe: stepping out into the road, danger be damned.

The rain was steady and cold now, falling in sheets across the windshield. Another car passed by; its tires sliced through a puddle, spraying water up against the side of their car. Their mother climbed back in, seeking reprieve from the storm as she wiped water from her face. She exhaled deeply and turned to check on the boys, still waiting quietly in the back seat.

"Is everything okay, Momma?" Caleb asked.

She gave him a worried but warm smile. "Everything's gonna be just fine, honey. Just a little hiccup, that's all," she said, shifting her body so she could see all three of them. "But y'all know what Momma says about hiccups, right?" she asked.

Michael grinned, proud to know the answer. "You take a spoonful of sugar… and smile while you wait," he said.

Their mother laughed, the kind of laugh that made everything okay for just a second. "That's right, baby. Don't ever forget it," she said, calm and steady.

Their father's voice called out, muffled through the rain. "Hey hun, can you come hold this real quick?" he shouted.

Their mother opened her door again, shielding herself from the downpour with her hands as she stepped back into the storm. The door slammed behind her with a loud *thunk*.

Inside the car it grew quiet again—just the three brothers and the sound of the rain. Kenny pressed his forehead against the window, watching the droplets race down the glass. His view from the back was obstructed by the front seat, but he wasn't scared. He was with the people who made everything better—his family.

Then everything changed.

It started with their father's voice—sharper this time, loud and urgent.

"Get back in the car, son!" he shouted through a rumble of thunder.

Kenny sat up straighter, confused. He saw headlights cutting through the rain, moving fast, coming around the bend.

Just then lightning cracked close by. Their mother shouted something he couldn't make out; her voice was tangled in panic.

His father's voice came again, but this time it was a name. "Michael!" he screamed.

Then there was a sound— the kind that doesn't leave you.

Tires screeched and brakes skidded across the wet pavement. There was a thud that echoed in Kenny's ears long after it was over. Kenny didn't see it as he sat frozen in the back seat.

But Caleb, Caleb had gotten out of the car. He'd gotten out to help his father hold the flashlight. Caleb saw it all.

He was standing near the edge of the road, soaked and shaking. He was watching helplessly as Michael—brave and selfless Michael—pushed him out of harm's way... and took his place instead.

The truck had tried to swerve. It wasn't enough.

Their father screamed. Their mother fell to her knees. And Caleb... Caleb watched it all. His eyes locked on the spot where his brother had been just a heartbeat ago.

Inside the car, Kenny gripped the edge of his seat and whispered Michael's name under his breath. Everything was different now, and nothing would ever be the same again.

Chapter Forty-Seven

As Kenny sat slouched inside the tall locker, his mind raced. Tonight was rough—but not hard. He'd seen hard, he'd lived it. Sleepless nights spent on the edge of his bed, a note tucked deep in his pocket as silence pressed in from all sides. Days when there was no game to win, only the next hour to survive.

He thought about his father, about Caleb, and about Michael. He thought about the mornings Ma made pancakes to help him choke down the sadness. He thought about the promise he made to himself when he came back to the team, about a job not finished.

Basketball had never been Kenny's life, but for or better or worse, it was a way back to it.

Kenny stood up amongst the silence of the locker room and spoke to his teammates, to his brothers.

"Guys...this is just a game"...He said calmly before continuing. "And if I'm bein' completely honest, I don't love it." The locker room remained hushed as his teammates and Coach Wills began to look at him. Kenny continued, "But I do love ya'll boys. And now, I've seen my fair share of pain in life," his voice steady, as his teammates eyes locked on him. "And this—this ain't pain man...This is just another excuse the world gets to tell us no. To tell us that we don't belong here...that we ain't good enough." The words poured out of him as his brothers soaked up every breath of it.

"I mean...life is hard. But tonight, this is real simple," he continued, steadying his breath. "So, either we believe we're not enough—not worthy to be here. Tell ourselves we're too broken, and we lay down and die...or we decide to be unbreakable."

For a moment, the locker room was silent. Until one by one, his teammates rose, shoulders back, eyes blazing.

"Let's do this for Caleb!" Deron shouted.

"For Kyrock!" another echoed.

Kenny pulled them all into a tight huddle, the kind that made one heartbeat. His eyes scanned his brothers before he said. "One. Two. Three..."

"Job not finished!" they roared in unison, fire in every word as they sprinted back toward the court.

The second half began with a completely different energy than the first. Kyrock had come out of the locker room like they had something to prove— because they did. With every possession, every pass, every dive for a loose ball, they clawed their way back into the game—led by none other than Kenny Bledsoe.

It started with a spark.

Kenny poked the ball loose at the top of the key and dove to the floor to grab it, launching a fast break layup. Then another steal—this time he jumped the passing lane and dished it ahead to Deron, who scooped in a shot with a sweet kiss off the glass.

Their full-court press was suffocating. Probably because it was led by a young man used to the world not allowing him to catch his breath.

The crowd sensed the shift, too. The noise built with every possession. Slowly, as the lead shrank, the arena had decided to favor David.

Ten points, eight, then five.

As the end of the third quarter buzzer sounded, the voice of the radio announcer rang through an old wooden radio in the Bledsoe home.

And going into the fourth, the lead is down to five. The Cinderella Knights from Kyrock aren't going quietly.

Ma and Pa leaned on the edge of their couch with their hands clasped, hardly breathing.

In the stands of Rupp Arena, Sara and Kate sat next to each other and yelled their hearts out.

The fourth quarter was war. Bodies flying, fouls mounting, and Kyrock kept chipping away.

The radio play-by-play continued during the final moments of the game.

Alright folks, under a minute to go here in Rupp Arena—Kyrock down by two. The ball is in Kenny Bledsoe's hands. He comes off a high screen at the top of the key... squares his feet... rises...—BANG! Kenny Bledsoe buries the three-pointer! The Knights take the lead with under a minute to play! Rupp Arena is electric!

Bledsoe put that thing in the bottom of the net. It's Kyrock 62. Louisville Christian 61. Our boys in black have come all the way back to take the lead. Christian has called their final timeout. And we will be right back with the finish of this fantastic ball game.

The fans in the arena were losing their minds. Everyone not wearing a Louisville Christian shirt was on their feet, shouting and screaming. Sara was doing her best to help prop Kate up as they both screamed until their throats were sore.

Back in Kyrock, Ma and Pa leapt off their couch as if they were seventeen again. The radio announcer continued now.

Twelve seconds on the clock. Here we go, folks. Louisville Christian has it. Parks takes it, dribbles hard toward the right corner... Kenny and Deron—double-team him! This is it; they've got him trapped! He's stuck—he's off-balance—

He flings it out! Oh, somehow the ball is back to Hill on the wing. He's got it, falling out of bounds—Hill puts it up— A desperate three-pointer.

Oh my, and it's good! Unbelievable! He put it in. And Louisville Christian is back on top with just seconds remaining! Louisville Christian 64. Kyrock 62. And Coach Wills will take his final timeout with just 2 seconds remaining.

The gym fell quiet—shocked. Only the Louisville Christian fans celebrated. The rest of the arena stood frozen, in disbelief that the fairy tale had come up short.

Back in the little blue house on Bledsoe hill, Ma and Pa sat quietly.

In the Knights' huddle Coach Wills was calm. Like he had made peace with whatever may come.

"It's okay to be nervous," Wills started. "That just means it matters. But let me tell you something, gentlemen. This ain't the most important night of your lives, not even close," he said looking at Kenny. "But when you're older, and your lyin' in bed next to the woman of your dreams..."

Kenny looked up into the stands. His eyes found Sara and Kate, standing together, arms linked tight.

"You'll be dreamin' of nights like tonight, moments like now," Wills continued.

He let the meaning of his words sink in as his gaze swept across the huddle. "Look around, gentlemen," he said, his voice steady but charged with something deeper. "It's here for the taking. Let's bring this one home, let's FINISH THE JOB!"

The team broke the huddle with fire in their eyes.

Back in Kyrock, the Bledsoe house sat in a quiet hush. Ma and Pa held each other tight as Betty Lou mouthed the words she'd said to her grandson thousands of times before.

However, back in Rupp Arena, inbounding the ball was chaos. Louisville Christian had every lane shut down. The five-second count was ticking fast. Just before the ref's whistle would blow, Deron heaved the ball toward midcourt.

It floated, suspended in time. Kenny ran and leapt high in the air catching it on the run just past half court. He took one dribble, gathered himself. He pulled up from deep—from somewhere back in Kyrock.

And....he let it fly.

As the buzzer echoed throughout Rupp Arena, the ball rose like a prayer. And although the game clock had expired, it was as if time itself stood still.

Chapter Forty-Eight

<<<<<

In the perfect light of a late Kentucky afternoon, two young boys played beneath a large white basketball goal nailed to the side of Ma and Pa's barn. The backboard was new. Pa had just put it up, and the net was long and crisp. To Kenny and Caleb, it was Rupp Arena. Every shot was for glory.

The ball bounced across the dirt and echoed against the barn walls with each dribble. Caleb pump-faked and spun around Kenny, tossing up a wild shot that clanged off the rim and rolled toward the barn door.

As the ball rolled away from the brothers it made its way to the feet of someone else.

Then came a voice, warm and full of life. "Y'all look like you could use a little help?" Michael asked as he stepped into view, grinning wide.

Both boys lit up. "Michael!" Kenny shouted. As their oldest brother scooped up the ball and jogged over to them with something dangling from his hand.

"Look what Ma gave me. My early birthday present," he said, holding it up high. A blue basketball pendant hung from a thin silver chain, catching the sunlight as it swayed.

"Whoa," Caleb gasped his eyes wide. "That's so cool."

"So cool," Kenny mimicked.

"Just like the ones we saw in the catalog." Caleb said, impressed.

Michael beamed with pride. "Yeah, well, Ma said it was 'so I can always carry the game in my heart.' Whatever that means," he said as he shrugged his small shoulders. "I just think it looks sweet," he joked.

The three brothers laughed, together.

"What's the score?" Michael asked.

"We're down two," Caleb said. "National championship. Last possession."

Michael bounced the ball once between his legs. "Well," he said with a wide grin, "let's run the play then."

Like clockwork, the brothers moved in rhythm, weaving, and cutting on that old patch of dirt as if it were polished hardwood. Michael dribbled toward the imaginary baseline and swung a pass over to Caleb, who faked a shot and then drove toward the basket.

"Four seconds left!" Michael shouted.

Caleb dribbled hard to his left, then pulled up and fired a pass to Kenny, who was wide open at the top of the imaginary key—marked not by paint, but by the scuffed-up earth of the Bledsoe land.

"Three... two... one..." Michael and Caleb counted down together.

"SHOOOOOT!" the older brothers shouted as Kenny launched the ball toward the hoop. The ball flew high into the air, spinning and climbing into the glow of the evening sky. The three watched as they held their breath.

Swish! The ball dropped clean through the hoop.

"HE HITS IT!" Michael shouted, as he lifted Kenny up off the ground.

The three whooped and jumped and ran in circles, celebrating their imaginary state championship with the joy only brothers can know.

"The Wildcats win the championship! Ahhhhhhhh!" the brothers echoed.

Caleb high-fived Kenny while Michael spun in a slow circle, holding his little brother high in the air, as high as their little hearts could lift.

In that moment, on that dirt court beside the old barn under a fading Kentucky sun, the three Bledsoe boys were inseparable.

Frozen in time—together forever.

Chapter Forty-Nine

The final bell screamed, delivering freedom for the students of Kyrock High. Kenny zipped up his backpack and glanced across the table at Kate. He caught her eye, wondering if she too had been waiting on the bell. They had just finished their group presentation, or at least what was left of their group. The third member of the trio, Sara, had been conspicuously absent.

Ms. Carter approached them as students trickled out of the classroom. "Kenny," she said gently, "did you hear back from Sara?"

Kenny shook his head as he slung his bag over one shoulder. "I have no idea what happened," he answered, a little worried.

"She got a phone call at lunch and ran out. I'm guessing it's somethin' with her dad," he continued.

As he moved toward the door, Ms. Carter's voice stopped him. "Oh, wait—I almost forgot," she said, as she reached into her desk. "You got another package last week," she said nonchalantly.

Kenny blinked. "Package?" he asked, confused.

Ms. Carter nodded. "Yes, Sara got the last one and said she'd give it to you. She said you didn't really want to talk about it though, so I didn't bring it up," she said.

Kenny froze. "She never gave me anything," he said, puzzled.

Ms. Carter paused, a little surprised. "Huh. Well, here's this one," she said as she handed him a small, sealed brown parcel.

Kenny stared at the package, turning it over in his hands. "Thanks," he mumbled.

As he stepped into the hallway his eyes were locked on the package as he tore the seal. Inside was a hardcover book and a folded letter. He unfolded it cautiously and began to read it.

My dearest Kenny,

I hope this letter finds its way to you. I've been trying—truly trying—to reach you. To find the right moment, the right words.

Ever since I got the news of Caleb... my heart's been breaking for you. For all of you. I wrote once before hoping maybe then was a good time, but Sara Grace wrote back and said you weren't ready. And I understood.

But I want you to know I'm here. I've always been here. Waiting and hoping. And if now still isn't the right time, that's okay, too. But if there's a chance you might be ready to see me... I would give anything for that moment.

I wanted you to know how proud I am of the man you've become. I've followed every story I could find of your team and of you. You've been so strong. If you'd allow it, I'd love to come see you.

The letter continued.

I wanted you to have something. Momma's story might have changed a bit since you last heard it but after all these years I finally found my title. Or maybe... it found me.

Love you, always, Momma

Kenny's hands trembled as he stared at the letter, the words echoed in his head. He swallowed hard and slowly turned the book over.

Bluegrass Kingdom by April Bledsoe-Hawkins

His mother's name, right there in bold print.

Kenny furiously flipped to the first page; his fingers were rough with the edges of the paper as he scanned the opening lines. His eyes darted across the words, soaking them in, committing them to memory.

The first few sentences hit like a whisper and a punch all at once: raw and unfamiliar, he stopped reading after the first paragraph. He couldn't bring himself to go on. His breath caught in his chest. His jaw clenched.

How dare she! How dare she write those words! How dare she call this "their" story—his story, as if it belonged to her. As if she'd been there; as if she hadn't left!

The book shook in his hands as he held it. His heart pounded. The words she'd written, the pages she'd filled... they weren't just ink and paper. They were ghosts. And Kenny wasn't sure if he wanted to run from them—or finally look into their eyes.

His knees buckled slightly as he pressed himself against a row of lockers for support. Everything felt like too much, too fast, too loud.

That's when Kate hobbled into the hallway, a single crutch under one arm. She spotted him immediately. "Kenny?" she called out, concerned.

But he was already moving, walking faster, then running—away from the letter, away from the crushing heaviness of it all—until he reached the gym. It was quiet there, familiar. He leaned forward with his hands on his knees, struggling to catch his breath.

Kate found him moments later as she limped to his side and placed her hand gently on his back.

"Just breathe," she said softly. "Just breathe," she whispered. Kenny did his best to try, shaky at first. Then again, steadier. "What happened?" she asked.

"I... I don't know," he said, his voice barely above a whisper. "It's a letter... from my mom. I didn't even know if she was still..." he trailed off behind a shaky breath as he showed Kate the book and letter.

"She wants to see me, she said she's proud. Said she's been trying to reconnect." He stared ahead blankly before his brokenness overwhelmed him. "What am I supposed to do now?" he asked.

Kate looked at him, her eyes soft. "Listen, I know it's none of my business, and it's an entirely different situation with your mother, but I'd give anything to talk to my mom just one more time. I mean, even if all you do is yell at her. Maybe you need that. But, you owe it to yourself to find out."

Kenny sat on the court trying to calm his breathing; Kate did her best to sit beside him, the gym quiet except for their breath.

"She left a number," he murmured. "I can't do it here; I need to go home," he said, panicked. "What should I do?" he asked as he looked up at Kate.

"I'm not going to tell you what to do. This is one of things you need to decide for yourself," she replied.

The panic on Kenny's face began to spread, his breath again became unsteady. "I could be there when you call her if you want me to be?" Kate offered.

Kenny looked over at her. "I'd like that," he said as a weak smile came to his lips.

Kenny got to his feet and then helped Kate stand up straight once again. The two stood together at center court for a beat, Kenny lingering—hoping, perhaps—for just a little more time.

High above the court his brother's jersey still hung in the rafters. And next to it, a brand-new banner that read:

Kyrock Knights: Kentucky Boys Basketball State Tournament, Runner Up

Out in the school parking lot the sky was cloudy, early spring in the air as he fumbled with his keys and tried his best to unlock the truck. He helped Kate up into the cab, gently, and tossed her crutch into the bed. He then climbed into the driver's seat and tore off through the parking lot.

Neither said much on the drive to Ma and Pa's. Some silences say everything. Kenny called Sara again. And again, nothing. Where was she? Was she okay?

Why would she hide something like this from him? A letter from his mother! She hadn't even told him. He didn't know whether to be angry, hurt, or something else entirely. All he knew was that he didn't know anything.

Did he even want to lay eyes on the woman who had walked out on him? Who had given up on him and his brother?

The questions turned in his mind as the truck wound its way up Bledsoe Hill. With every bump in the gravel road, Kenny's heart beat faster. What was he even going to say? What could he say to a woman he didn't know anymore? To someone he didn't really want to know.

When they reached the top of the hill, he saw it: Sara's vehicle parked crooked in front of Ma and Pa's house. Kenny didn't wait. He barely got the truck in park before he flung the door open and sprinted across the yard. Kate hobbled out behind him, slower.

As Kenny reached the porch Sara stepped outside of the house, her face pale and tight. Something in her eyes—fear, maybe. Shame perhaps. Maybe both.

"Sara," he called out. "What did you do?" his voice was tight.

"Kenny," she said, her voice catching. "I'm sorry. I didn't want you to—"

But he wasn't listening anymore. His attention had snapped to the figure emerging from the doorway behind her. A woman, curly-haired and middle-aged. Her eyes were wide as she stepped out onto the porch, clutching her hands together as if they were the only thing keeping her from falling apart.

As she neared the edge her voice trembled as she spoke. "Kenny," she said. "It's Momma..." She smiled—soft and hopeful. "It's good to see your face," she proclaimed.

Kenny stood frozen. His breath caught in his throat as time slowed. Then... another figure stepped out of the house and onto the porch. This one with curls too, but smaller and younger.

A young girl stood beside his mother with dark curly hair that bounced at her shoulders and a shy unsure look in her big brown eyes.

His mother turned and placed a gentle hand on the girl's shoulder and said, "Kenny... this is your little sister. This is Virginia."

The girl blinked at him, and she looked so much like the brothers he'd lost. Like a piece of something that might've been. Kenny stared at her as his heart pounded, all his words caught somewhere deep in his chest.

As the wind rustled through the blooming trees on Bledsoe Hill, a line from his mother's book repeated itself in his head over and over again—soft and distant, but clearer than anything he'd ever remembered.

The very first line:

Sometimes in life, like the cruel mistress it can be... sometimes your story ends, right where it should begin.

The End.

Bluegrass Nights
Coming 2026
Scan now for a sneak peek

Thank You

Wow, where do I even begin?

If you've made it this far, thank you. Thank you for sharing in a piece of my heart. A person much wiser than me once said, "Stories are only half-alive until someone reads them."

Eli and Micah, my wild boys. Never forget that your dad loves you beyond measure. This world will try to tell you you're not good enough, but don't listen too closely. You're already everything you need—brave, kind, curious, and more special than you could ever imagine. I love you both...Always.

Kayla, Melanie, Emily, and Mom—thank you all for taking this plunge with me. I'm so grateful to have people in my life who I can trust to tell me exactly how much I suck. (I think I *should've* used *whom* there, but I'm not really a 'whom' type of guy—and Elizabeth didn't edit this page.) I love you all.

Elizabeth, thank you for all of your hard work and patience. But most of all, thank you for being someone I can trust enough to hand a notebook to and say, "I wrote something... would you read it?" You will always be my first reader. I'd say *I love you* here, but now it just feels weird... so how about a high five?

Amanda, thank you for being my best friend and my biggest supporter, no matter how crazy my dreams might seem. You are, and will always be, my reason to keep chasing them. I'm thankful every single day that I somehow managed to trick you into marrying me. You are my home, and being with you will always be my favorite story.